The Cowboy's Texan

FOSTER RANCH
BOOK THREE

BA TORTUGA

BA's Cozy Cowboys

If y'all are interested in warm, joyous novels where the cowboys have kids and love saves the day, please check these BA Tortuga books out:

Back in the Saddle

Cowboy Haven

Cowboy in the Crosshairs

Cowboy Logic

Cowboy's Law

In the Morning Light

Ranch Manny

Security Detail: an AusTex novel

Silver Buckle Linings

The Cowboy Contract

The Cowboy Guardian

The Meaning of Life

Trial by Fire: an AusTex novel

Two Cowboys and a Baby

Two of a Kind

For Jay.

Chapter One

"I don't camp."

Nathan did a lot of things. He cooked, he cleaned, he planned, and he created amazing meals.

He did not camp.

Ryder Chiara blinked at him, then grinned, and it seemed like a wry one. "I get that. And it's not what you hired on to do, but we're in a real bind for the next two weeks until Jordan's replacement arrives."

"And it's not exactly camping." Kase, who was his other boss at the ranch, chimed in. "There's a shelter, a propane kitchen, beds. You'll also have a grill. Two meals and sack lunches for a dozen guys—it'll be a breeze."

"What about my job here?" Nathan's head was beginning to pound. "I have to put in orders, run food costs."

"I know. And I'll get you as much help as I can." Ryder blew out a breath. "I didn't expect my whole food team to quit all at once."

"Yeah." He chuckled softly and shook his head. That he understood, on a deep, personal level. "My job is still going to be here when I get back, right?"

Because he didn't know if he could handle another blow.

"Hell, yes. In fact, I bet we expand your job and give you a damn raise before you even start good."

"I can handle that." He was a chef. He thrived on that kind of stress.

Losing everything he owned? Not so much.

"So do I need to order in supplies? Is there a list?" He wasn't sure what the process was but he could do one hundred and fifty-six breakfasts, lunches, and suppers, plus snacks and the periodic desserts in his sleep, but he needed supplies to do that.

"Yes. I'll show you the ordering program. Well, Kase will. And there's lists of any food allergies and such."

"All right. I'll need your food—budget." They weren't selling the food, so he didn't have a food cost, so to speak. He was going to have a discussion with the chuck wagon guy at the rodeo, though. His food costs were damn near forty-five percent.

That was highway robbery for such simple fare.

"Sure. I know we have it all in a database." Ryder chuckled. "Kase can explain the rest of that to you, since he deals with it. One thing I do want to emphasize is the guys would live on Twinkies and beer if you let them. I would prefer more nutritious fare for them."

"Nutritious I can accomplish." He wasn't a health food nut, but he was good at creating meals that nourished. He was in this business to feed people.

"Good deal."

Kase grinned. "Okay, get out of the way, Ryder. We need to get to business."

"So you'll go up to camp?" Ryder asked, rising.

"This time to help, yes. I'll have time to plan the Fourth of July party food, then." It was his first big event here at the ranch, and it came right close to when he started his job in the kitchen full time.

Maybe in a year he'd be able to show his face in Austin again, hunt for a new investor.

"Yep." Kase grinned. "That will be a job and a half. The whole ranch and rodeo company turn out, and half the town comes in addition to our people."

"Well, we'll have to figure the budget out for that too so I can work up a few menus." That was way more up Nathan's alley than camping without Wi-Fi.

"Sure. I can show you what we did last year, and then we'll add on, because we have a guy who's coming up to write a magazine article about it this year. So we'll need a few luxury items for the VIP." Kase wrinkled his nose.

"No problem. We can have some amazing apps and sweet bites that fill that need." It kept food costs down, and it left an impression. All in all, it was a winning strategy.

"Cool deal."

Ryder nodded as if that was that. "I'll leave y'all to it. I need to talk to some of the road guys." And he was off, leaving him with Kase.

"Thanks for agreeing to take the high reaches for a couple of weeks. I know you were supposed to do a soft landing, but that's too often not how ranch life goes."

"Yeah." It wasn't how Nathan's life had gone lately, that was for sure. "I'm not the most outdoorsy person alive, but I know how to cook."

"That's what we need you for. And I'll assign someone to you to help out with your gear and all. A good hand." Kase opened up a database. "Here's where the ordering stuff is. This should be the easiest job ever. It'll be cool up in the high meadows, so oatmeal, eggs and biscuits, you know? Then sandwiches and such for bag lunches, and a hearty supper."

He might have to make clangers. He loved the idea of two-thirds savory and a third sweet. Those could be a hoot to experiment with. And they would surprise the hell out of cowboys, he would bet.

That might make him smile while he was going without a shower for two weeks.

Ugh.

God, he prayed he'd have a cell signal at least. He had work to do.

Kase gave him a sideways glance. "Questions about anything before we start with this?"

"What do the facilities look like up there?"

"Pump water. There's solar, and there's also a generator just in case. There's satellite internet because we need everyone to be connected."

Oh, thank God.

"I might survive." And he might not lose his mind. "What do I need to bring—work and personal?"

"Sturdy clothes. More than one pair of shoes, boots if you have them. Any cooking tools you need that aren't part of a standard trail kitchen. The inventory is here." Kase showed him a tab on the database. "Reading material. Days are long and the guys work as long as there's daylight sometimes."

"Okay. Well, I'll nap a lot." A lot.

He knew how to read, of course, and he'd bring some cookbooks, but really? He'd rest.

"I bet you could catch up on some sleep."

He squinted at Kase, wondering what that meant. What did Kase know?

"Uh, yeah. I was working sixty to eighty hours a week at the restaurant, sometimes more." Especially at the end of things—he had been lost and trying to put fires out.

"You said in your cover letter that you were looking for a more reasonable schedule." Kase's lips twisted. "And here we are, asking you to do a high camp your first month."

"I can do it. I mean, there's a camp shower, right?"

"Three." Kase chuckled. "I love it up there, but I'm not great at roughing it anymore. Bad crash."

"I'm sorry. That sucks. I hate to hear that." Car accidents were the worst. He'd known more than one guy who had been broken up and then couldn't work anymore.

"Yeah. It was a harsh thing. That bull stomped the living daylights out of me." Kase shook his head. "But I'm way better than I was when I showed up here. This place has a way about it, if you get me."

"A bull? Jesus Christ. Are you okay?" He had seen a couple of rodeos, but he didn't actually know any real-life rodeo people.

"Well, I had a crushed pelvis and some other massive breaks." Kase chuckled. "Took me months to get back on my feet, and then I ended up here because Ryder let me come. Rodeo is a young man's game. Animals are unpredictable sparring partners."

"Yeah. Yeah, but you still own a rodeo company? *Still*?"

"Well, technically, Ryder owned it when we got married. But yeah. I can't imagine not cowboying. And this way we can provide help for riders when they get hurt." Kase's fingers seemed a little gnarled already, even though he couldn't be near old enough to have hands like that.

Then again, Nathan had chef's hands. Cut and burned and bruised. He had scars that were bad enough they seemed like road maps.

Every job had its dangers.

But he'd never been kicked or stomped by a bull. Which made him wonder.

"So am I going to have to ride a horse up to the camp?"

"That would be the easiest way. Do you know how to ride?"

Motorcycles? Cars? Hang-gliders? Skidoos? Lovely men? Yes.

Horses? He was from Austin, for Chrissake. A city boy, for all he was from Texas.

"I guess I'll learn."

"We can get you a crash course. No pun intended. We've got some great gentle horses too."

"Yay." He chuckled. "I suppose it was too much to hope for a chuckwagon to ride on."

Kase grimaced. "Trust me, that's harder on the butt than the horse. And I'd let you take a side by side, but if it's wet up there at all, it will just get bogged down."

"Then lessons it is." He'd known when he signed on at a ranch that he might be roughing it some. He'd thought it might be more like that famous rancher TV show, was all.

Kase smiled at him, the expression gentle. "You're being a very good sport. The one thing I've learned about being at this ranch is that nothing is boring, and you have to be flexible. Animals and kids, right?"

"I'm trying, for sure." And he had no choice. His ex had taken everything and flushed it down the toilet, including the restaurant he'd worked so hard to build, his reputation as a chef, and his freaking house. All of it gone because of a bad investment Dan had made.

Thank God they hadn't been married.

As it was, he'd been humiliated, blackballed, and he'd had to leave the city and head to Nowhere, New Mexico to feed foster kids and cowboys.

At least he had control over what he was producing.

Kase studied him for a long moment. "Okay, man. Let's get you up to speed on this stuff. I know you're ready to get to work."

"You're absolutely right." Losing himself in his work made everything else bearable. And it was time to get to it.

Chapter Two

"I don't babysit." Ames Paulson stared at Ryder Chiara, a muscle ticking in his jaw. He was a full-time wrangler, and he worked cattle and horses.

He didn't give riding lessons to spoiled city chefs.

Ryder snorted. "If you want to move the cattle to the high reaches for the summer, you sure as hell do this week."

"We can survive off peanut butter and coffee. We'll be fine."

Ryder rolled his eyes. "Maybe you can, but Ed and George have diabetes, and there are a couple guys that are keto."

"Well, whose fault is that?" he snapped, then instantly felt like an ass. "Sorry, Boss. That was out of line. You took me by surprise with this."

"Look, the truth is I trust you to get to get him up to speed by the time you go up. And you guys need a cook."

"I can put him on a sled..." He might get shit on, but then Ames wouldn't have to teach him to ride.

"Ames."

He sighed. "Yeah, yeah. It was a thought."

"A bad one. No travois. Just give him enough lessons to get him to camp and back."

He shook his head and sighed. "All right. All right, Boss, but I got to tell you. He's going to run crying. Two weeks in the boonies with dogs and bugs? The city boy is going to quit."

"Mmm." Ryder leaned against the door of the stall he was in, arms crossed, a little grin on his face. "Don't be so sure. The city boy is here for a reason."

He didn't doubt that. The question was, what reason? He didn't really care—not enough to go hunting for information, anyway.

"I'll be professional."

"That's all I ask, cowboy. You can start this afternoon."

"Sure. You sending him to me?"

"I am. Thanks. Who knows, you might like it."

"Huh." He'd seen the guy. He doubted he had much fun doing anything but maybe getting ink. Not that he was against tattoos. He had a few himself. But damn.

This guy was like a freaking gang member or something, if the gang was filled with pasty white boys with a mass of dark red hair.

He was kinda hot, truth be told, but Ames wasn't going to admit that to anyone. Nope. He was going to hold out for the guy being a jerk.

He'd seen more than his fair share of city boys who thought they were special, that their shit didn't stink.

He didn't need it now.

"Make sure he has boots," he called after Ryder.

"I have boots." The man's voice was flat, and that lip was curled. "I'm not any happier than you are. I'm doing the Chiaras a favor."

Shit. He whirled around. "Let me see your boots. You could get hurt wearing the wrong kind."

The boots were simple, lace up, with a low shaft, and they weren't new. And they had enough heel to be safe in a stirrup.

Grudgingly, he nodded. "Well, come meet Lobo."

The son of a bitch didn't answer; he simply followed without a word, eyes the color of whiskey. Wary, too. And hell, Ames couldn't blame him. He'd been talking shit in earshot.

He fucking hated that.

He hated being caught out.

And now he was going to have to wait for the little prick to bring it up. Dammit.

"This is the gelding you'll be on. Lobo. He's twelve. Sure-footed. Smart. But gentle. Not mischievous." Not like his mare.

"Sounds good." That was the most insipid answer ever.

Ames gritted his teeth. "You might as well come meet him while he's still in his stall. Get to know him a bit. Talk to him." And he wanted to observe. Was the guy scared?

"What do you say to a horse?"

"You ever had a dog, man? A cat? You just talk to him. He's got ears, don't you, boy?"

Lobo's ears swiveled, the big gelding nodding in his stall like he was laughing.

"Um. Hey." The guy sidled closer, and Lobo put his head over the stall door, nose working as he hunted a treat.

"Here. Hold your hand open, fingers flat. I'll put a carrot on your palm. He'll like that." A little demon made him add. "If you curl them up, he could bite them off. I assume you need them in your line of work."

He got an ice-cold stare. "If I were you, I'd be more worried about the fact that I know where the tenderloin is located on a human and how to remove it while you're still alive."

Oh, touché. He didn't grin, though. He went with nodding sagely. "Secret is in the sauce. Go ahead. He's really in it for the carrots, not the fingers." Lobo loved carrots and apples more than oats, even. He had a sweet tooth, that gelding.

"I understand. I make an amazing carrot adobo. My carrot soup is worth Michelin stars." The cook wasn't talking to Ames. He was talking to Lobo.

Which was okay. Ames talked to horses better than he did people too.

Lobo lipped up the carrot, which made the guy laugh. "That tickled."

"It's all those nose hairs. Tells him where his head will fit, lets him sense things."

"Huh. Well, you have a huge head, man. Huge."

Lobo nodded again, then leaned farther out to head-bump the chef.

"What does that mean?"

"That he wants more carrots. I'm Ames by the way." He supposed he ought to know the guy by more than the chef.

"Nathan Greene. Most people call me Greene."

"Well, Greene. Lobo is ready for some exercise if you are. We're on a timeline."

"Yeah, Kase and Ryder both said."

"Add me to the list. We need to get the cows up before we have to worry about the southern pastures causing bloat and other problems due to the sun and temperature change."

"I won't pretend to understand what you said, but I do comprehend bloat."

"I guess, huh?" He chuckled. "It's about mold. Weeds. All sorts of things can kill cattle. Let me bring him out."

Greene backed off, and he opened the stall, then clipped a lead to Lobo's halter. The gelding knew this game, and he loved it. He was a working horse, through and through.

"He's big."

Ames almost felt sorry for the guy. Almost.

No one had made him take a job on a ranch. If he was scared of critters, he didn't belong here.

"You're a pretty tall guy. Trust me, you don't want a short horse. That's one reason I chose him for you. Now grab that blanket right behind you. It's already folded correctly, so you're going to put it over his back with the pattern going along his spine."

"Pattern going along his spine. Okay. Hey, there. I'm supposed to talk to you, so this is me. Talking. To you."

He watched Greene carefully, then showed him how to pull the blanket up. "Okay, smooth it all out. Wrinkles can cause him to chafe, so you want to make sure he's all good before we put on the saddle."

"Chafing? Ouch."

"Yeah, you've heard of a lathered horse?"

"Uh-huh."

"Well, horses sweat. And a blanket wrinkle can bunch up like our underwear or socks."

"That sounds unpleasant." Greene didn't sound sarcastic, but he didn't seem overjoyed either. "Well, I promise to try and keep you latherless."

That was pretty nice to hear. They didn't push the horses too hard on the Chiara outfit, so unless something weird happened, they would rest every few hours on the trail, but he liked Greene more for saying it.

"Let's deal with the saddle."

Greene blinked at the tack. "That thing is huge."

"Well, it has to fit him. And you." He grinned. "Here, I'll show you the trick." He grabbed the saddle, then swung it up from the side as if he was about to toss a feed sack. It settled on Lobo's back, light as a feather. "It's all about momentum."

"It doesn't hurt him? Landing on him like that?"

"Nope. And trust me, they'll let you know if you hurt

them. They're not shy that way." He rocked the saddle into a good spot, then lifted the stirrup so he could start cinching.

Greene watched him, standing there without a word. It was a little unnerving. Not that he was much for chatter, but damn. Not a comfy silence.

"You'll need to learn to do this, but the best way is on the trail."

"Oui. I'll figure it out. I'm determined."

"Yeah." He could kinda see that in the set of jaw and shoulders. "Okay, all cinched. Now, come hold out your arm to measure the stirrup."

"Okay?" Nathan went to him, expression one of utter concern.

He bit back another grin. "It's the easiest way. I'll adjust them when you mount up, but your arm is a good indication. So let him know you're coming with a hand on his neck..."

Chapter Three

Nathan was fixin' to die.

He'd be damned if he let a single one of these assholes know it, though.

Six hours on a horse was sheer hell, and his thighs were blistered, and he had to create supper and get the kitchen put together.

He wanted to lie down and expire.

"You need a hand?" That was one of the older guys. Ned, maybe? He thought that was the man's name. It was hard to remember. They called the horses by name more than they did each other.

"I'd appreciate it. That takes a lot out of the legs."

"You did good for your first time. You stayed standing when you stepped out of the saddle."

"Go me." He chuckled, but he remembered the first time he staged for a certain famous chef in France, and he worked the first three days without stopping, then slept four hours and got back up and did it again. That was a few years ago, but he did that then, and he would do this now. "Seriously, thank you for the offer. There's a lot to unload."

"No problem." Ned helped him unload the pack animals, and someone had gotten the fridge and freezer combo turned on and going by the time they had everything ready to put in it. Ned grinned at him. "I got a word of advice. We'll be setting up and tending animals for at least an hour and a half. Heat some water while there's still sun to run the solar heater and shower. Then cook."

He gave a wry chuckle. "I think I might at that."

"I know you have to be hurting. Tonight will suck, but the rest of the job should be a breeze. Ames is in charge of the rotation, so you'll have a hand on KP duty."

"Good deal." Woo. Ames seemed to think he was an asshole, but the simple fact was, he'd almost pissed himself when he'd seen Lobo walk out.

He'd never even had a goldfish. He'd grown up in an apartment in downtown Austin. He'd gone from culinary school to New York, then Paris, then Lisbon, then Los Angeles, and back home.

And Lobo was huge. He stood a foot above the other horses at the shoulder, and his dapple-gray back was wide as a frickin' Winnebago.

On the good side, he had seemed way more sedate than the other horses, and when Nathan had been so tired he could only hold on and not steer, Lobo had put himself nose-to-tail with the mare in front of them and plodded on in line, never showing any sign of bad temper.

He had an hour and a half, and if he took fifteen minutes to wash up, then he could make up a quick and dirty chicken piccata with angel hair pasta and green beans. Kase had guaranteed him that there would be a new load of produce and dairy in a week, so he was going to plan accordingly.

But he had canned goods. Durable fruits and veggies. And a fridge full of meat and such. So he was good to go right now.

He grabbed his pack and headed the way Ned had pointed

him. The shower was in a lean-to like at the beach, and it was pretty easy to figure out how to heat the water someone had pumped in. So he took a shower, much shorter than he wanted, but hot enough to melt his muscles, and took some Tylenol as he dressed. The only one who stuck around to watch was one of the old-timer's dogs, a one-eared heeler named Fred.

He refused to sit down. He started the process of creating his mise en place, using the familiar rhythm of the knife on the board as a comfort.

Lemon. Capers. Garlic. Parsley.

It smelled heavenly already.

He dried the chicken, then seasoned it before setting up his flouring station. He didn't bread piccata, but it needed the flour to crisp it up, and to thicken the sauce when he deglazed the pan. He could do this. He'd cooked on propane, fire, electric. None of that mattered when he was in the zone.

The water was on the stove, then he started trimming green beans before tossing them with shallots and a little black salt.

"What's for supper?"

He damn near sent the chicken flying when he jumped, his hand hitting the platter. Ames had startled the hell out of him.

"Please don't sneak up on me in the kitchen," he snapped. "Someone could get cut or burned."

"Yes, sir, Mr. Chef, sir." Ames shot back in a heartbeat. "I was coming to see if you needed anything."

He took a deep breath, then let it out. "No. Wait, yes. I need a basic schedule."

"Sure. I'll write one out for you. But for now, all the guys will be in for supper in an hour or so. Then half of them will head out to work the night with the herd. They'll need sandwiches and such. At seven in the morning, shifts change at breakfast, and the day guys will need lunch."

So he'd make twelve sandwiches for today, and then the clanger experience would start tomorrow night.

He'd start with chicken, spinach, and cheddar on one side and apple with cheddar on the other.

"No problem at all. Supper will be on time." And he'd manage to do a steel-cut oatmeal in the morning with a berry compote.

"Good deal. I'll leave you to it." Ames left, and he shook his head. There were three cowboys who had to be twice as old as Ames here. How did he get to be the manager?

"I'm setting up the dishwashing station," Ned told him, coming in to grab a little container of bleach. "Anything you need scrubbed right now?"

"No. I'll do my own knives, but do you guys do the pans?"

"Yep."

"Cool. Nothing scratchy on these two, okay?"

"You got it." Ned winked.

"So can I ask you something?"

"Sure." Ned paused, reaching down to rub Fred's ears.

"Are you not upset that Ames is the boss up here?"

"Shit no. No one likes the trail boss job. I mean, he gets paid more. But it's thankless. I would still be a day laborer if I could."

"Ah." He sort of got that. Not everyone wanted to be the head chef.

Especially once they realized that they paid for everything.

"Fair enough." What else was he supposed to say? He didn't love being the asshole on the bottom rung, so he'd fought and bit and scratched his way to the top. "Ames kind of seems like he would like the top rung, though."

"He does a damn good job. And he's fair. That's a great quality. And he'll cut loose with us now and again, but never in a bad way. The boys respect him."

Huh. Were they talking about the same guy? "Well, thanks for washing up. It will make my life easier."

"That's how we do it. The guy who feeds us does no dishes."

"Well, I intend to give y'all the best meals of your lives." It was all he did, day in and day out. Feed people.

"I can tell. It smells damn fine already. I reckon we're used to cans of chili and hot dogs."

"Oh, there's definitely a place for that. But not after a long day on the trail. You need a much tastier meal." And healthier. Starch, Protein. Veg. It would stick to the guys' ribs way better than soy-filled canned chili and fake meat logs.

Ryder had given him his instructions there.

"Fruit, Nathan. Fruit and vegetables and whole grains. No crap."

So that was what he intended to do. Feed the guys delicious, healthy food. And maybe the occasional treat. Hamburgers could be great since they had grass-fed meat. And he wasn't afraid of dessert. While he intended that to be fruit and such, for the most part, he could make a mean cobbler or dump cake, and s'mores were on the list. One of the guys had a birthday coming up this week, and that had been his request.

He put the chicken away and started boiling the noodles. The green beans wouldn't take long at all.

After he dropped the noodles, he began organizing the kitchen to his liking. He had a nice stock of canned goods from last week, and no mouse droppings, which was great. The flour, sugar, and other dry goods were in airtight containers, as were the spices. All in all, it wasn't bad for a camp kitchen.

He approved.

Before he knew it, he had twelve perfectly portioned plates. He'd eat off what was left. They appeared healthy, appetizing, and Insta-worthy.

"What is this?" Ames asked, peering at the plates as he walked into the kitchen.

"Chicken piccata. Enjoy."

"So it's fancy food?"

"Come on, even you have to know what chicken piccata is."

Ames made a face at him. "I do. But I guarantee Ned doesn't."

"It's okay. He'll learn." Lemon, chicken, yumminess. It was good.

The expression on Ames's face could have defined skepticism, but Nathan ignored it. This man was not going to get him down. Not one little bit.

His food had never been the problem, and it wasn't the problem now.

"Something smells damn good." One of the younger hands, or drovers, or wranglers—since they seemed to call them all sorts of things—drifted in, nose working.

"Chicken piccata," Nathan said.

"Should I ring the bell?"

"Is there really a bell?" He'd seen that in movies.

"Oh, hell yeah."

"Ring away. It's ready."

"Yay!" Well, someone was looking forward to his food, at least. The guy went out to the overhanging porch of the trail cabin and rang the triangle, just like on TV.

Okay, that was cool. He'd have to tell his buddy Kev about that. That would crack the man up.

The cowboys trooped in, all of them thanking him politely, a few making happy noises as they smelled the air. Ned beamed. "Chicken piccata. My momma made this."

"Yeah? Hopefully I've done it well enough." Food memory was a powerful thing. And so much for Ned having no idea what it was...

Ames gave Ned a glare, eyebrows raised.

"I would know that smell anywhere. Thanks, man. I appreciate it."

"Of course."

"Your momma, Ned?"

"Uh-huh. Her momma was Italian." Ned beamed. "Capers and lemon."

"You know it. It's my quick and easy go to."

"This is damn good," one of the guys said, forking up a bite.

Ames took his plate, then frowned. "Where's yours?"

"Hmm?" His what? He had angel food cake and berries for dessert, if anyone wanted it.

"Your food. You don't like this?" Ames waved at the chicken piccata.

"Love it. I have been nibbling, and there's enough left here." He wasn't used to meals. He spent his days tasting.

"Well, you need to eat with us." Ames sent a meaningful glance at the cowboys, who were sitting all over the main room of the cabin, chowing down.

Oh, for fuck's sake. One, he was busy. Two, he had to cut strawberries.

Three, and most important, if he sat down, he'd fall asleep and possibly never stand up again.

"Let me get the strawberries ready. I wasn't aware of that and didn't schedule accordingly."

Ames gave him a searching kind of look, then nodded. "It's good to have that feeling of camaraderie," he said, keeping his voice low. "That way if there's an emergency..."

"Got it." That was fair. "I'll work on it. I'm not used to leaving the kitchen. I never thought about it."

And that was true. Almost as true as his poor ass.

"Well, you'll have dessert with us, right?"

"Absolutely." He summoned a smile, because Ames seemed less growly.

He started hulling strawberries, chopping them to macerate them. The angel food cake had been pre-made so he wouldn't have to bake his first day, so all he had to do was whip cream.

At least his arm wasn't as tired as his ass.

He chuckled at that thought, but then he was done with dessert, and the guys were trading supper plates for bowls of berries. Nathan sat nearby to eat his.

It wasn't too sweet; it wasn't too tart. Actually, it was perfect.

He could feast on this, and he wasn't even a dessert guy.

"Yum." Ned licked his spoon. "Thanks, Chef. I loved that. I'm gonna go get the water working again."

"You're welcome." He was going to make up twelve sandwiches—goat cheese pesto chicken—and then a jar of rice salad and a lemon bar, which he'd made up yesterday. Then he was going to fall asleep and die.

Clangers would just have to wait.

Chapter Four

Ames had to admit, grudgingly, that Nathan Greene had done better than he'd expected. All the guys loved his food, he'd never once bitched about how tired and sore he was, and his meals were still pretty creative even though it was grocery delivery day.

The guys were getting more vegetable matter than they'd likely eaten since they were kids, the weird-assed pastry things had gone over like they were amazing, and everything had spices and herbs and shit.

It was maddening.

Then again, he'd never eaten so well himself, and he knew it, though he would never admit it.

He hadn't known that canned food and rice could make something spicy and creamy and amazing. He didn't know he liked foreign food that didn't sound like anything he understood.

He did know there was something about Nathan Greene that made his eyes cross and made him grumpy as hell.

He sighed, heading to the kitchen to collect his bag lunch for the day. "You all set for delivery?" he asked.

The man was relaxed, a bandana on his red head. "Oui. I'm set up. Should be a fun couple of days. I hope they found arugula and chard…"

"What the hell is chard?" Okay, he knew, but only because he watched *Top Chef* reruns.

"It's a leafy green. I'm going to make wali ya mboga. I've been reading about it, and it's gluten free."

"Is that anything that's real?" He thought it sounded like a movie.

"Which part? Gluten free, chard, or wali ya mboga?" Smartass.

"Just tell me what it is?" Ames cut a hand through the air.

"Rice and vegetables and chicken with spice, basically. It's East African, and I've been reading a lot about it while I've been here." Like that was normal. Who did that?

"Hmm. Is there going to be an alternate?"

"What? No. You all like chicken and rice. I will make it less spicy and give you the option to add more. I know there are some sensitive palates."

"Yeah. And bellies." Some of the guys had cast iron stomachs, but Hal, for example, had required surgery to remove part of his gut when a bull had gored him when he was in his twenties.

Nathan just chuckled, shook his head. "Yes. I was being delicate. Everyone deserves a seat at the table."

"Thanks." He sighed. "I'm on the herd today, but I'll be in for the night. Can we set up a meet to see what the menu reads like once you get supplies? You have free rein. I want to know what's what."

"Sure. Seven suppers, seven breakfasts, seven bag lunches, and three desserts. I'll make a menu once I see the produce." Nathan tilted his head. "You've been eating. Do you not enjoy the food?"

He had, sure, but he would kill for a steak or enchiladas, chili dogs, burgers. Something simple and familiar.

"I do enjoy it. But I want something American or Mexican. Those are my go-tos. Is that possible?" See him be reasonable.

"Oh, I wanted to make a mole poblano, but the food costs weren't great, so I settled on chiles en Nogada." Nathan hummed. "Poblanos stuffed with picadillo and covered in a walnut cream sauce, sprinkled with pomegranate seeds."

"Hmm. I mean, that sounds yummy, but I was wondering about green chile enchiladas. I'm New Mexican."

"If they send the ingredients, I'll see if I can fit them in." Nathan seemed a touch constipated. It was probably all that chard shit.

"Thanks, man. I really appreciate it." Ames relented some. "I dig your food, but it's a learning curve. And I crave a hamburger sometimes."

Nathan nodded, then handed him a bag lunch.

"Another one of them weird things?"

"No. Today you have turkey and muenster wraps with tomato, pine nuts, olive salad, and hummus."

"That's the bean mayo stuff."

"Yep." Nathan nodded, seeming more cheerful.

So he dared to tease. "No cookie?"

"No. Hand pie. Apricot and basil."

"I'll take it." He winked. "Thanks. I know it's annoying."

"It so is." Nathan deadpanned it, but his lips twitched.

Hopefully that was laughter Nathan was holding back.

"Is there more of that steel-cut oatmeal, Mr. Greene? It's the best stuff I've ever tasted." Cash, one of the younger hands, brought over his empty bowl.

"Of course. You want the blueberry-ginger compote or the rosehip one?"

This guy was corrupting his hands.

"Blueberry please." Cash beamed, then winked at him. "Mr. Greene is the best cook we've ever had."

"Yep." That was probably a true and fair statement. The guy got under his skin.

"I should hope so. I spent enough time at the CIA learning how to." The bowl of oats was like a piece of art, fruit arranged around one inside edge, nuts sprinkled atop, little bits of candied ginger glistening.

It was crazy-making.

"Okay, well, I'll see you tonight then." Ames turned on his heel and left before he snapped at anyone.

Everyone was chowing down, little bags of lunches close by. The night shift was acting like they were starving.

So Ames went to saddle his horse. At least *they* weren't eating Nathan's food.

Last thing they needed was gourmet sweet feed.

"Hey, Boss. How goes it?"

"Hey, Ned. I'm about to head out. You on with me today?"

"I am! It looks like it's going to be a gorgeous day. I do love this time of year."

"Me too, buddy." He grabbed his saddle and moved to gear up his gelding. He wished he knew why that chef guy got to him so bad.

The man wasn't a bitch. He wasn't whiny. He wasn't an asshole.

But there was something about him that set Ames's fucking teeth on edge. Maybe he reminded Ames of someone deep down in his subconscious, though for the life of him he couldn't think who.

Thank God he only had to deal with the man for another week. Then he'd be doing fancy shit for the Chiaras and their guests, and Ames be eating normal food again.

"Hey, you," he told Buck, settling the blanket into place on his back. "Let's have a good night tonight, huh?"

Buck whinnied, head tossing good and hard. Someone was ready to get to work.

Nathan was on the last day of his camping adventure.

All in all, it hadn't been bad. In fact, there had been certain things that had been fun as hell.

For instance, Mr. I Only Want Normal Foods?

Got a bowl of cereal—no fruit, thank you—for breakfast, a ham and cheese sandwich and a plastic-wrapped oatmeal cookie for lunch, and a hamburger on a bun and six tater tots for supper.

Every fucking day.

He wasn't a short order cook—not now, not ever. He would—and did—make eggs to order, and he cooked beef and lamb to the temperature requested, but he didn't dumb down his food.

If the boss called him on it, he could prove that Ames was getting the same amount of calories as everyone else.

He was only getting a quarter of the care.

To his credit, the man never said a word. After the first morning where Nathan stared Ames down at the incipient raised eyebrows when everyone else got frittata and fruit salad, and he got Chex, Ames wore no expression at all when he came to collect his meals.

The food wasn't bad, but it was exactly what had been asked for—normal, American food. With the least effort he had to put in, since he was already cooking four meals for each shift, essentially.

He wished he could say it wasn't that he was being an asshole because he knew he probably was. In fact, he most likely owed the guy an apology. Not that Nathan was going to give him one. Not right now. Not after everything that had happened.

Not by the cowboy. Ames wasn't who he was so goddamn angry at.

It just...it hadn't been all that long since he'd had the restaurant.

Since he'd been up for a James Beard Award.

Since he had been someone. And now he was what?

A fucking camp cook making Chex mix and hamburgers. Ham and cheese sandwiches. Cookies.

It hurt his soul in a deep way that made him worry he wasn't fixable. He knew no one really understood how or why, especially no one who wasn't in the business, but this was his passion.

Food was his life. He spent hours, days even, searching for the perfect recipe, the perfect ingredient, the perfect set of flavors he wanted to see people eat.

Feeding people was what he did.

Jesus, he'd been so proud of that damn restaurant. Magnolia Ink. It had been what they'd named it, decided while they were soaking in the bathtub, Dan's hand on his cock, bubbles up to his neck.

"It's going to be beautiful, angel," Dan had promised, and it had been.

Beautiful.

Decorated in deep purples. Not too many tables, a few sets of leather banquettes along the walls with one chef's table near the kitchen. It had been a place for the elite to go and have a cozy, intimate dinner. Something to linger over.

They did one seating a night, and his menu changed daily, depending on what was freshest, what was best, and what had turned him on.

And somehow now he was scared of being turned on? Of the thought of his soul waking from its sleep.

And that was it. He was fucking terrified of this whole thing.

Worse than that, he was ashamed.

He'd trusted his ex with more than his life. He'd offered Dan access to his business, to his career. He'd paid with his heart, with his soul, and...shit.

He'd sacrificed it all to keep Dan out of jail. The worst part of all though? It hadn't been worth it.

Nathan had lost everything, full stop. That son of a bitch had simply found another sucker. Promised him his love and a new restaurant and started over in Houston.

God, he was tired.

Maybe that was why Nathan'd come here. Because no one knew who he was, no one cared. No one had any idea that he was—had been—special. Talented. He had been a mentor, someone to look up to, someone to care for. Hell, even a protégé another chef might brag about. Now he was nothing but a cook.

Now instead of his million-dollar condo in Austin, he was sleeping in the tiny house attached to a commercial kitchen. No bathtub. No bubbles. Just a stand-up shower and the toilet. The kitchenette squatted under a loft bed.

He didn't have to pay for it, at least.

Nathan sighed. He was trying to focus on what they were going to have their last night here at camp. They were almost out of fresh vegetables, but there was enough.

Salad maybe? Navratan Korma? Vegetable soup and cornbread?

Come on. Nathan. You gotta figure this out. All you have to do is decide what to make for supper. You've already got everything ready for biscuits and gravy before you leave out in the morning. Easy peasy lemon squeezy.

Pasta. That would be fun. He enjoyed making fresh pasta. He could make up one hell of a sauce. That was what he needed.

And tomorrow they'd eat biscuits and gravy, and they would load and go. He might even let Ames have some. Especially if he used up all the milk for the biscuits and gravy.

He laughed. Yeah, it was mean. He admitted it, but they did give him a little bit of a happy. It made him feel the tiniest bit in control. And it wasn't like he was starving the man. He wouldn't do that.

Mostly.

Besides that, it was almost over. All he had to do was finish. Get through today.

Twelve breakfasts. Twelve sack lunches. Twelve Suppers. Three desserts.

That was it.

The food costs. Run the nutritional info data. Feed the cowboys. Go home.

And save every penny. And dream of better days.

Chapter Five

"Ames. There you are." Ryder caught him as he stepped out of the office where he'd been giving his report to Kase.

The herd up at the high pastures was someone else's problem for a month now. And there was a camp cook installed there with the crew who'd changed places with them.

But the last thing he wanted to do was talk to another boss. He wanted an hour-long shower, and then he was headed into town for a huge plate of Mexican food. Or a steak. Maybe an all-day breakfast of pancakes and a Denver omelet at the diner.

He was fucking starving.

It never occurred to him how quick and how bad a cook could fuck your world up, but damn, it didn't take much at all. He'd been polite, he thought, but apparently Nathan had taken offense to his request for normal food. So he'd had precisely measured tasteless crap for a week. And there hadn't even been a bag of Cheetos or an extra cookie in the kitchen at three a.m.

"Here I am," he agreed, trying for anything but snarky.

Maybe a deep-dish pizza.

"I need to speak with you. Come to my office?" Ryder's face was a thundercloud.

Fuck. Fuck, what had he done now? Had that cook asshole complained about him?

"Sure, Boss." He had no intention of asking what he was in trouble for. Go for innocence. That was his thing.

"Good deal." When they got there, Ryder closed the door. Dammit.

This was bad.

He sat when Ryder waved him to the chair across the desk, and he tried not to fidget or breathe too hard. Was he getting his ass fired? He sure as fuck hoped not. He was in his groove.

"I got a phone call from Jennifer—she's our social worker."

He nodded, tension easing from his shoulders. That had nothing to do with him. He'd taken the foster training like everyone else at the ranch, but he wasn't signed up as a potential parent.

"She says that she's afraid your aunt, Reba, has been killed in a car accident."

He sat back, his eyebrows flying up. "Jesus. Aunt Reba?" That was— "Wait. What does the social worker have to do with anything?"

"Your cousin, Sophia. She's heading this direction. Partially because you're the only family that anyone knows of, and partially because we have room for her, and she identifies as queer."

Holy shit. His cousin. The last time he'd seen her she'd been...what? Five? "I—wow. Sophia. She's okay? She wasn't in the accident?"

"No. No, she was in school. I'm going to have her brought here, but I wasn't sure how you wanted to play it."

"Of course she can come here. I mean..." He pondered the

situation. "But I'm the trail boss, and the gather is coming up. I'll be out for two, three weeks before I'm back for the branding for a while."

"Well, we can give her a room here, let her be settled. I mean, you have room for her, but she can't be on her own for weeks at a time..." Ryder shrugged, wincing a bit. "Not that I'm telling you how to deal with your cousin."

"No, I would appreciate that. It could be super awkward until we get to know each other again. I haven't seen her since she was little." It was a bit embarrassing.

"That's fine. You two can spend time together, but she can be here in the main house with the other guys—we have Jaime and Bea here, and 'Lijah, of course. They're all her age." Ryder gave him a wry smile, shook his head. "I am sorry for your loss, Ames."

"Thank you." He felt stunned, kind of stuck to the chair. "I mean, Reba was...she was difficult for me. But I know she loved Sophie."

"Well, I know Sophie told them to get you, but she wasn't sure your last name, so they were having trouble." Ryder's eyebrow lifted and he shrugged. "She told the social worker there that you worked at a big gay ranch. Jennifer happened to talk to her because we place LGBTQ kids, and—guess what?"

"Wow. I'm glad I have a not-average first name." He really was. "When will she be here?" *Please say tomorrow. I need a minute to breathe.*

"She'll be in Albuquerque late tonight or early tomorrow morning. Someone is bringing her to Albuquerque, and then Jennifer will bring her to us. I don't know about probate or anything, though. Do you need a lawyer?"

"I guess? I mean, I can see my mom going to war over the house and land Reba had. Not over Sophie, but her stuff, since she's not of age. I would want her to have it or have the sale money." She deserved anything Reba had left her for college.

Ryder's nostrils flared. "Then we'll get you with Roger. He's on retainer. He'll make sure to arrange everything for her."

"Thank you. I'll pay you back."

"You will not." Ryder cut a hand through the air. "We do foster care here. We deal with this stuff so the families don't have to, you included. Now, once you get her moved in with you, then you can decide what to do about those kinds of bills, but this is what Kase and I do."

His cheeks heated some, but he was also proud to work for an outfit like this. "Then I'll help out in other ways, Boss. You have my word."

"Thank you. I'll have one of the rooms made up for her. Her paperwork, a couple of suitcases, and the girl herself will be in hand by this time tomorrow, at the latest."

"Okay." He nodded. Okay. He could clean up. Get some stuff together for her at the store. Eat something so he was less of a bear. And then be around when she got in. "Okay, that's doable."

"Take the rest of the day off. Take care of what you need to. The work will be here tomorrow."

"Thanks, Boss. I was ready to go have a shower."

"We'll call you if she should get here early."

"Thanks." His belly rumbled loud enough to hear.

"Nathan's in the main kitchen. He's always got food for people that stop in. He's testing hors d'oeuvres for the Fourth of July party."

"Oh, I won't bother him." He would give Ames a bowl of cereal. "I'm sure he's glad to see the last of me. I dared to ask him for a hamburger." He chuckled, shaking his head.

"He seems much happier now that he's in a commercial kitchen. There are brisket egg rolls that are the finest thing I've ever eaten." Ryder actually licked his lips. "But suit yourself."

"Yeah. I don't know, Boss. I think I really pissed him off.

And I thought I was being diplomatic." Not his strong suit, he guessed. "And I'm craving pizza or enchiladas."

"You might see what's in our kitchen then...did you guys fight in the camp?"

"No. Not really." He might as well come clean. "We disagreed about everything, Boss. Every damn thing. And then asked him to put something normal on the menu. Steak. A burger. Just one meal... So I got cereal, ham sandwiches, and burgers. For a week. With six chips or six tater tots."

Ryder fought his amusement with everything he had, Ames could tell. Truth be told, it was pretty damn funny, if it wasn't happening to him.

"Yeah." He rubbed the back of his neck. "I'll order a pizza. See if the kids up at the Slice will deliver."

"They should have someone on tonight."

"That's my thought too." But then he needed to shop— He guessed he could order some stuff off Amazon.

"Whatever you need, man." Ryder stood. "Get some rest and some food."

"Yeah. Will do." He climbed to his feet. "Thanks for all of this, Boss." He would have been in a world of hurt if this had happened, and he wasn't at this ranch, and he knew it.

"I really am sorry for your loss, and don't stress the chef. He's had a hard row to hoe, and he was very raw when you two met."

"Sure. I get that." And he did. He'd been licking his own wounds when he'd showed up at the Chiara place, and they'd been good enough to let him recover. So he would do the same favor for the chef.

He would simply leave the guy alone.

Chapter Six

"Hey, Nathan. Can you do me a favor?" Kase met him in the kitchen, where he was working on cinnamon rolls, since Miz Alba had asked for them with orange and a little anise... Which was an intriguing proposition.

"Sure. What's up?" He hummed, sprinkling dough with nuts.

"I need a brunch for a fifteen-year-old. Her mom was killed in a car accident a week and a half ago, she's been uprooted, and she's coming this morning with her social worker."

"Ouch. Well, I'm making cinnamon rolls. Is she a meateater?"

"She is. Bacon, sausage, eggs, midnight pancakes. At least that's what Jennifer said."

"No problem. How many people?" Breakfast was comfort food. "Is Nanette okay?"

She usually cooked for the main house. Not that he minded, of course he didn't. He loved brunch.

"Just me and Ryder the Grans. Oh, and Ames. This girl is

his cousin. She's going to stay with us until they get to know each other again." Kase gave him a wry grin. "Nanette is at the zoo with the homeschool kids and Wat."

"Oh, wow. That's cool." He almost managed not to smile. "Do you think bacon is okay with Ames? It might be too fancy. I can have bran flakes brought in from town."

Kase gave him a stare. "I think Ames would be pleased to have some bacon rather than cereal." Then he got another grin. "Legendary, but to be fair, he thought he was being diplomatic asking for one meal a week."

"Mmm." Nathan wasn't sure he was ready to give Ames that. "I'll make sure he has plenty of real food since there's a teenager involved."

And he was a chef. He didn't criticize the way Ames did his job. He didn't create food that was inaccessible, he wasn't a bitch about it, but dammit, he was a professional. He didn't intend to dumb down his fucking skills to make the lowest common denominator happy.

That was not what he'd been hired for.

He'd been asked to create nutritious food at a certain food cost. Bingo-bango.

Kase nodded easily. "Cool. I mean, it's brunch. But I appreciate you, man."

"Cinnamon rolls, bacon, eggs, and a fruit salad ought to be a comfort." And he had some amazing berries today. Perfectly ripe and begging to be used.

"That sounds amazing. And we're out of juice. I can make some if you want, but I'll need to borrow some oranges. We do have milk, if she likes." Kase sounded a little worried.

"I bet milk will be a comfort. I can make hot chocolate too. No problem. I'll do the juice. A nice pineapple-orange ought to be right." He frowned over, confused as hell. "Why are you out of juice? Do you need some?"

He had room in the budget for juice, for fuck's sake.

"Ryder drank the whole bottle of orange juice last night with some Sprite. He was up late doing paperwork. And no one has gotten to the store today."

He blinked. "I do the food ordering now. Y'all don't have to make emergency grocery runs."

"Oh." Kase stared, then laughed. "We're all getting used to you yet. You're damn efficient."

"I'm insanely talented that way. I have a database. You can totally send me a text—you, Ryder, the ladies—and I'll get you set up. I'm a machine." And he was so fucking bored.

Kase studied him. "Are you okay, Nathan? I know this is far from your dream job, but—"

"I'm fine," he cut Kase off. "Don't worry about me."

"Oh, man, I worry about everyone. I know what it's like to have a life change."

"Yeah." Nope. No breaking down and wallowing in Kase's sympathy. "I'm cooking at least. That's what I do."

"Sure. Sure. I'm not trying to pry. Anyway, she should be here in the next hour and a half. I'll text you when she gets in."

"I'm good with that." The timeline would be about perfect. "I'll get the cinnamon rolls done and sent up first."

"No worries. Alba will wait now until that girl gets here. She takes her foster granny duties seriously."

"Yeah." Poor kid. It sank in what Kase had said. "Tell Ames I'm sorry for his loss."

"Oh, I imagine you'll get the chance to tell him..." Kase lifted a hand and left him to it.

He drew in a deep breath, glancing at his dough. It needed another short rise. Half an hour in the proofing box once he rolled it. But that would time out right with everything else.

He started the bacon in the oven, then got to work on the fruit. He turned the music back on, singing along with his morning playlist before he started making juice.

When all was said and done, he had a hell of a feast, and he kept everything warm until Kase texted.

Sending help to carry everything

I'm ready.

He got trays together, making them pretty. He wanted to wow the kid and, if he was honest, he wanted Ames to be impressed too.

Two of the cowboys he wasn't sure he knew came in to lug trays, and it wasn't long before he was setting up on the huge dining table in the main house. He had to admit, it was a nice canvas for his food, and the way the grans exclaimed over it made him feel ten-feet tall and bulletproof.

Ames walked in as he put the finishing touches on the last tray. He wore dark jeans and a pressed white shirt, his hat in his hand. His boots had been shined, and he smelled like Old Spice.

Oh, someone was stressed as hell.

He walked over, offering Ames a nod and a hand. "I'm sorry for your loss."

"Thanks. Aunt Reba was...well, she tried to be kind to me." Ames's shoulders were up around his ears. Family relations could be a bear.

"Are you worried about your niece?"

"I haven't seen her since she was five. Shit, the last time I sent a card she was ten. Reba didn't want me around her kid, you know?"

"How old is she now?"

"Sixteen."

Nathan winced. That was a hard age to lose your mom. "I'm sorry. That so sucks."

"Yeah." Ames sighed. "This is amazing, man. Thank you.

She'll love this. Who wouldn't?" Ames studied the cinnamon rolls. "Do I smell orange?"

"Yes. Miss Alba wanted orange and anise. I kept it light, because I didn't want to be too much for any young taste buds."

"They smell amazing, dude." Ames's eyes glinted with humor. "Even my weak palate might be able to take them."

"Heaven forbid. I asked if you wanted bran cereal."

"However will I keep myself regular?"

There was a stir at the kitchen door, and it opened, Ryder stepping back to let someone in.

A solid teenager with bright pink hair and blue eyes matching Ames' walked in, arms wrapped around herself. When she saw Ames, she gasped and ran to him.

"Uncle A! Oh my God! I found you." She started sobbing, the poor baby falling apart.

Nathan backed away, nice and careful, allowing Ames to deal with that little girl and her grief. He could go make coffee.

"Hey. Hey, kiddo. Wow. Look at you." Ames stroked her hair. "I got you. I'm so sorry. I am."

She sniffled, her shoulders shaking. "I was so scared. I thought—I'm so glad you're here."

"Me too. I'm so glad you were so smart."

"She said I can stay here. I can, right? I don't want to be on my own yet."

Nathan's heart was breaking for her.

"Of course you can."

A woman walked into the kitchen, putting down a heavy tote bag. "Whew. You move fast, kid. What smells so amazing?"

"Jennifer, meet Nathan, our new chef. Nathan, this is the social worker, Jenn." Ryder waved them at each other. "You've met Ames, Jenn."

"Ah. And you're the one who started the foster training, right, Nathan?"

"I'm about three-quarters of the way through, ma'am." It was actually pretty interesting stuff, and he didn't mind doing it at all.

"Good deal. I'm glad to hear it." She gave the cinnamon rolls a peek. Maybe he should have baked more.

"Is that all for me?" Sophie asked, looking at the table past Ames.

"Well, for all of us to share, but you get to sample anything you want." Ames wrapped an arm around her and turned her. "Nathan cooked."

"It's gorgeous. Did you make the cinnamon rolls too?"

"Yes, ma'am. They're orange and anise. I hope you enjoy." It was the best thing he knew to do—deliver with the food.

"I will. I'm starving." She dried her eyes. "Wow. This place is huge. What do you do here, Uncle Ames?"

"I'm the trail boss. I take groups of guys out to work the cattle year 'round." Ames puffed up a little with pride.

"Oh, wow. So...are you never home then? I mean..."

"Sure he is, honey, but we'll make you a room here for when he's up pasture," Kase offered her a gentle smile. "That way you're not at his house all alone. Fair?"

"Uh-huh." She glanced at Ames. "You don't have a dog?"

"Not right now. I had an Aussie named Tinker, but she passed last year."

Sophie gasped. "Tinker? Like the elephant I had when I was little?"

"Yep. You know why she was named Tinker? Your elephant and my dog."

"No?" She bit her lip.

"That was our grandpa's nickname for our grandma."

"Really?"

"Yeah. I know you don't remember them, but I do, and it was so funny to hear him say, 'oh, Tinker...'."

"That's too cool." She seemed like she would cry again, so Nathan dished up a cinnamon roll on a little plate to hand her, then poured her some juice.

"Sugar helps when emotions are high."

"It so does." She took a big bite, her eyes widening. "Holy cow, this is the best."

"Thank you. I'm experimenting with the—"

All of the sudden she blinked and squealed. "OMG! I saw you on the Food Network!"

Nathan flushed. He was going to die. "Did you?"

"Yes! You were on that best chefs in the country thing. You got nominated for best restaurant, um, South? Southwest? I love food TV."

"Texas, and yes. Thank you. I was honored to be nominated." And glad, at this point, not to have won. He would be miserable if the reporters had all shown up asking how he felt about losing everything. Like a douche.

He just grinned, handing out plates to people.

The teenager kept stealing glances at him, really exploring her food, the knife cuts, the plating. She was a foodie, no doubt. And if she loved her food shows, maybe he could teach her a thing or—

Nope. Not his place. He wasn't here to mentor anyone. Cook his little food, wash his little dishes.

Save his pennies and find a way to get his restaurant back, dammit.

Chapter Seven

"Hey, kiddo. Do you like your room?" Ames wasn't quite sure if he should sit or stand.

Sophie sat on the couch in the family room up at the big ranch house, playing a game on one of the Nintendo Switches the bosses kept for the foster kids.

"Yeah...are you sure no one minds? I just showed up..." She wouldn't quite look at him.

"Hey." He sat at the other end of the couch, facing her. "No one minds. I'm so glad you came. I'm sorry about your momma."

"Yeah. She—She was awful mad at me when she drove off, but I promise to God I didn't mean for anything bad to happen."

"Oh, honey." Damn. Had they had a fight? "It's not your fault."

"I feel like it was. I—I don't want to be that person, you know? The one that started shit." Her cheeks were red as fire, and she wouldn't meet his eyes. "She caught me making out with a girl a few months ago, and it's been hard. I'm not sorry for doing it, but it sucked anyway."

His ears went hot. "I know how that feels, kiddo. That's one reason I left home."

"Did you get caught?"

"With a guy? No. There was no one brave enough to take a chance. But with a stash of magazines, yes."

"Oh." Her face worked. "I only wish we didn't fight right before—"

"I know." He scooted over to grab her in a hug. "I know. That has to feel awful. But you didn't do anything wrong."

She held onto him, crying hard, the sweet baby sobbing. He didn't try to stop her. She was hurting bad, and she needed a friend. She needed to let it out, too.

That pent-up stuff would kill you if you let it, and he knew it.

And hell, his mom and dad were still alive.

He didn't think he'd ever forgive them for not taking this little girl in, dammit. She'd needed them, and while it was hard to be queer in such a closed-off town, she could have at least graduated with her friends in a year and then struck out on her own.

She didn't need to feel alone in the world, even for a short time.

"I got you. Tomorrow you can come see your room at my house. After the paperwork is all fixed, you'll stay with me most of the time, but I'm about to go out for the gather, so you'll have the room here while I do."

She nodded. "Miz Alba said that there are other teenagers here, and that it's really open, so I can have this room for now too. They're scary nice. They're not like...in a cult or anything, right?"

"Nope." He laughed. "I mean, they're cowboy folks, but they're lesbians, their grandson is married to a man, they have a genderqueer great-grandchild who is in a long-term relationship with a lesbian, and this whole outfit is queer-friendly." And if they weren't, they moved on fast.

"Wow. You—you found the big gay ranch."

That tickled the hell out of him.

"I did." He chuckled, squeezing her before he sat back. "So can I play too?"

"There's another Switch. Have you played the food-making games?"

He raised an eyebrow. "No."

"They're cool. I'm super good at focusing."

"Yeah? Good for you. I'm willing to learn, fair enough?"

"Sure. It's cooperative, not competitive."

"Cool."

"The pizza one is the best. Go grab the other console so we can go to online gaming."

"Yes, ma'am," he teased.

She winked at him. "I know. I just... Everything feels weird. Like, what about my stuff? Do I get it?"

"As much of it as we can get." He feared the worst there. "You know my momma..."

Sophie wrinkled her nose. "Mean as a stepped-on rattlesnake."

"Yeah, but we have a lawyer. We're going to get your things. No matter what." If he had to go down there and fist-fight someone to do it.

"Okay. I mean, I don't want her to toss it or burn it or anything."

"Well, ideally, the lawyers will stop her from doing anything with your mom's house. Aunt Reba owned it, and I'm sure it's meant to go to you."

"Yeah. Yeah, I want to sell it, but the stuff in my room is mine, plus some things that were my daddy's..."

"Of course." Her dad had been good to her. When he'd

died in a bull riding accident, poor Sophie had been devastated. So young to have lost both her parents.

She queued up the game, and sure enough, it was about assembling food. Put down a pizza crust. Put sauce on it. Then cheese and toppings.

It was kind of soothing, actually.

"So Nathan is a famous chef, huh?"

"Yeah! Cool, huh? He had this crazy seasonal menu fusion thing going on—so like Japanese tacos or brisket and spaghetti."

"Mmm." He kept it noncommittal. He'd seen the brisket egg rolls. They'd seemed great, but he was still skeptical.

"I know it sounds weird, but everyone raved about it. He was charging like two hundred dollars a plate!"

"Wow." So what had happened? How had Nathan ended up here? "Did he own his own place?"

"I don't think anyone does, not really. It's like an investor thing?"

"Ah." Okay, so he could see that. So what had lost Nathan his investors. "Burning!"

"Oop!" She opened the fake oven, and they laughed loud, which brought dogs, as well as Dani and Nell, who were Ryder and Kase's adopted daughters.

"Whatcha playin'?" Nell asked.

"Who are you? You missed the zoo. It was so much fun. I saw zebras and giraffes!" Dani's eyes were lit up, and she waved at him. "Cowboy Ames."

"I'm Sophie. I'm Ames's cousin. I'm here to stay with him."

"Oh. Cool. Daddy says you're staying here too because Cowboy Ames is the trail boss. Do you know how to ride a horse? Do you go to school? Do you like to read? Do you know my best friend Naomi? She goes to school like 'Lijah."

Sweet Dani. She seemed so much younger than she was.

Sophie glanced at him, and he nodded and grinned, handing off his controller to Dani, who piled up next to Sophie.

"I don't know anyone here but my Uncle, I mean Cousin Ames. But I do know how to ride. My mom sold my pony when my dad died, though. Said she was dangerous."

"Oh. Weird. We have lots of horses and dogs and everything. You'll be fine. We're pretty nice."

Nell smiled at her. "You have pretty hairs."

"Oh, thanks." She blushed dark and ducked her head. She rubbed one of the dogs' ears, and that puppy laid his head on Sophie's knee.

"We have good dogs," Dani said.

"You do." Sophie sniffed. "Sorry."

Nell's chin wobbled. No one cried alone around here. "Do you miss your momma? We miss ours. She had cancer."

"Mine was in a car accident. She died last week."

Nell threw herself in Sophie's arms. "Oh, poor girl! I'll be your friend forever!"

"Okay." Sophie sniffled harder, and they were crying together then while Dani frowned and tried to keep the pizza from burning on-screen.

So Ames took over the other controller and helped her.

Dani rolled her eyes, but she didn't say anything to the girls. She simply said, "Open the oven! The oven!"

"On it." He found the button for the oven, and they played until Nanette came to offer all the girls a snack. It was good timing, too. Brunch had been several hours ago.

"You okay, Ames?" Sophie asked.

"Uh-huh. I have to meet with the first wave of guys going out on the gather this evening, but otherwise I'm all yours until day after tomorrow. Want to play cards later?" Would she like cards? Their family had always played, but she'd been so young when he left.

"Okay. I know Uno and Skip-Bo. What else do you know?" Sophie tried to smooth her makeup. "Do I look okay?"

"You're fine."

She wiped her nose on her sleeve. "Do we go to the kitchen?"

"Uh-huh." Nell grabbed her hand. "Come on."

"I'll be right there." He took the Switch from Dani and put them both up to charge. Elijah was in the kitchen when he got there, spreading peanut butter on graham crackers and studying Sophie out of the corner of his eyes.

"You the new girl?"

"Yeah."

"I'm Ryder and Kase's son. You're Ames's niece?"

Sophie shook her head. "Cousin. But I call him Uncle."

"Wow." Elijah glanced at him. "I thought you were way old, Ames."

"Thanks, buddy. I'm thirty. She's sixteen. My mom was the older sister and had me at nineteen. Her mom was the younger and had her at twenty-eight."

"Huh." Elijah shrugged. "Want peanut butter crackers?"

"Sure. Soph?"

"Why not?" She shrugged, trying to smile. "This house is huge. How many people live here?"

"The grans, the dads, me and my sisters, you, and we have two fosters right now, but we can take ten at a time." Elijah didn't even blink.

"Whoa."

"Yeah. Apparently, the grans always hoped Dad's parents would have like, eighty kids."

He didn't have the heart to tell her that old adobes like this one seemed to grow, all of their own accord. Families in this part of the country tended to live with several generations in one house still.

"Are they nice?" Sophia asked.

"Who, the grans? Oh my God. Granny Chiara can be stern, but she's really a softy, and Granny Alba is like, something out of the best movie." He chuckled, shook his head. "Gram can make anything—clothes, food, blankets—and Nanette is like a kitchen witch. She runs the house here."

"This is a big place..." Sophie sounded more than a little scared.

"It is, but you get used to it. And Bea and Jamie are in the same bedroom wing you're in."

"They're at the school still. Softball practice. Are you a homeschool or a public-school person?"

"There's a choice?"

"Well, you got to go to school..." 'Lijah teased, "but yeah."

"Oh. Well, I went to public school." Sophie made a face. "It was hard."

"Wat isn't a breeze. Dani has to work as hard as I do."

"No, I mean people didn't like me. I did pretty good with classes."

"Ah. Well, screw them. We have assholes, but they tend to be few and far between." He handed out the crackers.

"Cool."

Ames poured himself a cup of coffee from the late afternoon pot and sat, waiting them out. It was good to let Elijah carry the conversation.

He didn't know what to say to a teenager who had just lost her mom. Who had lost her home.

She was reeling. Hurting. And he was about to leave for almost two weeks. But then he would make it up to her.

God, he felt like a bad man, a terrible uncle, a shitty human being.

Then Sophie gave him a slight smile while brushing peanut butter off her upper lip, and he felt better. She had a place thanks to him. She was safe. She'd put herself out there and found him. And he was proud of her.

She'd done so well.

She was a good kid.

She needed a place to lick her wounds and breathe, and he was going to give it to her. Or at least he was going to do the very best he could.

Chapter Eight

Every single time Nathan went outside, the new teenager was there.

Reading a cookbook.

Working in the herb garden.

Helping the cowboys unload the supplies.

Finally, he wore down, and he went to the picnic table and sat across from her. "Hey, you. You okay?"

"Uh-huh." She gave him an uncertain little smile. "How are you?"

"Good. So..." What do you want seemed rough. "Talk to me."

She took a deep breath. "Can you teach me to cook? I mean, I've been cooking for myself for a long time, and I've watched food shows and tried recipes I found online..."

Like he had time for that. Still... "What's your favorite thing to cook?"

How mean could he be to this lost kid?

Her eyes lit up. Her eyes were the same blue as Ames's. "So far? I've had to stick to stuff we had in the house, but I make a great kitchen sink pasta. And a good mac and cheese. Oh! And I made really good deep-dish pizza."

In other words, they had a lot of dried pasta, flour, and jarred red sauce. He remembered those days.

"All right. Come in and make the two of us lunch. I'm not judging, this isn't a competition. I simply want to see where you are. Fair?"

"Okay." She bit her lower lip, but he saw when she decided to take the bull by the horns and go for it. She hopped up to follow him into the kitchen. "What am I not allowed to touch?"

"This is my knife kit; it's off-limits. Also, let's avoid the mandolin, please." He didn't want to explain a lost fingertip.

"Okay. And that stuff is for supper?"

"Yep."

"Got it." She nodded, then grabbed an apron to tie it on. Then it was a little like watching *Chopped*.

He sat and watched her. Her knife cuts weren't amazing, and she needed to learn patience, but she had a decent palate, and she wasn't scared of spices.

When she served him his lunch, he had a creditable stir fry with sesame noodles, and he ate all of it.

"Okay. You're hired after school."

"Yeah?" She beamed at him.

"And over the summer, if you want. We have a big client for the Fourth of July party, so..."

"We do? Who is it?" She forked up the last of her noodles, slurping hard.

"Stefano Abruzzi. He's a journalist for a biggie-wow magazine and the bosses are worried." He wasn't worried.

"Wow. That's scary. Are you scared?"

"Are you kidding? I have a budget, a plan, and three hundred people to feed." He was terrified.

"Oh. Well, I can help." She perked up. "So can Uncle Ames. He'll be back by then."

He bit back a groan. "No, that's okay."

The last thing he needed was to serve grape jelly meatballs and pigs in a blanket.

Although...

Hrm...

He could totally serve elevated country finger food. Take the boy out of Texas, but not the Texas out of the boy, so to speak. He could make a going thing out of that for the fancy magazine guy, and the ranch folks would love it too.

"Mr. Greene? Chef? Are you okay?"

"Huh? Yes. Yes, you gave me a great idea. Tomorrow, bring in a notebook and a pen, also, closed-toe shoes, hmm?"

"Oui, Chef." She bounced and, thank God, she managed to run off without hugging him. That might have been one nicey-nice too many.

And now he had to start on supper for some hungry cowboys. He was lucky that Ames was out on the trail. Not a hamburger in sight.

In fact, tonight they were going to try moussaka. He thought the guys would like it.

He wouldn't warn them about the eggplant until after they'd eaten it. If they pressed him, well, he could say it was a ground beef casserole.

He grinned at the thought. It was a hoot, in fact. He would love to rub Ames's nose in that.

God, what was wrong with him? Seriously? One little pissy, I-don't-like-your-food comment, and he was going to be a bitch forever?

Really?

Nathan was going to have to have some thoughts about that, because that felt super fucking vindictive, and he wasn't.

He was a reasonable type. Nuturing-ish. Sort of logical.

So if that was the case, it had to be Ames. The man had an incredible effect on him. Like matches and gasoline. But why? Lots of people had been way meaner about his food. Hell, Ames had said he liked it. He'd wanted something more pedestrian once or twice a week. So why was it so annoying?

God, maybe he needed to call his therapist.

He was not going to be a bitch, and especially not to that little girl who wanted to cook.

Oh.

Cooking.

She needed knives, an apron. Was there a way to get those out here in twenty-four hours? If not, they could plan and work on egg cookery.

Scrambled eggs first. Then fried.

Ooh...ramen. They could so make ramen for tomorrow.

He wandered off, humming under his breath.

Noodles made everything better.

AMES FELT LIKE HE'D BEEN ON THE TRAIL FOR TWO years, not two weeks.

Little Danny Maines had broken his leg on the first day out, and they'd had to airlift him from a flat spot on one of the pastures.

They found a small herd of wild horses in with one of the groups of cattle, so it had taken them an extra damn day to sort those out and make sure they hadn't killed any calves.

And he'd been worried as hell about Sophie. He knew she wasn't alone, but he'd still hated leaving her and going off where he could only be reached by sat phone for a damn fortnight.

He headed in from the barns, wanting to get Sophie, take a shower, and then drive into town for Mexican food.

He was starving.

He popped into the main house, coming face-to-face with the housekeeper, Nanette. "Good afternoon, ma'am. I'm hunting for Sophie."

"She's working in the kitchen, Señor Ames."

"In the kitchen?" He was in the kitchen. So what the heck did Nanette mean?

"With Señor Nathan."

"What?" Working? What the fuck? She was just a kid.

Nanette nodded. "She's working hard. She made biscuits for breakfast this morning, I hear."

"I—Okay. Thank you, ma'am." He wasn't going to growl at Nanette. Not her fault. Nathan? Was going to get an earful.

He stormed out of the house and headed for the commercial kitchen, putting his feet down hard. This was the second time he'd gotten home wanting to relax and eat and Nathan had interfered...

Okay, so Nathan had nothing to do with the last one, but this time, he was smack in the middle.

The kitchen door opened, and Sophie ran out the big door. "Ames! Hey! How are you?"

"Hey, kiddo." He held out his arms and she hugged him, grinning hard. "I was looking for you."

"Yeah? I was making some tortillas."

"Why?" He shook his head when she frowned. "I mean, yay, but you know you don't have to work to earn your keep."

"Huh? Chef Nathan is offering to teach me! Like for free! He bought me knives and an apron, and a copy of his favorite cookbook, too. He says I have a great palate, and that I'm a natural."

"Oh." Well, shit. She was wreathed in smiles. "You get along with him?"

"He's so nice. He doesn't fuss at me when I mess up, and

he tries all my food. This is... I never ever thought I'd be doing this *now*."

"Wow." He bit back all his protests, because she was so excited, and if Nathan was good to her, what could he say? "You got time to go to supper with me tonight?"

"Of course! Yes. Chef said to go on and spend time with you. I—I made biscuits this morning. Want to come try one? I saved it for you."

"I do." He would brave the chef's den for her and hope his ass didn't get kicked out.

"Chef! Chef, can I fix Ames a biscuit?"

"Oui, Sophie, tu peux."

"Merci, Chef."

Okay, this was weird.

Nathan nodded to him, knife sliding through bell peppers that sure looked burned. "Have a seat. How was the drive?"

"Long and dusty." He perched on a stool at the non-business side of the through bar.

"It's getting warm, hmm?" Nathan passed him a cold bottle of lemonade from a huge fridge.

"It is. But we did pretty well. Not much loss this year." Were they having a conversation? Did three or four sentences make an actual talk?

"Excellent." The knife started moving again, almost flying.

He watched, fascinated, as Nathan chopped while Sophie put him together a plate. Surely he wasn't letting her do...that.

"Do you want butter, whipped honey butter, butter and jam?"

"Honey butter, thanks." That sounded amazing.

"Cool! I can do that." She seemed so happy. "We ran out of gravy."

"Mmm. But now you know how to make it."

"Yes, Chef. I can totally do it. It's so good, too."

"Yay." This was the weirdest fucking situation ever. He

took the plate Sophie handed him, having a big bite of biscuit. "Oh, yum." It was flaky and a touch salty.

She actually bounced. "That's right. Yum. Go team me."

"You're amazing, kiddo. I'm proud of you."

Nathan gave him an approving glance over Sophie's head, the first he'd ever seen from the guy.

"Thanks. Chef Nathan is teaching me so much. I'm going to be in charge of one of the apps for the Fourth of July party."

"Wow. That's really cool, kiddo." He would have to talk to Nathan about that in private. She needed to be able to be a kid and enjoy the party.

"Better than." She beamed at him. "Is there anything you need from me, Chef?"

"No. Not at all. You go hang out with your family."

"Thanks!" Sophie was all smiles. "I'll see you in the morning."

"Whenever you have the time and inclination, Soph."

Sophie nodded, then came to take his hand. "You got it, Chef. You need a shower, Ames."

"I do. I thought we'd go up to my house. You can check out your room there and tell me what all you need. I can take a shower, and then we can go get pizza or Mexican food."

"Yum." She laughed. "Chef is being so nice. I know I'm probably a pain, but I want to learn all sorts of stuff."

"So, you—is he paying you?"

"Huh? No. Nope, he talked to the Chiaras, and they talked to Mr. Wat. Chef says that I have a lot of time to do this for money, but learning is great. So I keep records of how many hours I'm in the kitchen, and Chef tells the skills I've worked on, and I get school credit."

"Oh." Well, that was good, right? Really good. And that made him feel better about the whole thing. Now he felt like he needed to thank the guy.

"Right? Like I told you, he says that I show promise, and that I've got a good palate. Can you believe it? He bought me a knife kit of my own! Like a real chef. They're expensive and so cool!"

"That's super kind of him. I wouldn't think he had it in him."

"What? He's amazing. Seriously, Ames. You would like him. He makes these brisket tacos with yuzu that are amazing."

"He and I didn't hit it off too well, kiddo. I think he'd rather not like me." He led her to his truck.

"Oh, yeah. I mean, you mean the camping thing. He was so scared. I heard him talking to Mr. Wat."

"He was scared?" Ames blinked. He'd sure never let on. Not once.

"He'd never seen a horse up close before. He's never even had a cat or a dog or *anything*."

"Oh, man." Shit. He'd known Nathan had never ridden, but damn.

"I know, right? It's, like, insane, but he grew up in a little apartment in Austin, and it wasn't an option."

"I gotta admit, I feel bad now." They headed to his place, and he was pondering his next move with Nathan. Apologize? Let it go and be nicer? Go on like before?

"Don't be. He's cool. I want to get him a kitten or something."

"A kitten? On a ranch? Nah. We'll get him a dog." A purse dog. With a bow.

"Okay! That would rock. Thanks!" She hopped into his truck.

He chuckled. Lord have mercy. "So what's your feeling on pan pizza?"

"Pan pizza rocks my world. Can we have sausage on it?"

"We can." He grinned. This kid got him. "And they have this salad wagon..." Man, he could murder that.

"Oh, yum. Mom hated salad." Her chin quivered a moment. "So I always got the salad bar at The Chuck Wagon."

The Wagon was their hometown's answer to a sit-down restaurant.

"Well, then, we'll have pizza and salad, and you can tell me all about your time here. Are you settled at the main house?"

"Yes, sir. It's nice. There are two other teenagers besides 'Lijah. We're all friends. So, am I going to have two rooms? Am I going to be alone when you're gone now?" She sounded worried, but she was trying not to be.

"Ryder and Kase and I agree that your room at their house is yours. When I'm on the trail, you'll stay with them. And there might be times when you stay down there when I'm home, because of late hours at the branding or something." She needed to comfy and confident.

"Is that...selfish?"

"What?"

"Well, to have two rooms when there are kids here that have nothing? I mean, I see how hard everyone works..."

"I think it's fine as long as the room is available." He glanced at her sideways. "And you help out, right?"

"Oh sure. Dani and Nell think they're keeping me company, but really, I watch them for Nanette sometimes." She shrugged and smiled. "And Charlie shows me all sorts of weird things I can do. She's home for, like, two months, and then she's moving to Albuquerque. She's going to UNM. Cool, huh?"

"It is. She's a good kid." He could remember that Charlie had given Kase and Ryder a few worries, but she seemed to be on the right track now. He was glad Sophie liked her.

"Yeah. I'm going to culinary school. I'm going to make it

happen. I'm going to be a chef and own my own restaurant one day."

"What kind of restaurant?" The drive to his place didn't take long. His was one of about seven houses at the edge of the ranch before the road curved into town. Two bedrooms, two baths, and a bonus room he used as a gym right now…

"Honestly? I'm thinking upscale comfort food—so biscuits and gravy, but with amazing ingredients and fancy sausages."

"Nice. I can see that." Someplace not here, anyway.

"Yeah. Or maybe green chile sausages… I wonder if Chef would let me do that."

"I'm sure he would. You mean, like, grind sausage meat?" His dad was a hunter; he'd taught Ames how to do that.

"Yeah. I mean, yeah. I would so try…"

"I can help to begin with, and then Chef Nathan can streamline it with you, if you want. I have a hand grinder."

"Oh yeah? For real?" She grinned at him. "Cool. I want to be able to experiment, huh?"

"Yes. We'll get some pork shoulder and some good fat at the store. And I have green chile out my wazoo in the freezer, already roasted."

"You rock. Thanks." She grinned at him, and he felt like he might be on the right track.

"Thanks, kiddo." He pulled into the cool little tract of houses, all with three- or four-acre yards. Well, not lawns. Cactus and scrub and a garden… "So this is my place back here. Our place."

"Oh. It's pretty! You need roses and an herb garden, okay?"

"We can work on it this summer." He had places to put stuff like that. He'd never had a reason to bother. And he'd have to make it puppy-proof if he was getting one for Nathan… And for him.

"Oh, cool! I'd love that. I mean, it's totally sweet that you're letting me in."

"Hey, it gives me a reason to do stuff. The yard is terrifying," he teased. "Tumbleweed city."

"Yeah, but things will grow, right? I mean, growing things are good."

"They will. We get water and fertilizer to roses, and they'll thrive. The herbs we'll do in raised beds." Their granny had loved gardening, so it felt nice to do this with Sophie.

"Yeah? I'm so in. I want to make this a little more home and less 'I'm a big single guy'."

"Cool." He laughed. "Come on. Your room, huh?" He led her in, showing her the neat, if dusty, main room and kitchen, the dining nook and hall bath. "This is your room, kiddo."

It wasn't fancy, but it was a blank slate for her to decorate as she wanted.

She wandered around, eyes a little misty. "Can I have my things from my house?"

"You can." Dammit, he was going to get them. The boss said the lawyer had waded in, arms swinging.

"Oh, you rock. I was...there's special stuff, you know? Those were my things. No one else's." Her eyes filled with tears.

"I know. And you need that stuff." In fact, he would see about driving up to get her stuff as soon as he could. He'd call the lawyer tomorrow. "Do you have...anyone important you'd like to talk to in person?"

She pinked and shrugged. "We chat. She's in Ruidoso. We met in church camp."

They shared a knowing glance, because that could be damn tough for people like them.

"Ah. Well, cool. You let me know if you need to talk." He wasn't wordy guy, but for her, he would do it. He'd wished so many times to have someone to just ask shit.

"Can she come visit maybe? Like before school starts?"

"If her folks say yes, and I'm home, I don't see why not."

"Okay, cool." She tested the bed. "I mean, I can see why you wouldn't want to put that on the big house."

"Yep. You're my cousin."

"I am. I'm like your...orphan?" She rolled her eyes. "Little Orphan Sophie."

"Well, maybe? I mean, what does that make me? The weird gay cousin who disappeared one day, and they find him buried in the garden?"

"Ooh...that would be very Wednesday Addams of you."

"Thank you. I like her better than Pugsley." He grinned. "I'm gonna go de-stink. There's a big screen and a Switch in the front room."

"I'm gonna go see where I might want to put the herb garden." She shrugged, the move well-and-often practiced. "And I want to snoop. It's a thing."

"You got it. Snoop away." He winked, then headed for his bedroom. He was pretty much an open book.

This day had been—well, more confusing and off-putting than he'd expected. Hell, he hadn't expected it to be any of that, to be honest.

He scrubbed up pretty quick, got dressed, and grabbed his wallet. "Pizza time!"

"Cool. I'm ready." Her eyes reflected the blue of her tank top.

He paused, so proud of her it hurt. "You're a good egg, kiddo."

"I'm trying. I keep trying hard, you know?" Her lips tightened, quivering.

"I know. It's tough, and I'm sorry." He offered a hug, and she took it. Then he guided her back out to the truck. "Less stinky?"

"Much, thank God." She winked at him. "I mean, whoa, horsey."

"Yeah. Well, I spent more time with horses and cows on the trail than I did people."

"Of course. It's a big herd, huh?"

"It is. And it's not even the largest share of what we do on this ranch." Ames shook his head in admiration. "This is a damn big outfit. I love it. It's a challenge."

"So...how did you end up here? I mean, did they advertise 'big gay ranch' in the cowboy newspaper or something?"

"Or something. I got my ass handed to me at a ranch about an hour north. Some guy took exception to my choice of reading material. Which he had to sneak into my bag to find." Man, that had sucked. "Anyway, a day laborer there told me I might like the company here better, and the Chiaras took me right in, bruises and all."

"That's cool and it sucks, all at the same time." She sighed and shook her head. "I mean, will people always be assholes?"

"I think some of them will. It's already better than when I was your age." Sometimes. Sometimes it got scary, but she knew that. He didn't need to tell her.

"Yeah. And maybe in a hundred years it'll be better again, huh?"

A hundred years. Christ.

"I sure hope so, kiddo. I mean, I hate the idea of fighting the same battles over and over again, but as a species, we sure do that." Good thing they also made things like pan pizza. Buttery, crunchy goodness.

"Right. But there's also super crazy delicious food and music and stuff."

"Exactly." Great minds thought alike.

"I'm glad you're back from the gather, Ames." She grinned over at him as they made their way back to the road into town.

"Me too, kiddo. Me too."

Chapter Nine

Nathan finished his work week, which was Friday's midday meal, and then he headed toward his baby tiny house.

He was exhausted, all the way to the bone, and he was going to take a long, cold shower, and then crash and burn like a crashing, burning thing.

Jesus, some days were harder than others. He'd done all the inventory and ordering, made up a million box lunches, cooked two breakfast shifts, and taught the little bit to make pain perdu before she'd gone to a little summer school catch-up at Wat's.

He stumbled to the kitchen door of his house, and he almost let out a girlish shriek when someone stepped up next to him. He barely managed to hold it in.

Sophie's cousin, Ames, appeared like a ghost, big and tall and rustic.

"Shit!" He stumbled, bouncing against the door hard enough to jostle himself and rattle his teeth.

"Whoa. Whoa, sorry." Ames caught him as he staggered, holding him up. "Sorry. I didn't mean to startle you. I saw you head out, and I wanted to talk for a sec. Then I'll let you have your downtime."

"Oh. Sure. Sure, you want to come in?" The sun was blazing down, and, while he wasn't hot, it was drying him out from the outside in.

Ames gave him a searching type of once-over, then nodded. "Sure. Thanks. I appreciate it. Man, you look a little peaked."

"Just need some water." He smiled, hoping it seemed honest. "Still grappling with the lack of humidity."

"Crap. I bet you are. You gotta love a swamp cooler then, huh?"

"Yes. Yeah—I'd never seen such a thing before, but it's amazing." He headed for the fridge and a pitcher of icy water with lemon and ginger steeped in. "Would you like a glass?"

"I would, thanks." Ames leaned on the wee kitchen counter. "Anyway, I wanted to thank you for teaching Sophie about cooking. She's really into it, and it's been an amazing distraction for her."

"She's a crazy cool kid, and she's got real talent. I think it's one of a chef's biggest responsibilities—mentoring." He grabbed two glasses and the ice trays out of the freezer. "She seems to be calming down, especially now that her things are here."

Sophie had told him how much of a drama that had been —how Ames's mother had tried to steal the girl's things, the house. It sounded like drama to the nth degree.

"She is. That was a battle and a half." Ames's mouth flattened into a straight line. "My mother is a hard woman."

"I'm sorry. Mine had been—not mean, just desperate." He frowned at himself. *Shut up, man.*

"About what?" Ames sat down in one of the two chairs he'd squeezed into the kitchenette.

"Hmm? Oh, she worked three jobs, had three kids in a

one-bedroom kind of thing." He'd been dirt poor, but he hadn't been miserable. Austin was a great place to grow up.

"Ah. Hardscrabble. I get that." Ames gave him a remembering kind of smile. "I was lucky that way. We didn't have a pot to piss in, but we had some land and a lot of family."

"We were in the city, so we had kids to play with." It hadn't been a miserable life; it had been hard.

Ames hooted, a sound that made him smile with how wry it was. "My older cousins and I spent a lot of time poking each other with cattle prods. They weren't terribly fond, but that was okay. I had the animals."

They'd played with toys they'd dumpster dived for, and there were always tons of them.

"Anyway," Ames took the glass Nathan handed him. "It means a lot that you're willing to help her out, and I apologize for being such an ass your first week here."

"No problem. I wasn't at my best." He still wasn't at his best, to be honest, but he was better.

"You having an easier time?"

"Tired." He was drooping.

"Oh, shit." Ames drank part of his drink. "I'll get out of your hair."

"You want to sit? I have two chairs." He didn't mind company. He only wanted to sit on his ass.

"Sure. I would love that." Ames moved with him to the other room, sitting opposite him.

He was embarrassed that he didn't have his old condo, his art, but it was all gone to pay creditors. All of it.

Ames didn't seem to notice. He sipped his water, then hummed. "I really like the lemon and..."

"Ginger."

"Nice touch."

"Thanks. I find it...comforting?"

"Sure. I can see that." Ames glanced around. "Are you

okay with this? The tiny home thing? There are other options."

"This comes with the job."

"I guess it does." Ames studied him again. "Do you want something to eat?"

He sighed and shook his head, his cheeks heating. "I was considering ordering onion rings and green chile and pepperoni pizza."

"No shit?" Ames eyes went wide. "I mean, you wanna? Sophie is going out with Elijah and his friend Sean and Sean's mom after the makeup session is over today."

"God, yes. Sometimes I want to eat something someone else made." And he didn't want to think. He wanted something greasy and spicy and crunchy.

"I bet." Ames grinned. "I was going to offer to make one of my few specialties. Pancakes. But pizza is always a good option. And onion rings? Oh yeah."

"I love them." He hated frying them, and he was supposed to be super-duper healthy chef man right now, but he wanted them today.

"Cool. You want me to order? I know all the delivery kids."

"Hell, yeah. I'm in. Do they just come in, or do I have to meet them somewhere?"

"They'll come to the ranch. I'll tell them which house you are. They all know how to get in the gate."

He chuckled. "You're a handy guy."

"I try." Ames shot him a look. "Do I get to tease you about trashy food?"

"Sure. I won't listen, though."

"Of course not." Ames chuckled. "That's okay. Sophie cooked chicken cordon bleu for me last night. It was good. You're great with her, did I mention?"

"She's a sweetheart, and she's been dealt a couple vicious blows." And he loved people who loved food.

Ames nodded, his expression serious. "I'm sorry her momma died, but I'll be honest. She's better off out of that place." He pulled out his phone, calling in their pizza order.

Ouch.

That sucked.

Sophie didn't say much about her past or her mother, so he didn't push either. It seemed the best.

"Pizza procured. And onion rings." Ames winked, his smile easier than Nathan had ever seen, he thought. "So did you really never have a pet?"

"What?" He grinned and shrugged one shoulder, not sure where Ames would have heard that. Still, it was true. "I didn't. We didn't have the money or the room, then I was in college, and then I was working sixteen hours a day."

And drinking and fucking around for ninety percent of the rest, if he were honest.

"That's wild to me. I mean, not the working. Just...kids without pets. I'm so damn country, I guess." Ames made a wry face. "We made pets out of everything."

"We had pet rocks. No shit. Mom glued googly eyes on them." His had been named Oscar.

"Easy care, huh?" Ames shrugged. "A busy mom. I can see it."

He nodded. "We did fine. We were all creative."

Stacey had her MFA in ceramics, Olivia played violin in a symphony in Oregon, and he cooked.

"I bet. You put stuff together I've never even heard of. And that's not an insult."

"Fusion isn't hip right now, but there's something about the balance that does it for me." And it was fun—cooking, putting flavors and experiences together for diners.

"I'm trying to be more open, if nothing else for Sophie's

sake. Your food is good, man. I've never been all that adventurous." Ames seemed so much more...relaxed. It was interesting.

"I get that. My pride was hurt." And he was still hurt—it was improving, but it still hurt. This wasn't what he was meant to be doing. This wasn't his calling.

Thank God that the Chiaras seemed to understand, that they really tried to let him be himself, or he'd shatter.

"I'm sorry for that."

He chewed his lower lip for a moment. "It wasn't just you."

"I wondered about that. I mean, you're an award-winning chef according to Sophie. I decided you had to be licking some wounds." Ames gave him a steady stare. "This is a good place for it."

"It is what it is. I had a restaurant I loved. It's gone, and I'm here. There's a learning curve." Altitude was a thing. Hell, water boiled at one hundred and ninety-five degrees here.

"I'm sorry." Ames seemed sincere, so he was going to take it at face value.

"Me too. Thank you for letting Sophie experience her passion." That was important. Even if Sophie didn't become a chef, that didn't matter. The passion mattered.

"I'm not gonna tell her no on anything that's reasonable. On the other hand, if she starts doing stuff that puts her in danger." That got him a glinting grin. "Now, she is a teenager. She might rebound and become stupid anytime."

Hell, teenagers did come in size stupid more often than not, so he got that.

"Oh, I do understand that on a personal level, and I have the feeling, Mr. Paulson, that you do too." He'd, in fact, had a ton of stupid human tricks under his belt.

"Oh, I do." Ames laughed, the sound merry as hell. "I was not even a teenager when I did a lot of my shit."

"Early bloomer, were you? Well, damn. I was in a kitchen

at thirteen, and I grew up there." He winked, drinking down another water. "Did you know you can't deep-fry a shirt?"

"Nope. I know eggs will explode." Ames leaned forward. "What happens to the shirt?"

He threw his hands up, dramatic as all get out. "Nothing! I was so damn disappointed. Spaghetti noodles curl up, though. Totally cool."

"Oh, I'll have to try that with Sophie." Ames laughed again, and they chatted until the pizza came, which Ames got up to pay for.

He was feeling better, too. Less exhausted. Happier.

He would put in for his half, no problem. "Do you want some remoulade to dip your onion rings?"

"Now that I've heard of but never tried. Sure. I've never been a ketchup guy. Ranch, yes? Mostly chipotle ranch."

"Spicy!" He winked. He got that. He was a Texan, after all. "I make a wasabi ranch that is amazing."

Especially on a spicy tuna taco...

"I like wasabi."

"You eat sushi?"

"When I get to Santa Fe or Albuquerque, yeah. We don't really even have grocery store sushi up here." Ames opened the pizza box and grabbed a slice.

"No? That's wild. I've made it a few times. I'm no master, but I can make a hand roll." He put a bowl of remoulade down between them. "But like pizza, I'd rather eat it out."

The onion rings were still hot, still crispy, and he might have moaned over the first bite. Loud.

"I get that. It's like there are certain things that you can't make taste the same at home, right?"

"That's it." He dipped an onion ring. Still holding up even though they'd traveled. Amazing. "And then there's the whole standing over the fryer. That's one of my least favorite things."

"Just too hot, or is it the burning?" Ames licked at the sauce. "That's nice."

"Thanks. It's one of my favorite dips." He licked his fingers clean. "It's the smell of the hot oil. So greasy and sweaty, you know?"

"I do. I feel that way about branding season, not to put you off your food. The smell is intense, and all I can smell for weeks is that."

"Oh, gross. Burned hair is the worst. The absolute worst!" He got that. There was stuff that happened in the creation of a job that sucked.

"But this pizza is exceptional tonight."

It really was. The green chile was spicy, the pepperoni a little greasy; it was amazing.

"It's perfect. Just what I was craving." The camaraderie was even better. He wasn't used to being alone all the time. He was grateful Ames had decided to bury the hatchet, at least for now. That way he had company for a meal.

"Yeah. Yeah, I think so too. I do love a green chile pizza." Ames grinned at him. "I didn't think you were going to be nice."

"Ditto." He sighed. "But we decided to try."

"We did. I like it."

Oh. Oh, good. "Well, me too."

Ames dipped another onion ring. "This was a great idea, man."

"Yes." He was enjoying this a lot, and that was weird. "So, do you work on the weekends?"

"Depends on who's on vacation. Usually not, but the guys all get family time off, and I'll fill in here and there. As a rule the newest guys work weekends with someone on call to help out."

"Ah, but you have a family now, hmm? You'll be having those times off too?"

"I guess?" Ames blinked at that. "I mean, it will only be a few years before she goes off to school." Ames shrugged. "And Kase and Ryder love her already, so she can stay with them anytime. But I would like to take her somewhere on vacation."

"Oh, cool." He loved traveling, and he'd be willing to do that again soon. Maybe in five years or so. He hadn't done it in a long time... "Where would you go?"

"Someplace foodie but west... San Francisco, maybe? Portland or Seattle?" Ames shrugged. "I'd love to take her to Texas, but—"

"Yeah. I get you."

"It'll be good, I hope."

"I bet. I have some thoughts about Seattle." Nathan said.

"You do?" Ames gave him an encouraging glance. "I'm down for the help."

"Cool. She'll love Pike's Place market."

"That's the place with the fish tossing?" Ames asked.

"You have no idea..."

Chapter Ten

"Ames!" Sophie came pelting across the drive from the big house, the rainbow laces in her sneakers flopping.

"Hey, kiddo. Don't hurt yourself."

"Sorry!" She skidded to a halt. "You remember that thing you asked me to ask Kase last week?"

"Uh-huh." He was not going to let the summer go by without getting a dog, and he really did want to get one for Nathan, who was turning out to be a decent type. So he'd asked Sophie to talk to Kase about who might have some puppies up in their neck of the woods.

"He had a friend who has border collie bloodhound mixes."

"No shit?" That was a mix and a half.

"Nope. Says when they're twelve weeks, they'll be ready to go to homes, and he would want the shots covered."

"That's exceptional kiddo. I'll talk to him in the morning."

"Cool." She twirled.

"You about ready for the big Fourth thing?" It was less than a week away.

"I am! I've practiced all the things. Brisket sliders with homemade pickles. Tex-Mex eggrolls. And artichoke and mushroom tostadas."

"Wow. That sounds amazing." He tried not to lift his arm and sniff his pit. He'd worked his ass off in the heat all day.

"Thanks. Do you want to come to dinner with me and Nathan tonight?"

"Uh…" That caught him flat-footed. "Sure. I need a shower."

"Cool. Can we cook at your house?"

"Our house," he reminded her, gently.

"Right. Can we cook at our house?" She wrinkled her nose. "His kitchen sucks. I saw it through the door."

"Through the door?" he asked.

She nodded. "He says that it's not really cool to have a teenager in his space, just the two of us. He says this way, there's no chance of impropriety."

"Of course." Nathan had no real kitchen or dining room to speak of. And Nathan had never been to their house. "You gonna show him how to get there?"

"Uh-huh. And help him carry food. He shopped a lot."

"Ooooh." He chuckled. "Okay. I'll make sure we didn't leave a ton of clothes on the washer in the kitchen."

"You rock. Thanks. You want—half an hour?" She was beaming at him.

"I do. I really need to scrub myself up."

"That's cool." She grabbed his arms and jumped up and down.

He wondered if he'd ever been that energetic.

"We're going to get a puppy!" she whispered. "I'm so excited!"

"Are you now? Are you still going to be excited when you're cleaning up poop every day?"

"Uh-huh. Because loving on it will be amazing."

"I'm looking forward to it too. It's been a while. Okay, I'll go clean up. You two come on." Anticipation curled in him. He was getting to like when he was able to spend time with Nathan.

It was fucking weird, how fascinating the chef was. Maybe it was how kind he was to Sophie. Maybe it was the sadness in Nathan's weird light brown eyes. Maybe it was the way he wielded that big knife.

That was oddly hot.

He raised his hand when Kase waved at him, nodding when Kase made the call-me motion with his hand to his ear. So he dialed Kase when he got in the truck.

"Hey."

"Hey, Boss. I hear you have a line on puppies."

"I do. What happens if Nathan leaves without it?"

"Then I take both of them. I love dogs."

"Fair enough. You want males or females—they have three of each available."

"One of each." He would see which one appealed more to Sophie. He liked both, though his last dog had been a female. But that way there wouldn't be too much rivalry. And he'd get them fixed.

"I'm on it. She was over the moon. You're a brave man, Ames."

"Don't I know it?"

"You decide Greene isn't out to starve you to death?" Kase teased.

"I did. We called a truce, and I bought him a pizza."

"Ah, good choice. Glad to hear it. Sophie is fond."

"She is," Ames agreed. "They're cooking me supper."

"Oh, that's cool. I'm jealous. I hear Sophie's perfecting chicken katsu."

"Chicken what?"

"Fried chicken with rice and this soy and ketchup-y sauce. I had it in Hawai'i. So tasty. You'll like it."

"Cool. I love fried chicken." And he was learning to love Nathan's weird sauces. "Thanks, Boss. For everything."

"You got it," Kase said, laughing. "Go get clean."

"God, yes." He smelled like death walking, and he headed home, tickled as shit.

He'd actually hired one of the cowboy's partners to clean the house every other Friday, so the place was sparkly. He managed to jump in the shower and get clean, redressed, and pour himself a Coke before Nathan pulled up in his little red SUV.

"Ames! We're heeeeereeee!" Sophie laughed, carrying a bunch of grocery bags up to the kitchen.

"Let me have those. Nathan, you need help?"

"Just hold the door?"

"You know it. Come on in." He took Sophie's bags and let her get the door for Nathan, so he would feel safe and welcome.

"Thanks! Happy Friday." Nathan seemed easier in his skin this Friday, casual and simple in jeans and a Led Zeppelin T-shirt, the bags under his eyes lessened. Ames'd bet his bottom dollar someone had snuck in a nap.

"You too, man. I'm glad to have the weekend off." He was gonna sleep all day tomorrow. Okay, not really, but he did think he was gonna be a bum and potter around the house and maybe watch movies. He'd make pancakes for breakfast.

"Me too. I'm thinking about running to the farmer's market. It seems promising, if small." Nathan grinned. "I'm craving fresh tomatoes, radishes, and I need some seeds for sprouting."

"This time of year, there's a great bunch of fruit and veg at the market in town."

"Can we go, Ames?"

"Sure, kiddo. The best time is pretty early, maybe seven-thirty, eight?" Ames poked through bags. There were chicken breasts, Panko, soy sauce, cabbage, sesame seeds…ooh, ice cream.

He did love ice cream.

He grinned. "Fridge or freezer?" It depended on the plan for the ice cream, really. Milkshakes could be fridge.

"Is there room in the fridge? This is a rock from being in the deep freeze."

"Yep." He and Sophie ate with the cowboys a lot. They also ate a lot of pancakes and such. They only got enough fresh fruit and veg that wouldn't go bad in a week.

"Excellent. How goes it, man? Good week?" Nathan carefully organized his groceries, acting as if this was important, something worthy.

"Not bad at all. It was hot out there, but we got a lot done. How are you doing?" He watched, fascinated, Nathan's hands pulling his gaze.

"Good. We're ramping up for the party. Sophie had a couple of ideas she's running point on."

"She told me. I like the sound of the eggrolls."

"Yeah. She got the idea from some old menus I had, but she's totally putting her spin on it."

"I am. I'm going to make them tomorrow. And maybe three or four or five more times before the party…" Sophie gave him a half-grin.

"Practice makes perfect." Ames had to laugh. "And I'll eat any and all attempts."

"All right. Mise en place, first, hmm?" Nathan smiled at Sophie. "Are you doing proteins and sauces or sides?"

"Sauces and sides! I want you to do the protein."

"I'm on the chicken then. Go ahead and start putting your cabbage slaw together. Don't forget to taste."

"Yes, Chef!"

He watched Sophie shred cabbage and carrots, chopping a jalapeno superfine and making a dressing of rice wine vinegar, soy, sesame oil, and sesame seeds. The last thing she added was green onions. He was super impressed.

"That smells amazing," he told her. He couldn't believe how they moved around the kitchen, working together like they'd been doing it for years.

Nathan was banging on chicken breasts, heating oil, creating these little stations with flour, milk, egg, and breadcrumbs.

"So where did you learn to make katsu? Is that how you say it?"

"It is." Nathan shrugged. "I had a friend who was part Japanese. He taught me. It's so crispy. Just totally yummy." He got a bright grin. "For me? It's the sauce. I love this sauce."

"Tell me about it." He wanted to hear Nathan talk food.

"It's sweet and savory—think a Japanese barbecue sauce. There's a ton of umami in it. It's good on pork, chicken, shrimp." Nathan put rice in a bowl and ran water in it and left it on the counter.

"What does that do to the rice?"

"Sophie?"

"Oh, Nathan told me rice is gross. It can have arsenic, even! So you always soak it and then rinse it until it runs clean."

Nathan nodded. "It also helps to make it fluffy. It's nicer all over."

"Huh. I had no idea about the rice. I usually microwave a bag."

"Heathen." Nathan winked at him, that smile so damn surprising. Nathan's smile lines were hot.

"Yeah, yeah, yeah—Have you ever smelled burned rice?"

Nathan's laughter filled the room. "A thousand times, buddy. Get you a microwave cooker—cheap and easy."

"Okay. We can do that, huh. Sophie?"

"Yep. Nathan showed me on Amazon."

"Cool. We'll grab one then."

"I told him about the gross Spanish rice."

Ames groaned. "I have no food secrets. That stuff was foul."

"Yeah. Sophie knows how to make a tomato-based rice, and we'll work on an annatto-based one as well."

"With peas and carrots, like Tequila's," Sophie said.

"Cool. You know I love that." He could watch Nathan cook all damn day. It was kinda nuts, how fast his opinion of the guy had shifted.

It was the confidence. He'd thought it was arrogance, but now he thought it was passion, confidence, and joy.

This man knew what he was doing, and he loved it.

"Here, Ames. Stir." Sophie handed him the slaw and some tongs, and he stirred while she made sauce. It felt very much like a family night meal, all of them working together, which was so rare for him.

The rice was started, the chicken went into one of the bowls, and he went to turn on some music and set the table.

"Can I ask a question?" Sophie asked. "Why... I mean, this is like a family. This is like what people want. How come I didn't have it?"

Damn. That broke his heart. He glanced at Nathan, who was suddenly busy with chicken, head down.

"Your mom had it rough growing up. I think... Maybe if your dad had lived, she might have been happier. And you might have. But she was really unhappy, and it's hard to share yourself when you're like that, kiddo."

And his mom was heartless—he didn't understand why, and maybe it didn't matter, but it was the truth, so...

"It makes me angry." She glanced at Nathan. "What about you?"

"My mom passed away—heart attack—but I have two sisters that I adore."

Sophie pelted Nathan with questions about his sisters while Ames tried to process all this. He felt awful for Sophie. He felt like he should have checked on her over the years, but he'd been wrapped up in his own shit. And there was no way he could have gone back to that crappy little town. Just no way.

Recriminations did no good. It was what it was, but he was in her life now, and he intended to see her through school and into adulthood. Then he would still be there whenever she needed him.

He was her family, and she was his, dammit, and he owed her a little happiness.

"What was your jam in school, Ames?"

"Huh?" He realized the conversation had shifted without him when Nathan asked that. "Uh. Sports."

"What about school subjects?" Sophie demanded.

"History, actually. I loved the Wild West."

"History is cool. I like English. Chef?"

"I did best in languages, believe it or not."

"Which ones?"

"French and Spanish. I knew those were the language of food and the language of line cooks."

"You were focused at an early age."

"I was," Nathan agreed. "I mean, so were you."

"Oh yeah. I never wanted to be anything but a cowboy."

"I knew I wanted to be a chef. I wanted to run a restaurant." Nathan shrugged. "It's a calling."

"So is that what you're saving up to do again?" Sophie asked.

Ames waited, curious to hear the answer and surprised at how grumpy the idea of Nathan leaving made him.

"Well, I'm a restaurant chef. So I want a place—maybe

nothing the size of what I had, but something where I can do my food. It's going to take me time, though, to save up enough to get financing."

"This is a good place to lick your wounds."

Nathan nodded. "I feel like I'm starting to get a rhythm. I mean, some days are long, but the guys are decent about everything." Nathan grinned at him. "And the weekends off are stellar. Stellar."

Sophie cracked up. "But you took other days off, didn't you?"

"I didn't feel like I ever got time off, kiddo."

"Owning a business is tough," Ames told her. "Ryder and Kase hardly ever got time off back in the day. Now they've learned to hire more managers."

"Yeah, and it's a labor of love. I was doing it with the guy I thought I was going to marry, but...well, it didn't work out."

"The guy?"

"Yeah. The guy, the restaurant, the guy and the restaurant..."

There was a story there, and Ames wanted to ask, but he wouldn't do it in front of Sophie. Maybe someday soon over a beer.

"You were going to get married?" Sophie asked. "Wow."

"Uh-huh. It didn't happen." Nathan got a pan set up for the chicken.

"I'm sorry. I mean, obviously he wasn't right for you, because...right?"

Nathan snorted. "He is an asshole. Not right for me. Not at all."

"Ouch." Ames shook his head. "Well, I guess if you hit the bottom, up is your only direction."

"That's what they tell me." There was that smile again—a little wry, a little bittersweet, a lot wicked. "It's over. Now I have a new adventure going for me. I can ride a horse, sort of."

"You should take lessons with me," Sophie said. "I would love to teach you stuff too."

"Aw, thanks. Maybe I will."

Ames thought that maybe he ought to do the teaching. He'd started the whole thing after all, hadn't he?

"We could all go on a nice, gentle trail ride if you want. Get you more used to it." He grinned, challenging Nathan with his eyes.

"Yeah... I did sort of do a trial by fire." Nathan shook his head. "I swear to God, I thought I was going to die that first night. I laid in the bed and cried like a baby."

"You never let on, though. I gotta give you that."

"I could barely walk, and then I had to cook."

Ames chuckled. "Welcome to the world of cowboys, man. We all lie in bed and cry like babies some nights."

But at least they had someone to cook for them, he guessed.

"I'm not sure I'm cowboy material, but everyone has been kind about the food, really."

"It's so good," Sophie said. "I mean really."

"She's right." Ames was big enough to admit it. "And you even made burgers the other day."

"I did, and they were amazing, right Sophie?"

"God yes. Fried egg, brioche bun, bacon. Uhn."

Nathan cracked up, and Ames had to smile too.

"I was all over that." He set the slaw aside, and clearly it met Sophie's approval because she stuck it in the fridge.

"Kase says we're allowed one unhealthy meal per week, so —" Nathan winked at him.

"Ah. Well, then. I vote for spaghetti and meatballs soon. With garlic bread." He gave Nathan his best butter-won't-melt-in-my-mouth expression.

"Sure. I love to make pasta. I bet albondigas with a nice pasta and tomato salsa with green chile would be amazing..."

"Oh. Oh, Chef!" Sophie bounced on her toes. "Chef, you could put it in an arepa!"

"Oh—good suggestion! Do you think there should be cheese?"

"Cotija? Queso fresco?"

Oh, God help him. He'd have to get that from the pizza place, he guessed.

"Maybe a bit of both, hrm? Good thoughts. You should write it out, and we'll do some testing."

Sophie was glowing. "Thanks, Chef."

"So is that the recipe process?" Ames asked.

"You mean, brainstorm, write it, test it, re-write it? Yes."

"That's wild." Ames tasted the sauce from the spoon Sophie handed him.

"Wow. Do you ever just experiment?"

Nathan chuckled softly. "Every meal. Every single one. I'm learning so much being here."

"Neat." He breathed deep. "Man, I'm hungry."

"It's close. Finish up the sauce, Sophie."

From there, dinner came together fast. Fluffy rice, golden-brown chicken, slaw, and sauce.

He was drooling for it.

And it was so good. Crunchy chicken with a bite, the slaw spicy but also cooling, the rice taking everything down a notch...

It was perfect.

And he let them know. "You two are amazing. This is the best meal I've had in ages. Thank you." Ames patted his belly to help emphasize his words.

"And we're going to have milkshakes later!" Sophie grinned and motioned toward the living room. "Want to watch a movie?"

"I'll wash up while you guys go sit and find something, if

you want." He had a dishwasher they hardly ever used. "I promise not to mess with your knives."

"We'll clean those first, right, Soph?"

"It'll go fastest with all of us anyway. That's the best."

And suddenly they were cleaning up the kitchen and laughing and Ames was soaring. This was...well, it was warm, happy, and he wanted to kiss Nathan.

Badly.

What the fuck was wrong with him? Had he had a stroke over supper?

He glanced at Nathan. No, that wasn't fair. Neither of them had been willing to bend when they met, but they were getting to know each other. And God knew Ames was gay. Like rainbow flag-waving glory hallelujah gay.

"Okay, let's cool off and sit, and then we'll do milkshakes." Ames led them to the living room, and everyone had sat down when a knock came to the door.

"I'll get it." Sophie hopped up, and a couple of teenagers were at the threshold, giggles sounding. There was a muffled conversation, and Sophie called out, "Ames, is it okay if I go to the big house to go swimming?"

"Of course it is, kiddo. Thanks for supper."

"Let me go get my bag!" She raced back to her room.

Nathan met his gaze and whispered, "That's super good, isn't it?"

"Crazy good. This is the first time. It's about time that she feels good enough to go out. She's so much more confident. A lot of that is down to you."

"Ha." Nathan scoffed. "You're the one who's given her a solid base. A home she can count on. It's way easier to feel like you're on an even keel when you have someone at your back."

He nodded. "That's your problem right now, huh? You lost the floor right out from under you." He wasn't being a dick; he thought it was so obvious to him at this point.

"Like you can't imagine, man." Nathan's words stopped short as Sophie came back in.

"I have my phone! I'll call if I'm later than ten?"

"That works for me, kiddo. Have fun." He waited for her to leave, then texted Kase and Ryder.

> the kids are all coming to swim. did they clear that with you?

> Totally. They're having a party—music, Cokes, tacos, no booze.

> Good deal. Call me if I need to come get Sophie

He tossed his phone on the table. "Does this mean we get more ice cream?"

"Absolutely. Everything good? Is it okay if I stay, or would you rather I head out?"

"Oh, man, don't leave me alone and worrying about the girl." He winked. "I'm not scared she'll do anything stupid, just that she'll get wigged-out and need me to come get her. It only takes one weird comment or bad memory."

"Yes. She's got some healing to do, but you're helping. It takes time, though, you know?"

"It does." He sat back, not really watching the movie that was starting. "It took me a long time to settle once I left home. I started out shy, then I went to fighting, and then I finally decided I could be me." Ames waved a hand. "This place had a lot to do with that."

"Kase and Ryder are stunning men. Honestly, I love how giving they are. They make me tired, with how busy they can be."

"Yeah." But Ames wanted to know what had happened to Nathan. "Do you mind if I'm nosy?"

Nathan glanced at him sideways. "I'll tell you if I do mind."

"What happened with your restaurant? And your ex, I guess. They seem all tied up."

"They were." Nathan shrugged and sighed, and it was a sad, soft sound. "It's all out there in the public. My ex—boyfriend-slash-fiancé, not husband, thank God—was my business partner, and he embezzled from our investors. Think in the millions, not the thousands. I ended up having to sell everything and pay back what I could. It was an embarrassment and a disaster."

"Shit, man. You didn't take him to court?"

"No. My whole financial life was tied up with that crap. I would have been the one to end up in jail, knowing my luck. It caught me totally flat-footed."

"So you took the first job that came along?"

"No one wanted me. He's already with another chef in Houston. I went with the job that had room and board, freedom, privacy, and that wasn't in fine dining. I needed a fresh start."

Oh.

Oh, that didn't sound as bad, did it?

"I think that sounds really smart, man. Get out, really get some new experience and perspective." He was being all rah-rah cheerleader, but Nathan seemed like he needed it.

"Yes. I needed a new mindset. New folks to feed. New kitchen. New challenges. Even the budgeting part of this is different." Nathan met his eyes, cheeks bright red. "I know that I'm not everyone's cup of tea, but I'm trying to experiment, show folks new things, right?"

"You are. And the guys are into it." He grinned. "I mean, a few of them are still carting cans of beanie weenies up to the trail, but that's just stubborn tradition."

Nathan snorted. "You mean you?"

"Nope. Not even when I was schlepping turkey and chips."

Nathan rolled his eyes. "Yeah. Hurt feelings. Hurt pride. I just—all I have are my skills. I have no Michelin stars, no good reputation, no restaurant. I'm a little tender, I guess."

"You have a right to be." He could be the one to give some. He'd worked out his tenderness already. Mostly. He had his cowboy pride, but really, Nathan had given as good as he got.

Ames could respect that all to hell.

"Do you play cards? This movie is boring as all get out." Ames didn't want tonight to end, not yet.

"I do. I can play pretty much anything you throw at me..." Nathan's expression went tickled like he had a feather up his butt. "I love games. What's your poison?"

"For two people? Cribbage or Skip-Bo. Or I have backgammon if you want a board and dice game." He beamed. For the most part, the other cowboys liked poker. He was more of an old fuddy-duddy game man.

"Oh, God. I haven't played backgammon in eons. Do you mind if we play that? I used to love it. I played with this Scottish guy in culinary school."

A tiny spurt of what had to be jealousy went through him. Ames would tuck that away for later when he was alone. No need to examine that now. "Let me get the board out. I love backgammon too, man. The guys all want to play cards, though."

"Is that weird? You being the boss?"

"When we're on the trail, no. Here at the ranch, yeah. I don't live in the bunkhouse, so it's odd if I invade their space."

"Yeah, okay. I can see that," Nathan admitted. "I have to say that it's a tad strange staying in the little house there by the kitchen. Not awful. I'm not complaining."

Nathan's eyes went wide, as if he had surprised himself by admitting maybe something that was a touch too personal.

That was odd given what they had just talked about, all the weirdness with Nathan's ex and everything but, still he supposed that was normal. After all, this was here, and everything that had happened before at least to Ames was like some story, something totally intangible, that he had no real connection to.

"Nobody said you were complaining. It's okay. This isn't going to get to the bosses or anything."

He wasn't a snitch, and besides folks got to bitch about things. It was part of life. If everything was hunky-dory they wouldn't call it work.

"Right, right." Nathan kind of chuckled a little bit. "Okay, cool. I mean, there's nothing wrong with the little house. It's just..." Nathan rolled his eyes. "You have to understand. This condo that I had in Austin, it was like one of those weird architectural magazine kind of things, you know, super glass and formal and fancy and..." He sighed. "Not really weird, but if you came in the front door, you sure weren't going to touch anything, and I *lived* there."

"Was it like a museum?"

"More like a showroom. The ex wanted to be sure anyone who came to see us got a distinct impression."

Ames glanced around at his well-worn couch and his weird old 1940s coffee table that he'd refinished. "Yeah, I wonder what my house says? Early American junkyard?"

"Cool. Well, let me start by saying you have an amazing kitchen. Especially for someone who obviously doesn't cook. I absolutely love it."

Ames almost popped off with a sarcastic, "Thanks," but he didn't get a chance.

"It is totally ergonomic, easy to cook in, clean. I approve." Nathan searched around the house like he was seeing it for the first time.

Really? They'd been in the front room for, what? Almost

an hour and the kitchen was the only thing that Nathan had actually seen?

Ames wasn't sure if that was weird or wonderful.

It was probably odd.

"I don't think that your house says junkyard. I think it says home. I mean, it could use a little color maybe? Like, I could see if you wanted to paint a wall bright red or purple. That would rock, but really, this is just...like a house that's a place where people live and are happy." Nathan blinked, then rolled his eyes. "I mean, you are happy here, right?"

That was sort of a personal question.

"I'd say I'm...content. It's been nice to have Sophie so I'm not rattling around by myself." Cowboys were cowboys, gay or straight. He thought about how nice it would be to have a family. A lot. It didn't seem to be in the cards.

"I bet. She's an amazing kid. I can see why you'd like that. I've never lived alone before."

Surely Nathan was exaggerating. "Never?"

"Nope." Nathan's cheeks went rosy. "I moved from home with sibs to roommate after roommate to live-in boyfriends. It wasn't on purpose. It simply happened that way."

Wow. No wonder the tiny house seemed strange. For some damn reason, it quivered on the edge of his tongue to tell Nathan he could crash on the couch anytime he got lonely or freaked out by himself, but he stopped it. Ames figured that was something else he would have to tuck away to glare at later.

He got the board set up, handing Nathan his dice.

No thinking. It was time to play.

Chapter Eleven

"Come on, Sophie, get it together."

Nathan knew how hard this was. This was the first time the teenager had dealt with wait staff who had worked with other chefs in a commercial kitchen space. Had dealt with the fact that there were at least twenty-five million people out there who were eating like they'd never been served a meal in their entire lives.

The kitchen brigade was refilling plates as fast as they could, and still the wait staff was coming back with, "The bosses say we need more food."

They'd served the egg rolls, the brisket nachos. The shrimp. The chicken. The ceviche. The meatballs.

It wasn't going to be long before they were reduced to cheese on Ritz crackers. Not even good cheese.

Not even pimento cheese.

Just like processed cheese food out of a plastic wrapper slapped on it.

No, not even Ritz crackers. Saltines.

Plastic cheese, saltines, and, if the sons of bitches were lucky, an olive.

"I'm sorry, it's just everything is moving so fast." Sophie was trying, but there had been more than one round of tears already. And Nathan was losing his patience.

Nathan took a deep breath. Let it out. Then he took another one. Just to be, you know, sure nothing that was going to come out of his mouth would get him fired, get him beat up or get him put on the Gordon Ramsay scale of asshole. "You're fine, girl. Just breathe. You've got this. We got to find something to make more food out of."

"Right. Okay. Yes."

Luckily there were cowboys out manning the grills, so there were burgers. There were hot dogs. There were ribs. There was sausage. All of the main food had been taken care of and the sides were on the buffet line.

The problem was the VIPs.

Somehow, a small VIP section of ten to fifteen had become a gigantic VIP section of anywhere between seventy-five and seven hundred thousand, and they were trying to make up the difference.

God help him if one of the bosses walked in right now.

"We've got chicken breasts thawed. There's hamburger meat. There's steak. We've got peppers, onions, some kind of a fajita thing, maybe?" Sophie offered.

"For an appetizer, okay, okay, thank you. That's not bad, Sophie. That's not bad." He closed his eyes. Okay, fajitas. *Fajitas appetizer. Think man. Think fajita appetizer. Could you make fajitas on a stick?*

Sophie's fingers flew on her phone. "Do we have potatoes? There's a recipe here for fajita potato bites. Or fajita-filled wontons."

"Oh! We have wonton skins. Okay. Prep mode. You chop onions and peppers. I'll run the chicken out to the guys on the grill. It will be done in a flash out there."

Ames chose that moment to poke his head through the

door. "What can I do to help?" He wore a bandana under his hat to catch sweat because he'd been on grill duty.

"Oh, thank God." Nathan threw his arms up in the air. "You are a savior. Chicken. I need chicken fajita meat, and I need it now."

He grabbed the wrapped-up container of meat and shoved it at Ames. "You'll be my hero if you can get this to me. I swear we are completely in the weeds."

Sophie nodded. "Yeah, Uncle. Like, totally in the weeds."

It tickled Nathan to death that Sophie was calling Ames "uncle" even though they were cousins.

She'd explained that saying cousin sounded kind of weird and a little slang. And what did she call it? Sketch.

It was sketch.

Still, it made Nathan happy.

Whatever, it made Ames over the moon.

And that didn't matter right now.

"Fajita chicken. All right, girl. Peppers and onions. Peppers and onions." He had to think of a thing for the cheese and the toppings. Oh, maybe a cup with all of the accoutrements together. Like the cheese, the guacamole, sour cream and the salsa all whipped up like a dip.

A dip.

All right, praise Jesus. He had this.

They were going to survive this, and if they didn't, he was going to kill somebody.

And he was going to start with Ryder.

"Hand me the fajita seasoning," Ames said.

Nathan picked up the industrial bottle of mixed spices and tossed it at the back door. Ames caught it deftly and disappeared.

He grabbed wonton skins out of the big fridge, then started whipping up dip. He added some ranch powder to the sour cream, cheese, tomatoes, black olives and salsa. These folks loved their ranch as much as Texans did.

Woo. That was money.

He checked on Sophie's knife cuts, then peeked out the door to make sure Ames was seasoning the meat. The man had it under control, so he went back to the rest of his prep. No sense opening wontons yet.

Okay, next they could send out grilled pineapple, shrimp, and a nice bite of ham. It wasn't top-shelf, but it was food. Season it with a touch of brown sugar and mustard to make a sweet and sour, and boom. Tropical yum.

Ames came back in right about the perfect time, the tray of perfectly grilled chicken enough to put a grin on his face. "Good deal."

"You need me to help cut or wrap?" Ames offered.

"It's probably cooler out there than it is in here," Nathan warned.

"I can drink Gatorade. They don't need me out there, but you look like you do."

"Do I?" He snorted. Because it was one hundred percent true. This party was kicking his butt.

He was used to doing one hundred and twenty covers a night, not a buffet for twelve thousand one hundred and sixty-seven people.

That sort of thing sucked.

"It would rock if you could help. Sophie, show him how we want these things cut, would you? I'm gonna start skewering."

They got to work and, along with the other two people they had helping, they managed to bust out some more appetizers.

After the last set of hors d'ouvres went out, and he could hear the buffet line really getting started, he slumped against the counter for a second, breathing. Thank God all of the desserts were coming from some bakery in town that needed a boost.

He could make a cookie, but he was no pastry chef.

"Thanks for your help." He nodded, heading to the refrigerator to pass out another round of Gatorade.

He promised himself a glass of wine after this was done.

And not some shitty house wine they were serving out there, either.

No.

He wanted something full and round, something that he could drink the entire bottle, nice and slow for the rest of the night, possibly while soaking in his nonexistent bathtub because he didn't have one of those.

Ames glanced at him. "I see the smoke coming out of your ears."

"Yeah, I was wishing for a hot tub or a bathtub. Or any tub later. I might go get one and put my feet in it and pretend."

"Hey, if that's what you're after, I got a hot tub." Ames's expression stayed completely unreadable as he made the offer. "You're welcome to come soak if you need to."

Oh, wow. Okay. "Can I bring a bottle of wine?"

"If you want that instead of beer? Yeah. Because that's all I've got. Trust me, once the VIPs leave, you'll be glad you're not down here near the bunkhouse. You can crash on my couch."

"Yeah? Does it get rowdy?"

Ames made a face. "It stays pretty family friendly, but it gets loud and there are a lot of big booms."

"I will absolutely, positively provide the wine." Ames had a hot tub. Nathan thought maybe there really was a God, and maybe that God didn't hate him. "Do you really have a hot tub?"

"I really have a hot tub." Ames shot him a shit-eating grin.

"The bosses got, like, this crazy deal from this company that was going out of business. I swear to you, we are the hot tubbingest place on earth."

"You are aware you live in the desert, right?"

Ames's lips quirked, like he was fighting the world's biggest grin, before shooting back with, "You do understand how the whole water reclamation cycle works, don't you?"

Nathan gave up, like surrendered with his belly up in the air. Arguing didn't matter. He didn't give a shit. "I will bring wine and food if you need me to bring some."

"There's plenty of food, and I think that I have cheesecake..."

Oh, fuck him. Wine and cheesecake. "I'll bring an overnight bag. I really appreciate this."

Sophie stared at them both for a second, then she rolled her eyes. "I'm staying here. We're having a party. Remember Uncle Ames?"

"I remember."

"Good, because I don't want anything to do with something that involves wine, cheesecake, two hairy old men, and a hot tub."

"Whoa. Whoa." He held up his hands. "I am not hairy."

Sophie started to giggle. "Yes, Chef."

He stared at Ames. "Did you hear her call me hairy?"

Ames crossed his arms over his chest and leaned, tilting his head and giving him the hairy eyeball. "Is this where I say yes, Chef?"

"I'm gonna kick all y'all's asses."

Ames chuckled. "You're gonna try. Okay, what is it you call it? Brigade. What are we doing next? Clean-up?"

"We need to make sure the runners keep the buffet filled." He jerked his head at the big fridge. "Luckily, everyone is eating mains off the grill, and we have cold sides for both the VIPs and the family and cowboys."

"And we clean up, right, guys?" Sophie said to the two kids who had been a godsend this whole time.

"Damn right we do," one of the kids grinned at him, looking like a monkey the way his teeth stuck out. Adorable. "The bosses said that we get twenty dollars an hour. Twenty dollars an hour! We're saving up for a truck. We need that money."

Nathan thought this was a great idea—this whole him not having to participate in the cleaning up part. "Sounds good, guys. Sophie, you'll make sure that everything gets put back in the place where it needs to go?"

While this wasn't part of her job, it was an important part of learning about how a kitchen should be left at the end of the day. Not that he didn't trust her. This girl was as into this as he ever had been, and she made him proud.

That he could be called her mentor.

"Yes, Chef, I've got it. I know this." She glanced at Ames. "Just so that we're clear, I'm staying here at the main house tonight."

Ames nodded. "Yes. No drinking. No smoking. Nothing that could get me in trouble with the bosses."

"Uncle!" She gave him a glare that, if it hadn't been so quick, would have seemed like an affectation. "I am not a screwup. I have the sense God gave a goat."

It took everything Nathan had not to laugh. There was no way that he would hurt her feelings by doing so, but God, he wanted to.

He hadn't been around teenagers since he'd been one, and they were fascinating with the way their moods changed on a dime. They had the passion of adulthood, and the delicacy of a child, and he was fascinated.

He understood why Ryder and Kase did this, now. He got it. Teenagers were wild and weird and uncomfortable and odd, but really freaking cool.

Especially Sophie. Sophie was the most special.

Ames nodded. "Good deal. I'll be down here in the morning to deliver doughnuts. Kase ordered a whole truckload of them for all of us for all the work we put in today. So I'll pick you up then."

"Okay." She grinned. "Do you want me to clean your knives, Chef?"

"I'll do that right now. You take care of yours."

"Yessir." She saluted, and he washed up while Ames helped the other kids send out one more tray full of potato salad and coleslaw, as well as the grilled corn and avocado salad and New Mexican pasta salad for the VIPs.

"All set," he told Ames when his knives were back in their case.

"Go grab an overnight bag and your wine, then. My truck is over in the overflow parking."

"Are you sure I'm not keeping you from the party?" It seemed only polite to ask, but if Ames cancelled on him, he might hit the man in the nose.

Not too hard. Not hard enough to bruise. Just enough.

Hard enough to sting. Bad.

"Go get your bag, asshole." Ames chuckled and shook his head. "We're gonna bubble."

"I like to bubble."

His little house was literally a dozen steps away from the kitchen. So he hurried over, threw some swim trunks, a pair of shorts, and a T-shirt in his bag along with deodorant, a toothbrush, and a hair brush, just in case.

He probably wasn't going to spend the night, but he might. Surely Ames would let him borrow a towel.

Nathan found two good bottles of wine, the box of rose chocolate and passion fruit truffles, plus a bag of Doritos and the cheesecake.

Sometimes it was good to have a snack stash.

He headed over to find Ames at his truck, and it was wild the number of vehicles that were here. This place was as packed as any county fair. In fact, speaking of county fairs, was that a Ferris wheel?

Did Fourth of July parties have a Ferris wheel?

He gaped, kind of wandering, and he bounced off the bumper of a vehicle, damn near going ass over teakettle before Ames grabbed him by the arm. "You okay?"

"Is that a Ferris wheel?"

"Yes." Ames stared at him like a goat looking at a new fence. "They do have Ferris wheels in Austin, don't they?"

"Well, not as a rule, no, but that's not the point. This is not a county fair. This is a ranch's Fourth of July party."

"It's a big ranch."

He stopped, stared at Ames. "Yes, Cowboy, I know. I feed y'all every goddamn day. That doesn't mean that, by definition, there has to be a Ferris wheel."

"Do you need to eat? Maybe you're just too hot. We're very close to the sun here, way closer than in Austin. Get in the truck." Ames felt of his forehead.

Nathan thought about that pop to the nose, and then thought no.

Hot tub.

This man had a hot tub.

Seemed like every cowboy in New Mexico had his own personal hot tub.

He didn't even have a bathtub, but he wasn't a cowboy. He was a cook.

But he wanted in the bubbles.

So he got in the truck.

Ames eased out, making sure not to mow down any of the huge number of people milling about, and Nathan breathed a sigh of relief when they left the busy part of the ranch behind, heading up to Ames's house. They parked out by the kitchen door, and he peered around, trying to spot the hot tub.

"It's out by the bedroom part of the patio. The backyard needs some work, but that area I sank some time into."

"Oh, cool." Did he have to go through the bedroom? Was that weird?

"Come on in. I'm gonna go start the hot tub warming while you get changed. The ensuite's right through there."

"Listen to you, ensuite, very fancy." Of course, when he went in through the door that Ames pointed him through, it actually was elaborate for a cowboy bathroom.

Incredibly adorable.

There was a glass enclosed shower. There was a double sink vanity, and there was a claw-foot tub, as well as an antique radiator underneath a towel bar. This thing was charming as hell, and possibly the size of his little house.

Nathan decided that he wouldn't be jealous.

He also decided that if at any time he got the offer to come over and bathe in the claw-foot tub, he was going to say yes.

Not that those sorts of offers seemed to be a thing, but should they occur? His answer would be yes.

He stripped down into his swim trunks and a T-shirt before padding out. He wasn't sure if he was supposed to take a bath towel, or if he should have brought his own towel, or if there were Jacuzzi towels, or if there was such a thing as Jacuzzi towels because you know—pool towels were a thing.

Ames looked him up and down, nodded once. "Good deal. I'll go get changed and grab some towels."

"Thanks." And not only for being nice, but honestly, having the towel thing answered worked very well for him.

The back of Ames's property shot out through the high desert like an arrow toward the mountains. There was a barn and some random outbuilding, but beyond that it was fence and scrub. It had to be, what? Two or three acres, he'd guessed.

He wasn't particularly practiced at that sort of thing, but it seemed like that was a reasonable size for a decent lot. He began to chuckle at himself, because really, he was a giant, certified dork trying to pretend he had any idea about anything in this strange, new wonderful place, even after the months he'd been here.

He was out of his league, in every way except for where it pertained to the kitchen.

Possibly how it pertained in another man's bedroom.

But that wasn't open for public discussion was it? Nope. Not notty not not.

The patio, though, now it was way swankier back here by the bedroom. The other half had a cobbled together outdoor kitchen. Two grills, one gas, one charcoal. A smoker. A foot pump sink. A table and chairs. He would so redo all that if it was his place.

But the little deck with the hot tub built in? It was like the bathroom. Fan-cy. He could see where Ames's priorities laid.

This man was into his bubbles.

While he was waiting. Nathan wandered over to explore the outdoor kitchen, finding it well-cleaned and in pretty damn good repair. He liked the fact there was both a charcoal grill and a gas grill, because sometimes a cook needed that exact temperature control, sometimes he wanted to stretch himself a little bit and see how the charcoal did him.

Also the smoker. That he could get into.

He was pondering the whole idea of smoking tofu when Ames came out on the patio, and Nathan's entire world sort of stopped.

Because damn.

It was a sin to hide all of that body in dirty jeans and filthy button-down shirts.

A mortal sin.

Ames was lean like all the cowboys were, his muscles

designed to do exactly what they needed to do, not to bulk up. But he had broad shoulders, a narrow waist, and defined pecs with little brown nipples. And that belly. Holy mother of God, that belly was ripped within an inch of its life, the serious eight-pack marching right up.

Nathan was going to die.

He forced himself not to stare, but God, he wanted to. That was fucking unreasonable. So utterly unfair.

God was testing him. He wasn't sure exactly what the exam was, but he was ninety-nine-point nine nine percent sure he was failing it.

"Are you going to get in the hot tub, or are you gonna stand there and stare?"

"I'm gonna stand here and stare." That broke him out of his weird-ass fantasy dream, and he stuck his tongue out at Ames. "I would like to point out that it is completely unfair that you have a belly like a goddamn rock star. *And* you eat crap food."

"See?" Ames gave him a wicked little shit-eating grin. Then he climbed up into the hot tub, settling into the bubbles. "I told you that Doritos and hamburgers were a reasonable diet."

"I hate you." After he took off his shirt, Nathan managed to get in without one, falling, or two, seeming like too much of a daddy longlegs or one of those creepy green stick bugs with the great big spindly legs. "This is absolutely unfair."

"What?" Ames glanced at him, squinting in the fading sun. "Will you get settled and enjoy the water, you lunatic?"

Nathan had to admit that the water felt amazing. He moaned, leaning back, letting his head rest on the padded neck roll this tub had. So cushy. "Okay, I forgive you for your awful processed diet. This is amazing." His muscles started to melt.

"Well, I do appreciate that." Ames's tone was dry as dust,

but he did get a naughty little grin. "I know it's not a pool or anything, but it sure doesn't suck."

"No, it absolutely does not suck." He curled his toes tight, tensing his leg muscles, and then let it go. The tension released, and he sank deeper. "So be honest. How many hours a day do you spend in here?"

"It really depends, I reckon. I can tell you that there are days when I'm out—especially in the wintertime—on a horse all day, and I want to get back and get my happy ass in the water."

"That sounds cold."

"It gets cold here." That sounded rather dire. "To be honest, it's not getting in the hot water that's the problem. In fact, there's something amazingly cool about it snowing. Having the snow fall on the water, I mean." Ames shook his head. "Man, the hard part is the getting out."

"Dude." Nathan could only imagine. That had to suck. "Hmm. I wonder if there's like a thing that you could make to have something warm on your way in. Like a heated sidewalk or—uh..." He wracked his brain. There had to be a thing— something warming for the outside. It had to be a business. "You could look it up on Amazon, I bet."

"You're funny."

"What? It's true! Online shopping is the best, especially here given your options, which, while, while they don't suck, are not super huge. You have to admit, you have limitations."

"And you didn't in Austin?"

"Those limitations were totally different. It had nothing to do with shopping."

Ames tilted his head. "No. What did they have to do with?"

How to explain it to Ames...

"Weirdly enough, freedom. The competition there is kind of huge. For everything: for jobs, for condos, for men. Just everything. Yeah. I guess it's sort of like being in a big school of fish. And you have to be the brightest fish, and the sparkliest fish, and the fish with the biggest teeth. But when you are that man? You're also the fish that everybody wants to catch, and you're the fish that's easiest to see, and you're the fish that the other fish hate and want to eat. And... I don't know."

He was being stupid.

"Do you miss it?"

"I miss my restaurant. I miss my bathtub. I miss really good Wi-Fi." He pondered that. "That's really it."

"Did you not have friends?"

"Sure. But really, it's not like I can't see them on Skype whenever I want to. It's not like we ever had any time. We were all busy working our asses off all the time. The most we ever got was a twenty-minute cup of coffee or, you know, texts. That's it."

"That sounds...a little nuts. I'm used to a slower pace. I mean, there are times... You saw how the branding was. But there's a definite rhythm to life up here."

He got that he guessed, but—well, he'd never seen Ames hang out with buddies. "What about you? You said it was awkward here at the ranch, being the boss."

"Mostly because I'm not married, so the married guys feel awkward inviting me over, but I have this place, so the bunkhouse guys don't want me around." The grin turned wry. Maybe a little wistful. "But this place is so accepting. It's a good place."

"I hear you, man. Seriously, I understand what you're saying." Nathan leaned his head back and gazed up at the sky. A big old raven or hawk or possibly an owl—he didn't know—flew overhead. "I have to admit. I didn't think I was going to like it here."

"No? Why not?"

"Well, you know, there's the city mouse, country mouse

part. There's the I-don't-know-anything-about-snow part. There's the I-don't-know-anything-about-being-in-the-desert part. But mainly there is the I'm-in-a-bad-place, and I thought it would be really hard to make friends." Nathan shrugged, not looking at Ames. "I can't help it. I think it..." He sighed. He needed to shut the fuck up. "I don't know. I think it's dumb. I just...have a couple of raw spots."

"I hear you." Ames sucked in a deep breath and let it out nice and slow. "I've always been here; I've always lived here. I don't have a whole lot of idea how to live anywhere else."

"It suits you." It really did. The whole rugged, outdoor, hard work and sunshine thing was like...perfect for Ames. He was a Wrangler ad come to life. The ones that talked about cowboys living on forever or whatever.

And he had the best smile lines...

He told himself he wasn't ready to do this again.

To think sexy, bouncy thoughts about anybody, especially not about somebody he worked with.

Especially *especially* not with someone who was the uncle-cousin of his mentee. That whole situation could be a nightmare.

But it was even worse than that, Nathan wasn't sure his heart was healed enough to wake back up at all.

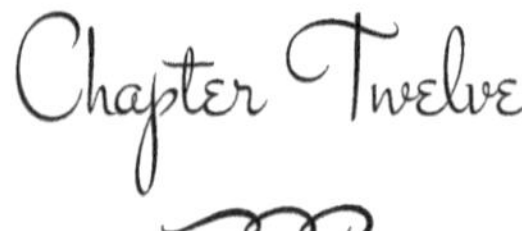

Chapter Twelve

Nathan was sacked out on his couch.

That was a novel damn thing, so Ames paused for a moment on the way from the bedroom to the kitchen to stare at him.

He wore a pair of boxer briefs and a soft T-shirt that did nothing to hide his body at all. Which was fine. Oh, Nathan wasn't a gym rat, he could tell. But this was a guy who worked on his feet, who was strong enough to break down a side of beef, but whose hands were delicate enough to slice the thinnest pieces of cheese or vegetables without mangling them.

Dammit. He didn't need to be staring. That wasn't polite. So he trundled in to the kitchen to start coffee. He was up early, but he needed to go on that doughnut run.

Nathan didn't work on the weekends, he knew, and since the Fourth had fallen on a Thursday, he was getting three-day weekends for all of July with comp time.

It worked out pretty good, really, because the guys were all out and about, not spending a ton of time on the ranch.

Hell, it was Cowboy Christmas. Most of the guys were off at rodeos now the big party was finished.

He got lazy and made a cup of coffee in the K cup thing. He had both that and a regular pot, but he was going to get good coffee at the doughnut shop.

When he turned around, he damn near jumped out of his skin, because Nathan was standing in the kitchen pass-through, hair wildly tousled. "You gonna make me one too?"

"Sure. Travel mug so you can come with me, or regular one? I can come back and get you on the way to drop the doughnuts at the big house."

"Travel mug. I mean, assuming you're not embarrassed to be seen with me in jeans and the T-shirt that I slept in. It's possible you might be." Nathan tried to smooth his hair, and it kept making it worse. It kept getting taller. "I think after I get back, I'm going to take my car and head into town and do some explor-ing. I haven't really had a chance to go wander and see things. Maybe I'll go to Santa Fe. Have you ever been to Santa Fe?"

Ames blinked at Nathan. "Who hasn't been to Santa Fe?"

Nathan raised his hand in slow-motion.

"How can you not have been to Santa Fe?"

Nathan held both his hands open like he was doing inter-pretive dance. "What do you want me to say? I've been lots of places. Just not lots of places *here*. I've been to LA. Houston, Dallas. San Francisco, Boston. New York City. London, Milan..."

"Okay. I get it."

Still, it was ridiculous that Nathan had never been to Santa Fe. There was something wrong with that whole idea.

He pursed his lips, thought for a second. "I don't suppose you want company?"

Nathan gave him the hairy eyeball. "I'm assuming you're talking about your type of company, like *you* company."

"Well, I'm not talking about asking Kase and Ryder."

"What about Sophie?" Nathan asked.

Ames shook his head, rolled his eyes. "They're having some sort of a makeover-slash-slumber-weekend-slash-pool thing. I don't even want to know, but what I do know is that the grannies are supervising it."

"Whoa."

"Indeed." Ames winked. He thought if Nathan had learned anything in the short time he'd been there, it was not thwart the grannies Chiara.

"Well, then. Santa Fe it is. But you have to let me pick where we have lunch," Nathan said.

"Okay. All I ask is not Geronimo."

Nathan tilted his head as if he recognized that one. "Why not?"

"Because that's a once-a-year dinner kind of place, not lunch. I mean, one of those four-course meal with wine pairing places for a hundred and fifty a pop. We need like, the Plaza Cafe, or the Shed."

"Oh God no. No, that is not what I'm thinking about." Nathan shook his head, motioning toward the coffee with this hopeful little grin. "Look, I like food—real people food. I cook dishes from all sorts of cultures. I like exploring food. I like exploring flavors. But I'm not looking to blow a paycheck. I want to eat really good food and explore stuff." Nathan leaned in and offered him a wicked little grin. "We could even share one of those Frito pies in the bag. I'm incredibly intrigued."

Ames couldn't have stopped his smile for love or money. It just happened, swelling from him like the sun over the mountains.

Suddenly, he wanted to kiss Nathan so bad. The urge was wild. There was something about that little grin, that spark that was coming out more and more often. This was a man who was supposed to be happy. Not knocked down. Not in hiding. Not bruised or broken.

He fixed Nathan's coffee the way he knew Nathan liked it —heavy on the sugar and the cream. Then he screwed the lid tight onto the travel mug.

"Well, I tell you what. At some point today, you and I will share Frito pie in a bag. As well as a Mexican Coke."

"Oh, Mexican Cokes. Those I like, a lot." Nathan took his coffee with a smile. "To be honest, there's very little wrong with Frito pie, in general. I've had it at football concession stands, and I've had it in Texas. From what I understand here, it's a totally different ball game."

"No shit?" How could Frito pie possibly be different?

Nathan leaned forward, as if he was sharing a secret, almost coming, nose to nose with him. "In Texas, they're baked."

He tilted his head the slightest bit. "'Baked'."

Nathan leaned a little more. "Baked."

"Are you gonna scream if I kiss you?" Ames knew he shouldn't ask, but he wanted to know.

"Only if you promise not to get scream if I kiss you back."

"That's totally fair." Nathan brought their lips together and the touch was—not electric. More like a tiny ember which filled him with this slow-growing warmth. It wasn't like anything he'd ever experienced.

It felt like coming home.

Nathan didn't close his eyes, and from here Ames could see the flecks of gold down in the brown. God help him, they were beautiful.

He stepped closer, and the coffee mug got trapped, keeping that little space between them. Jesus Christ, wasn't that the hottest thing he'd ever felt?

It was like being a teenager and knowing that if you

danced too close, somebody would notice, somebody would stop you.

Their lips parted, and Nathan stared at him. "Whoa."

"Yeah, buddy."

"I'm not sure I'm ready to start dating," Nathan admitted. "But you're freaking hot, man."

"That's okay, baby. I don't know that I know how to date myself. But whatever this is, I'm gonna hunt it."

Chapter Thirteen

"Oh my God, I will never eat again." Nathan put his hand on his belly as he climbed into Ames's truck. They'd spent a whole day in Santa Fe, driving down after they'd dropped off doughnuts and checked in with Sophie.

There had been a Frito chili pie and Mexican Coke at this little touristy drug store right off the Plaza. A shared bowl of mole at the Plaza Cafe. A cup of chocolate and some truffles at the Kakawa Chocolate house, which served indigenous-style chocolates and Mayan hot chocolate of joy. A slice of pizza at this place called Upper Crust, which was right next to the San Miguel mission, the oldest church in Santa Fe.

Maybe in the damn country.

And since they'd walked everywhere, he'd worked it off.

They'd finished up at this funky hotel bar he'd seen on the way back to the truck, splitting some parmesan truffle fries and a tequila lime tart. He'd also had a smoked sage margarita that was like...a revelation from the gods.

Even Ames had declared it freaking amazing, despite having a Dos Equis instead.

"I take it you approve."

"I feel like a snake that swallowed a—something bigger than a sheep. A gnu. A gnu is bigger than sheep, right?"

Ames chuckled at him. "You are a lightweight and yeah, gnu are way bigger. Hairy damn things too."

"You ever met one?"

"Well, sure." Ames started the truck, "I mean. I've never dated one."

Oh, that was how it was gonna be. Fine. He got his seat belt on and leaned back. "So what kind of livestock have you dated, cowboy?"

"Well, I didn't know...there was this roper this one time. I'm about one hundred percent sure after having seen his back that he was at least part buffalo."

"Okay, that's relatively gross." Seriously, he wasn't all that shallow, but hard-core back hair. Umm. Not his kink.

"It is. That really wasn't the worst part about him, though. The worst part about him was the smell. Have you ever heard that if you didn't like the way someone smelled, you couldn't really be compatible in bed?"

Nathan nodded. "I have indeed heard that."

"Did you like how your ex smelled?" Ames asked.

"Oh, that's a good question." Nathan frowned, trying to remember. "I don't know that I *didn't* like how he smelled. Does that count?"

Ames nodded. "Yes, but only if you like the way I smell. If you don't like the way I smell, then no, it doesn't count at all."

That got Nathan to grinning. "Ah, I see how it is. Give me your hand."

"What?"

"Your right hand, the one you're not driving with, give it to me."

"Okay... Is this some weird city thing?"

Nathan rolled his eyes. "No dork. I'm going to see if you smell good."

He took Ames's hand, leaned down and smelled right where the hand met the arm, that wrist where the veins were so close to the skin. It was rich and musky and just right.

"You totally pass."

Ames's fingers curled, and a smile kicked up the corner of his lips. "Good to know. I'm surprised I don't smell like pizza and truffle fries."

"Well, you do kind of. But that's okay. I'm a chef. I find that sexy." Did he say that out loud? Was that stupid?

Ames turned his hand to grab Nathan's, squeezing, and he didn't think he'd made an error. No, he thought Ames liked that.

"Well, good." Ames chuckled. "Anyway, happy food tour of Santa Fe day."

"It was a great day," he admitted, closing his eyes as they drove. "Thank you. Tell me, what's your perfect date?"

"Do you mean like a date-date?" Ames asked.

"No, asshole. I know what a perfect date-date is like. They're sweet and a little crunchy. Incredibly good in a milkshake. That's not what I'm asking."

Ames snorted. "Remind me why I'm taking up with the chef again?"

"Because I make the perfect blue and bacon burger. And I can make your life a living hell, which turns you on."

"Right." Okay, that made him smile. "So what was the question again?" Ames pulled up at a stop sign, the lights of Santa Fe like a rainbow to his kinda tipsy self. "So, a perfect date... Would it be, like, incredibly cowboy of me to say I like to go camping?"

Nathan stared at Ames. Camping. Of course it was camping. Camping involved things like bugs and possibly rattlesnakes and pooping on the ground, which was kind of weird. Cooking outside was all right though, and…

Hell, what did he know?

He'd never gone camping.

The closest thing he'd ever done to camping was his first two weeks here at the ranch.

"I'd try camping with you."

"Yeah? That would be cool." Ames grinned at him in a sideways kind of way. "Literally. We could run up to some-place like Durango and do some hiking…"

"No horses?" That was kind of an awesome idea. He'd thought that Ames meant going up to one of the upper camps on the ranch, and while he would have done it…

"Not the first time." Ames actually laughed. "I'd go easy on you and get a cabin or a platform tent, even."

"Oh now, that's love there." As soon as the words left his mouth, Nathan's cheeks went red hot, and he was glad that Ames couldn't see his face.

"It's something all right…" Ames chuckled, the sound warm, not mean at all and Nathan was glad for it. "Honestly? We could totally get a little rustic cabin. Something where you could shit in glorious privacy and actually have a shower. Maybe."

"Is that actually camping?" He could probably be okay with a place to go to the bathroom and shower.

Probably.

Maybe a cabin was the best thing for a first time, he didn't know. "You arrange it, and you let me know. I'm in."

"I'm on it." Ames sounded tickled.

"I have Fridays off for the next three weeks, for sure, and I do get vacation time." Which was a little weird, honestly.

He'd never had vacation time before. Not really. After all, when a man owned his own restaurant, it was working all the time. There was no vacationing. There was just working. And

Lord knows dishwashers and line cooks, they got what they got.

"I do too. I'll square it with the bosses. And with Sophie."

"Cool." He knew they'd hired a camp cook. She was a stocky little lesbian who made the best potato soup. If Layla wasn't up at the high camp, she could fill in for him...

He'd agreed to go camping.

Nathan wasn't sure what to think about that, given that he'd never even had a yard. Or a place to grow things. Or really any opportunity to.

Now he was living in...the freaking Wild West.

He hadn't known this world had really, truly existed. The high desert was fascinating and weird and the most beautiful and terrifying place he'd ever seen.

He wasn't sure he belonged here, but he wasn't sure he didn't.

So far, for the most part, everyone had been very decent. Even kind.

And it hadn't been the backwater, bullshit kind of job that he had expected.

Maybe at first.

That whole up in the mountains thing had been hard.

On the other hand, he thought he could do it again.

If he practiced.

On the horse for a few weeks. Maybe for fifteen minutes at a time.

He didn't hate the horses, right? Okay, so they might scare the living shit out of him...

"Why did you decide to become a cowboy?" he asked Ames, "Speaking of horses." Which they hadn't been, but in his head he had, so it was a fair question.

"Oh, that's really all I know. I mean, my people are more dirt farmers than anything, but all I saw growing up were cowboys. I wanted to be one so bad." Ames shrugged. "And I kept getting told that wasn't possible, so I guess it was a say I won't kind of situation."

"Okay. Will you totally do it?" That was a stupid thing to say, but he wasn't sure what else to say. Obviously Ames was, like, the ultimate cowboy.

Different than Ryder and Kase though.

Yeah.

Nathan was beginning to understand that there were different kinds of cowboys, which seemed ridiculous, but it was true.

There were the ones who rode in the rodeo. There were the ones who owned the rodeo. There were the ones who worked the land, the ones who owned the land, the ones who liked horses, the ones who liked cows, the ones who liked other things that weren't either horses or cows.

The rodeo itself had like five million different working pieces—absolutely none of which Nathan understood.

Then there was the support staff, and he wasn't a hundred percent sure whether or not they were cowboys, and whether cowboy was an official designation.

Was it something that if you worked around the ranch and you wore the hat and you did all the things, did it qualify you?

Because that seemed odd.

Nathan was relatively sure he wasn't a cowboy, but then he didn't have a hat. And he did own boots, but they weren't the pointy-toed kind. That was a totally different thing.

Also, he didn't wear Wranglers, although he did really, really like the look of a man's butt in that particular brand of jeans.

He supposed he was more cowboy adjacent-adjacent.

"Well, you can't tell me nothin', honey. So, say I won't, and I probably will." That little grin lurking on Ames's mouth made him chuckle.

"I can see you being stubborn."

"Me? Nah." Then Ames shook his head. "I never wanted to do anything else. So I left home and started hunting for a job."

Now that, Nathan understood.

"I hear you. I did basically the same thing. I started washing dishes and then moved up and up. Once I was eighteen, I went to culinary school."

Ames glanced over at him. "Where did you go to school?"

"I got my first degree in Austin, and then I continued working and cooking and exploring."

"Yeah, the bosses said that you've worked all over."

"I have!" He'd traveled, explored as much as possible. "I've staged all over the place. It's one of my favorite things. I really enjoyed learning about new restaurants and new cuisines, techniques." He shrugged. "I guess it's one of the reasons I came here, you know. This is totally not in my current skill set, and so it's been interesting."

"Where will you go after this?" Ames asked, his tone careful.

"I want a restaurant. I want to run a restaurant. Nothing huge. Nothing—I won't say nothing fancy, because I do like my fine dining, but I want something with, you know. Maybe four or five tabletops. Something with the menu changing on a daily basis depending on what's in season. Or what simply sounds good, or what the farmer's market has. Something where you could have another chef come in and... And maybe cook for a night. Wouldn't that be cool? You know, a guest chef."

He trailed off as he understood that he was waxing poetic about something that Ames cared about very little.

"That's really cool. I mean, that's a good goal."

"Yeah. I signed a contract for a year, so I'm solid here for a bit."

Ames seemed to relax. "That's good for me. I eat well with you here."

"Look at you, finally admitting it."

"I know! We're a stubborn breed, cowboys."

"I heard that." It was weird, how well they were getting along. When he stopped to breathe, he liked Ames a lot. He was rock-solid, kind, and he at least acted interested when Nathan talked.

That wasn't even acknowledging the kiss. Which had made him weak at the knees. It hadn't been super sexy or anything, but it had been intimate as all get-out.

He was hoping to try again, in fact.

He wasn't sure how much further they should go beyond that.

All right, that wasn't exactly true.

He knew exactly how much further he wanted to go.

But he had to remember that he had to work with these people. Also, he wasn't exactly sure how that functioned in this universe.

Where he was from a hookup was a hookup was a hookup. Of course, he subscribed to the rule of you didn't shit where you eat, so to speak. So, he never ever slept with employees.

It wasn't out of the question, before he was taken, of course, to find a guy who was willing to settle for a quickie.

It seemed as if it would be different here, and he didn't want people to think poorly of him. He didn't know how exactly to ask either.

Hey, Ames, how do you feel about fucking around?

Yo, Ames, if we had a one-off, would that be cool? And also, if it's really good, could we have a two-off or maybe a twelve-off?

Dear, Ames, I know that you have a kid who lives in your house so we can come do the dirty at my little house.

But was that going to be one of those *Brokeback Mountain* type of things? It didn't feel that way because they had married queer people running the show, but Ames had never come out and said, "Yeah, I'm up to bumping uglies."

Nathan grinned at himself.

Ames had been, however, incredibly clear with the kiss.

Not to mention it hadn't been the kiss of someone who had never done it before, so he was going to make the assumption that, one, Ames was queer, and two, Ames wasn't a virgin.

Hopefully both of those were true.

"I can smell the smoke," Ames told him.

"Huh?"

"From you thinking so hard. You're lost in there somewhere." Ames slanted him a concerned glance. "Did thinking about a restaurant upset you?"

"What? No. God no. I was just..." Pondering kissing Ames again. "Woolgathering."

"Mmm. Maybe dozing off because of all the food."

"As long as you're not dozing off while you're driving," Nathan teased. "I was actually thinking about you."

"Oh, do tell?" Ames glanced over again and then back to the road. "Were they good thoughts?"

"They were. Define 'good'." He had to tease.

"Define good. Okay." Ames chuckled and kind of rolled his shoulders like he was about to get into an altercation.

Like he was getting himself ready.

It was hot enough to make Nathan pant like a dog.

"In this case good would be defined by thinking about me in a sensual sort of way." A little grin played on the corner of Ames's lips.

"Sensual, huh? Okay. Well, that's fair then. Yes, I was totally in the arena of good possibly. More than, but totally in that positive space."

"I like a good headspace," Ames said, and Nathan then raised his eyebrow.

"And what do you know about headspace?"

"What? I read. I know things. I explore things." Ames waved one hand, swinging it in a circle from the wrist. "I mean not like in real physical time, but on a reading level, you understand."

"Oh, I see..." Nathan was going to die. "Well, yes, I do understand both reading and exploring and... Trust me. Whips and chains are not in my personal repertoire."

"Oh thank God." The words sort of burst out of Ames. "I wasn't sure what I was going to do if you told me that we were fixing to get all spanky and shit."

"No, that seems one, like a lot of work and two, sort of loud given that you don't live alone. And I have walls that are literally like two layers of drywall thick. Besides, I'm pretty sure that that sort of equipment wouldn't fit where I live right now, and those are questions you don't need asked by a certain teenager, if you get my drift."

"I hear you. I cannot express to you how much I hear you."

There was a long moment of silence before the hysterical laughter started, and when it did, it sort of exploded out of both of them, filling the cab up with sound and merriment.

"You know, man, we're both idiots." Ames managed through his chuckles. "I mean, we ain't even touched hardly at all, and we've already figured out that neither one of us are kinky."

"Boundaries are important." He nodded. "Boundaries are super important. Especially in situations like ours."

"So what exactly is our situation?" Ames asked. "I mean, are we exploring this thing? Because I'm feeling a thing."

"Are you?" That made something tighten up deep in his belly. "I am too, but we work together."

"Well, I been thinking on that, and I reckon we're not really co-workers."

"No?" He was curious now. "How do you figure that?"

"We work for the same guys—but they're a corporation. It's like if I worked for McDonald's, and you worked for... Uh...some other company that McDonald's owned..."

Nathan snorted. "That's an awfully thin hair to split. But I can see it. So we're allowed to fraternize."

"Hell yes. It's not like we live in the bunkhouse or anything."

"No. No, I think that might have been a bridge too far, even for me." While Nathan could accept the fall from gorgeous condo loft to tiny house behind the kitchen, sharing a bunkhouse with a bunch of stinky cowboys was simply not going to happen.

He'd done his time. He'd dealt with the weird shower thing for two weeks. No more.

Although he had agreed to go camping.

"Are you saying that you wouldn't wanna hang out with a bunch of the guys for hours on end, watching them cut their toenails and scratch their watches and wind their butts?"

"I will hurt you." Nathan warned. "I don't. I don't do mess."

"And yet you're here, working on a ranch. You know how much shit is on this ranch? I mean, like, literal poop. Like manure. You ever seen one of those bulls up close?"

"No. I saw the horses. That's got to be enough."

"Have you seen the donkeys?"

Nathan kind of sat up. "You mean real donkeys, like hee-haw, hee-haw?"

Ames laughed. "Listen to you. You must have had a See 'n Say when you were little. Yes, like those kind of donkeys. We have an entire little herd. One of them girls talked the bosses into getting miniature ones for 4-H. They're like dogs. They're they are the cutest things."

"Did you know there's a convent outside of Bonham that has miniature horses? It's right near an ice cream factory."

"No shit? Well, we do not have a herd yet. We do have three females and a male. So a herd is imminent."

"Be honest." Nathan leaned forward, closer to Ames. "Is it weird to watch them? You know. Do The Dirty?"

Because they seemed like baby critters. It seemed kind of nasty.

"You are a strange little man. I like you." Ames started chuckling. "But yeah, it's sort of like when the dogs go after it. There's a part of you that kind of goes, eurgh."

"I figured." He sat back. "But I'm glad to hear you say that."

"Another kink worry you can mark off your list. Totally not into that."

"So what are you into?" He felt daring asking.

"You, man. I'm still kind of reeling from the change in attitude. Mine, not yours. But I am super into you." Ames held out a hand, not meeting his eyes at all.

He took that hand and held on, because Ames seemed perfectly okay driving with one hand, and he loved the heat and callused roughness of Ames's skin.

"Is it weird to admit that this is a little scary?" Nathan kept holding on. "I mean, I really thought... I really thought he was the one. Like in that stupid monogamous, long-term, adopt babies, and run restaurants. The write-cookbooks-and-have-photo-shoots-at-the-house kind of way."

"Do you think that's real?"

Nathan managed not to snarl at Ames, because really? It hadn't been, had it? Not a bit of it was real. "No. It isn't real. It's all a lie."

Ames shrugged, his fingers curling further around the steering wheel and sliding a little. "I'm not a lie. Ranch. It's not a lie. It's dirty and dusty. Folks get hurt. Folks get hungry. It's all truth."

"I guess so. My restaurant was real. I loved it. And he fucked it all up." Nathan sighed. "Somehow the fact that you didn't like me to begin with is comforting."

Ames snorted. "Well, that's messed up. But I get you. That means the chemistry is there, and it's not just an easy con job."

"Exactly. If it was all smooth sailing and smiles, I would be suspicious."

"Anybody ever told you that you were weird?"

"All the time." That didn't bother him. "Anybody ever tell you that you are grumpy?"

Ames grinned. "All the time."

It was fair enough. "I think we'll figure something out."

And if they didn't figure it out today? They had nothing but time.

It was going to take a while to save up for a restaurant.

He could afford to be patient.

Chapter Fourteen

Ames grinned at Sophie, who was poring over a list of classes she could take at the local high school. She had to sign up soon if she was going, but she'd been given the opportunity to homeschool, too. Wat thought he could come up with a great curriculum for her.

"So you think I could make school credit if I keep working with Nathan?" She was on her stomach on the floor with her tablet, one foot up in the air while she scrolled.

"I don't know. We'd have to ask Wat." And Nathan, because he would be leaving before the school year officially ended, if he only stayed for his year. Hell, school hadn't even started yet, but the thought of Nathan leaving in the spring made him queasy.

So, they'd come home from Santa Fe and walked into—not really a shit show—but, the fancy pants magazine dude had stayed and wanted to talk to Nathan about his *"process"*. 'process',

Whatever the hell that meant.

So Ryder and the Grannies and Nathan had spent all of Sunday showing off the kitchen, cooking, and having pictures taken. They'd even done filming for some sort of a little segment for the local news morning show.

Sophie had watched with wide eyes, and when Nathan had asked her to join him on-screen as his sous chef, she'd almost vibrated apart.

Ames guessed it was cool.

Would have been more cool if they'd've been able to spend the night together at least once. Possibly gotten naked.

That didn't happen, though.

He had hopes that maybe he would get to see Nathan today. He'd been slammed, busy all week himself with all the guys in and out, enjoying their Cowboy Christmas and making their money.

So they were a bit shorthanded, and he had to admit he'd fallen into bed absolutely exhausted every night.

However, it was Friday, Nathan had the day off, he was done with work, so Ames kind of cleaned up some. He put on some smell-good, just in case.

"I really think, Uncle, that I want to work with Chef and get some credits for it. Maybe do homeschooling, and that would give me some flexibility. You think that's stupid?" Sophie looked up to him, and it hit him all of a sudden that this little girl was trusting in him to know what the hell he was doing.

Which he did not.

Not even, like remotely. He didn't have any idea about going to culinary school or what someone needed or...

It was hard to be a good parent. He wasn't supposed to do this.

But he damn well was going to do it.

Sophie believed in him.

Damn it.

So he would talk to Wat with her about her choices, and

he would ask Nathan about culinary programs. How much did they cost? What did she need to get into one?

See? That gave him a reason to see Nathan.

"Okay, kiddo. If that's what you want, we'll find a way to make it happen. If anyone can build you a curriculum for that in homeschooling, it's Wat."

"Thanks!" She set the tablet aside. "I want to try to finish my brown butter chocolate chip cookies today. It's a King Arthur Flour recipe, and there's a bake-along for charity on the Alzheimer's association, so I'll be busy this afternoon..." She gave him a glinting grin.

"As long as you save some for me and Nathan."

"That's why I'll bake them here and not down at the kitchen on the ranch. The hands smell cookies, and it's all over."

"You know it. Well, you need a ride anywhere..."

"I'll call Elijah. He's just doing work around the house today, so I can text him. Go do weird uncle things."

"I will." He winked, then headed out to the truck.

He texted Nathan while he walked.

Wanna go into town and get lunch?

Nathan had never tried their local Mexican place. Or the diner, for that matter.

It took no time at all for Nathan to text him back with

I would love to>

All right then. He checked his shirt—no stains, not too fancy, but also nice enough to go out to town. Then he texted back.

Pick you up.

Is it OK if I drive out to you? I can bring my
swim trunks.

There was a pause.

And a toothbrush.

See you soon.

Ames was going to have to go to the bathroom and kind of
thump his poor prick because this was the most exciting series
of texts in the history of the Earth for all that they were kid-
appropriate.

"Mr. Nathan's going to come over, and then we're going
to go to town. When we get back, we're going to enjoy cookies
and have a soak in the hot tub tonight."

Sophie applauded. "Go you, Uncle. Getting you some!"

He cracked up. "Oh girl, shut up."

His cheeks were hot, though, weren't they? Damn.

Didn't he hope that she was right, though? He didn't
want some. He wanted lots.

Maybe all of it.

It felt like heaven when Nathan pulled up in his little SUV
and hopped out. The man was fine as frog hair split three ways
—black T-shirt, jeans, ball cap.

Ames had to admit that he approved all the way.

"Hey, man, thanks for letting me come over. I-I'm free
until Sunday night. Monday morning."

"Well, listen to that. I think I am too." He gave Nathan a
grin. "What do you think about Mexican food?"

"I believe Mexican food is proof that there is a God, and
that he loves us with all of his heart. Especially if chips and
salsa are involved." Nathan rolled his eyes. "I understand that
it's not high-class, but it is one of my fondest things on earth.

Dipping things. I love to dip: guacamole, queso, salsa. I'm a dipper."

Every so often, Nathan said that sort of thing, and it made him fall in love a little bit.

In fact, Ames was very afraid that he was falling for Nathan a lot. That scared him kind of. But he could do scary things. He grabbed his own hat, and they headed out to the truck.

He liked the salsa at Tequila's. So he figured Nathan would like it too, and they had decent queso. Sometimes it was a tiny bit too hot, but hey, who was he to say? He was so totally a gringo.

He glanced over as he got them moving. "So you're gonna stay the night tonight? I don't wanna be all hopeful if I'm on the wrong page."

Nathan granted him. "Yeah. You've got the right idea."

"Perfect. That way we know what we're getting into from the start. Sophie is making cookies. We'll have dessert when we get home."

Nathan seemed somewhat panicky at that idea. "So is she gonna be there?"

"Nah. She's probably gonna go spend the night with somebody. She didn't want to make cookies down at the kitchen because she was afraid that the hands would clean her out before she even got them done."

"Smart girl. Those hands can eat some cookies."

"Yeah, no kidding. I understand. I can too."

"Well, I would love to try her cookies."

"She says they're gonna be brown butter chocolate chip." Ames wasn't sure what browning the butter had to do with it.

Nathan smacked his lips. "Those are the best kind, if she's using the King Arthur Flour recipe."

"She says she is," Ames agreed.

"Great, I'll eat half a dozen."

"Hey, you'll have to fight me for them."

"Oh, cookie-wrestling in the hot tub. That sounds kinky." Nathan waggled his eyebrows.

Ames laughed out loud. "I thought we'd discussed this whole kink thing. Right? Right."

"We have. I think that we have a running joke now—you, me, in the truck, talking kink."

Ames had to chuckle. "You're a butthead. How was your week?"

"It was good. It was weirdly good. We got some nice publicity from the TV spot and the article. I think that the bosses are pleased."

"Well, why wouldn't they be? You're kind of famous."

"More infamous." Nathan shrugged. "It was nice to be able to do what I do. Sophie was an absolute doll, so it worked out."

Right. He'd asked the man out for a reason. "Speaking of Sophie, she's thinking about homeschooling so that she can work with you and get credits for culinary school. She asked for my advice, but I got nothing, man. I don't know what to tell her."

"Well, Watson should be able to tell for sure, one way or the other, about culinary school and credits. So we will defer to him on that, I think. But if you're good with it, and that's what she wants, I'm willing to work with her. I think she has real talent, and I wouldn't say that to you, if I didn't believe it." Nathan got quiet for a second. "Now don't get me wrong, this is not an easy life. It's long hours, it's hard work. It's getting burned and cut and being around a lot of alcohol and some people that are not necessarily savory—pun intended— especially if you're in the fine-dining world. It can get real cutthroat real fast. But if it's a passion, then it is what it is. People don't become chefs to get rich. People become chefs because they love to cook, and they love to feed people."

"That's awesome, man. I mean, if you think she can do some of the work now."

"Oh well, I know there's all sorts of equivalencies and stuff with work and credit. I know that a lot of the culinary schools will take that kind of thing from like, a vocational school. So like I said, I bet Wat could come up with something no problem."

"Cool. Thanks. Sometimes this parenting thing is, like, really tough." And he hadn't even had to do it for very long, so he needed to shut up.

"I think you're doing a great job. She's an amazing kid, and she really admires you. And I think that she could really do well in culinary school," Nathan said. "I think that she has what it takes."

"That means a lot to me," Ames told him. "You're really good at what you do, so if you think that she's got it in her, I want her to go for it. I don't want to discourage her like many people did with me."

Nathan gave him a searching look. "They really did a number on you, huh?"

"Yeah, I guess they did. I mean, they told me all the time that I couldn't be what I wanted to be, and that I wasn't good enough."

"I'm glad my mom didn't do that to me." Nathan kind of grinned. "She was a hard worker, and she didn't exactly know what to do with me, but she never put me or my sisters down." Nathan reached over and grabbed his arm, sort of squeezing. "I think you're pretty awesome."

"Yeah? You didn't think so to begin with," Ames had to tease. He always had to tease about that. The way they'd started out had been rocky at best, but now he kind of figured they had it going on, and hopefully tonight they would have it going on way more. He was really excited about that idea.

Mexican food first, but still.

"I've had time to form a new opinion. And you've been way nicer to me lately."

"You inspire me, what can I say. I needed time to get to know you." That wasn't a tease. It was true.

"I am a bit of an acquired taste. Like Uni."

"Okay. What's a Uni?" Ames asked.

"It's sea urchin. Tastes like the ocean, buttery, lots of umami. It's incredibly popular right now, very hot."

Yummy. "Do you cook with that much?"

"If I had a purveyor that happened to have it, and I thought that I had a recipe that I needed it in, sure. But that's not really my schtick. I tend to elevate comfort food, and I also am very into comfort foods from other cultures. Like feijoada or…"

"That I know. In fact, I can get you that."

Nathan blinked over at him. "No shit?"

"Dude. Bull riders, Brazilians. They can make some feijoada like a bitch." He loved it—meat, black beans, stew? He was in.

"I would love to learn from somebody who learned from a grandma. That would rock my world. I've already hit Granny Chiara up for her Sunday sauce."

"So your deal is you take these things that are like a hamburger, and you make them…better than a hamburger?"

"No, not exactly. I make them more upscale than a hamburger." Nathan settled in to chat with him. "So let's say we're having a hamburger. I might make a patty out of the best beef with cubes of cheese in it… Oh, maybe the best Irish cheddar and perfectly pickled cucumbers and heirloom tomatoes on a brioche bun that was handmade that morning. Then I'd serve it with truffle fries. That sort of thing. Or maybe I would say take a hamburger and instead of making hamburger I would make meatballs out of it and have a meatball salad that tastes like a hamburger when you eat it!"

Ames loved listening to Nathan talk about cooking.

Not because he cared about the cooking; he didn't. But he cared about the way the man's entire body lit up and sort of rejoiced at the idea that there was the chance that a meatball could taste like a hamburger.

It was his personal opinion that meatballs tasted like meatballs, and hamburgers tasted like hamburgers, and there was a reason for that.

But he was also smart enough to understand that this was not the appropriate time to bring that up, and it might harm his chances of getting laid. So maybe he would keep that opinion to himself.

He pulled in at Tequila's, the smell of chiles already making his mouth water. "Well, I do like me a meatball," was what he settled on. "Hell, I like food."

Nathan laughed. "I know. And you've been venturing outside your comfort zone lately, which I appreciate. I know you did it for Sophie to begin with."

"Yeah, but then I started dating a chef."

Nathan's lips parted when he glanced over to see how he took that comment.

"'Dating'… That's kind of wild, man."

"Uh-huh. Wait until we get to the sleeping-with-the-chef part." He was determined to do that, dammit.

"Hopefully it doesn't take us so long to get from dating to fucking, as it did from meeting to dating." Butter wouldn't melt in Nathan's mouth.

"Listen to you. Do you kiss your mother with that mouth?"

"Not anymore, I don't." Those pretty lips quirked, giving him a half smile. "But you should see what I can do with my mouth. I'll turn your ass inside out."

Then Nathan got out of the truck and headed toward the restaurant.

"I'm gonna kill him."

They headed inside, and Ames worried for a minute about Nathan not loving the tacky décor, the scratched-up tables, the menus that were peeling a little at the corners and had seen better days. But Nathan let himself be seated and took the menu with a grin. "Oh, I do love a good dive."

Ames tilted his head. "Yeah?"

"God, yeah, this is where the food is. I mean, don't get me wrong—exceptional restaurants, Michelin-star restaurants? They can be amazing. They can be transformative. But this is food." Nathan waved one hand in an expansive sweep. "This is let's have supper. Let's sit and chat and have a beer and be relaxed. These are two different experiences. One's not necessarily better than the other."

It was fascinating to see Nathan settle in, talk to him like he was...worth sharing shit with.

"It's sort of like listening to classical music or listening to country music. Or reading some fancy-assed literature, hardbacked book thing, versus reading like some dog-eared horror novel. They're all good. Sometimes you need one, sometimes you need the other. Most of the time, you need the other. And that's okay."

Ames stared at Nathan, trying to decide if he should go for glib or for serious, because his instinct was to kind of blow Nathan off.

However, something in him thought that this was the same man who'd gotten on a horse when he'd never even had a dog. Who'd ridden for four hours and never once complained about it.

"Well, I can tell you that this place has the best salsa in three counties. And that the cook has a secret love for seafood enchiladas, which are actually really good." He sat across from Nathan, staring at him, because something about that dark red hair and those sherry-colored eyes was so arresting. He'd thought it was an odd combo to begin with, but now he thought Nathan was the hottest damn thing he could imagine.

"Hola, amigos. Señor Ames, how are you? You want a Modelo?"

"Yes, please. Thanks, Leo. This is Nathan."

"Hola, hola. Beinvenidos."

"Gracias, Leo. Do you have Dos Equis?"

"I do. And water? I'll be right back."

Nathan glanced at the menu. "So what do you get when you're here?"

"I've eaten almost everything on the menu," he admitted. "But my absolute favorite are the chicken fajita chimichangas covered in chile con queso. I only have it like once a quarter because you know, there's no way that it's any good for you."

"Oh man. Yeah, cheese, chicken flour, tortilla, fried, smothered in queso with rice and beans. Oh my God." Nathan's eyes rolled." That sounds so good, but so do the flautas. Ooh...how's their guacamole?"

"Not as good as yours," he admitted, "but damn good nonetheless."

Nathan beamed at him. "Good to know. I think I'm going to try the combo plate to kind of get a feel for the whole thing. Can we share guacamole as an app?"

"Sure, babe. Whatever you want." He was going to go for enchiladas with an egg on top. That suited him down to the bone. "So now that the Fourth of July party is over, what's your next big thing?"

"I'm assuming I do have a Labor Day type of situation, and really, I would assume we start fairly early with any sort of holiday preparations. Although Nanette has explained to me, very clearly, that she and the grannies do Thanksgiving and Christmas and that I would not be required to do that. So. That's gonna be kind of odd."

"Yeah, they're very into that being family time, especially with the kids. Everybody sort of does their own thing."

"Huh. Well, I suppose, if everybody's doing their own thing, should I do like an Orphan's Thanksgiving?"

"I don't know; everyone's welcome at the Chiara's table on Thanksgiving. There's always turkeys and hams and everything in the smokers, I mean, we all kind of get a plate. We set out those long tables, and sort of, you know, make it happen."

"So am I the first full-time chef here then?"

"Yeah, besides the camp cooks. Really you are." Ames wasn't sure what that expression on Nathan's face meant exactly.

Was he pleased? Was he worried? Was he constipated?

"I bet if you talked to the grans and offered to help in a family way, you and Sophie, you'd be welcome. The ranch really is like a big family."

Nathan chewed his lip, then finally nodded. "Sure. I can do that. I mean, I don't want everyone to think I'm too snooty to do it."

"Babe, I don't think anyone thinks you're snooty. I think you've been too busy to really meet anyone." And he was going to remedy that. Nathan was going to assimilate.

"Well, I'll feel them out. If they want me to help, I can, and if they don't, I totally understand. I mean, I can just eat at home."

"You will not. You don't have to." He shook his head. "Everything's going to be fine."

Nathan's eyebrow flew up. "You're sure of that are you?"

"Yes, I'm sure of it." The grannies would love to have help, and he knew it. He had to kind of tread carefully—at least with Nathan; the grannies would be easy. Maybe they could make it a big potluck.

Charlie would be home from school, and God knew she made some weird things. Their family had obviously done lots and lots of strange vegetable boards with ranch dip and French onion dip and chips.

Those kids were all about the pre-dinner munchies.

"You've got months to start worrying about that," he told Nathan.

"Fair enough. I'm looking forward to experiencing winter out here. I've never really had to deal with snow."

"Well, you're going to get experience, that's for sure, more than 'kind of'. Do you have the things that you need? Boots, a good winter coat, that sort of thing? Because it gets bitter, and it will stay that way for a while." Ames made a note to check the insulation on that tiny house because he didn't want his cook to freeze. Or for the pipes to freeze, for that matter.

"Ames, you've seen my boots. Do you think I need different ones? Or maybe better socks? Buying a heavy winter coat is on my plan for while I'm up here. I figured I would have better luck finding something that was suitable up here, where it's actually cold."

"Yeah. Yeah, the best place for that is the local outfitters. It's like a feed store meets Ace Hardware." Bobby Garcia would be able to hook Nathan up with all he needed. He'd need boot socks and gloves and all too.

Leo brought drinks and took their food order, and Nathan peppered him with questions about winter in Northern New Mexico.

"Oh, man, I can't wait for you to see it at Christmas. We do up the farolitos and you gotta learn to make biscochitos and posole, babe. It's amazing up here then. The ranch does it up right. We even have a sleigh."

"No shit? I've never been on a sleigh." Nathan actually bounced in his seat. "And I do not know what biscochitos are, but posole I am familiar with, so we're good there. I have also been researching green chile everything because, apparently, that's one of my jobs. Green chile everything. Nanette is going to give me lessons."

"So what do you use in Texas? If you don't have green chile, I mean."

Nathan chuckled, the sound soft. "Jalapeno everything, man. Jalapeno *everything*. Candied Jalapenos. Pickled jalapenos, stuffed jalapenos."

Ames stopped him. "You're not serious. Candy jalapenos?"

"I shit you not. They're really nice. You pour them over cream cheese, and you serve them with crackers. It's sweet and spicy and creamy and really delicious. I've also made a kind of preserve that has peaches and jalapenos and sugar..."

"Huh. I mean my mom used to do prickly pear and red chile on cream cheese..."

Nathan's eyes lit up. "No shit? Is it good?"

"It is. I can see if I can remember how she did it. Maybe Sophie would know. She was there a lot more recently than me." Ames shrugged. It wasn't like he could call his mom and get the recipe.

"Hey, all we have to do is remember how you started it, then we experiment. That's how recipes are made."

"Yeah?" That made him feel a little bit better.

"Totally. It's strange because you think that recipes are like these eternal things, that they never change. You know, I remember this potato soup my mom used to make, all the time, and I loved it. Then, when I got old enough, I started making it, and I told everyone, 'this is my mom's famous potato soup'." Nathan rolled his eyes like thrown dice. "And before she died, she made me some. And, I have to tell you, it wasn't the same. I mean not the same at all."

"Really?" That had to have been weird as hell.

"Really. I mean, I'm talking there wasn't anything that was the same about it. Except for maybe the memory of it. So, we start the recipe, and we make a memory of it—you and me and Sophie." Nathan blinked and leaned back, glancing down at his hands. "Jesus, I'm sorry. I'm not trying to insert myself, get myself into your family or anything, because that's creepy and weird. I just meant that..."

"Hey." Ames held up one hand. "Look, babe. You don't have to get all ashamed. You're not inserting yourself in anything." No, if anything. Nathan was rescuing him— rescuing a memory for them maybe? He didn't know, but he did know that Nathan was not putting himself anywhere he didn't deserve to be.

"Well, if you're sure. I'll take it. I'd love to know your favorite recipes and try to recreate them with you."

"I get it," he admitted. "I'm gonna teach you how to ride better and, you know, share that with you."

And now it was him who was blushing because. Nathan had a point. This felt ridiculous and intimate and weird. Not to mention they were in a restaurant, and there were going to be people coming in that they knew, and...

"We're going camping, right? Are we bringing horses to camping?"

That sounded like a bad idea. "Probably not this first time. Let's start slow. I'll teach you how to camp. You can teach Sophie how to cook."

"And I'll teach you how to enjoy eating."

Ames thought that was fair because he was like most of the people he knew, just a shoveler. There was food, it was there. It was tasty. He ate it.

Sophie and Nathan paid attention to the food and how it was put together and how it tasted and how one thing tasted against the other thing. And that was very much a different ballgame.

The chips and guacamole salsa came, and Nathan sighed happily. "Ah. This is heaven."

"On that, babe, you and I are of the same mind." He tilted his head. "Do you like anything besides cooking?"

"There are things besides cooking?" Nathan winked and scooped up some salsa with a chip. "I kid. Baseball. Legos. And garage sales."

"'Legos'?"

Nathan nodded his head. "I have an entire storage building full of them. It was like one of my things, I guess. I couldn't afford them when I was a kid, and when I grew up, and I could afford to, so I bought them. Then it was something I could do when I got off work at two in the morning, and I couldn't go to sleep right away. You know, I'd be up, I'd be sitting there, and I could click bricks together." Nathan pushed the guacamole closer, offering it to him. "So what about you? You've got to have some kind of a hobby that you're embarrassed to tell your rough-and-tumble cowboy friends."

"I know how to crochet."

And he was really good at it, too. It was peaceful, and it ended up making things that were useful, and he liked that. He liked things that made other things.

"My grandpa could knit."

"Oh yeah?"

"Yeah, he said it was a skill that he'd been taught, he knew how to do, it and it was useful, so he did it. He loved it. He could spend hours. He made all sorts of hats and scarves and sweaters and shit. I never could quite get it, but I kind of remember the sound of the needles sliding together."

"Were they Texans?"

"They were. Their parents had both come to the United States. From Nova Scotia."

"My people have been from New Mexico for a long time. They're like old, conservative New Mexico." Ames grinned. "And Mom has people who claim to be from Spain."

"Ah. So old New Mexican that they don't speak Spanish? I knew people like that in Texas." Nathan munched and sipped his beer in turns.

"Yep. I do speak Spanish, though. Six years in school, and I worked on a place up in Chama where no one spoke English at all. That will brush up your skills fast." Ames remembered the Dominguez family so fondly.

"My kitchen Spanish is exceptional. So is my kitchen French."

Kitchen Spanish. Ha. "So did you learn French in school?"

"Nope." Nathan shook his head. "I staged in a restaurant outside of Nice. You want to talk about being dunked into a language. I had no idea what I was doing, and Chef didn't care."

"Okay, so what's this *stodge*? It sounds gross."

"It's sort of like an internship, really. You go for a certain period of time, and you work in a kitchen. You learn about the chef's style, and you learn about the chef's food. It's not a permanent position, and you're not even looking for a permanent position a lot of the time. It's a place to go and learn from somebody who really knows what they're doing."

"Dude, that's kind of cool. We do something in that vein, kind of. You have to learn how to rodeo, right? You have to learn how to cowboy. There's not rules for it so much as it's just a thing."

"I think that's like how it is in most of life, right? Most trades—all this is, is a trade—you have to learn from somebody, and you can't learn it from a book."

Ames liked that. "You gonna write a cookbook one day."

"I doubt it, but I never say never. I have notebooks and notebooks filled with recipes, of experiments, of disasters and successes, you know."

He did know, because he watched Sophie carry that damn notebook of hers around all the time, scribbling and writing in it, so serious. "Chef gave me this book," she'd tell him. "It's for me to take my notes in so that I know what I'm doing. You have to be able to replicate your work."

"Has it been hard coming here?" The words kind of slipped out of his mouth, and he hadn't intended to say them.

Because he wasn't absolutely sure he wanted to know what the answer was.

Nathan shrugged. "There was a culture shock, for sure. But I think I'm starting to kind of fit in a little bit. It's hard, though. When you have a kitchen brigade, you have a built-in family, friends. Folks you can go to the bar with after work or go have pancakes at midnight. Here, if I want pancakes at midnight, I have to open up the kitchen and make a mess and turn on lights—so I don't."

"Shit, man. I am the king of midnight pancakes. You can come to my place anytime. Or call me. I'll run you out to the truck stop. There's one about twenty miles north. It doesn't take but a few to get there. It's twenty-four-seven." Ames could and would provide late-night food if it kept Nathan here longer.

"Yeah. Well. I'll take you up on that."

Not maybe I'll take you up on that.

Not oh, that's neat

Or where's that truck stop.

I'll take you up on that.

This was feeling more and more like a thing.

Hopefully it was a good thing. Because he wasn't sure his heart could handle losing his good thing.

# Chapter Fifteen

They were in the hot tub. They'd had a beer. All the lights were out.

Even the house was dark, Sophie gone to bed.

His phone was playing the *Oh Do Me Now* playlist.

They were alone.

The water was bubbling.

Nathan figured if they didn't do the deed now, they were never going to.

There would never be orgasms. This would be an orgasmless relationship.

Nathan would be perfectly honest—orgasms were one of the best parts of relationships. Not the only part, sure, but a big, fun, delicious part. But they weren't getting over that hump, so to speak.

Maybe Ames was shy.

Maybe he was a virgin. Did they make virgin cowboys? They'd probably made gay virginal cowboys. Virgin cowboy gays?

Regardless, Nathan was tired of waiting. He slipped off his swim trunks, leaving them at the bottom of the hot tub, and then he floated closer, making sure that some or all of the appropriate parts touched some or all of themselves on Ames so that it was totally clear he was naked.

"Hey, stranger."

It wasn't *nice boots wanna fuck*, but it was close enough. And well, Ames didn't have on any boots.

Ames blinked at him. Twice. Then he grinned like the Cheshire Cat.

"Hello. Did your trunks explode?" Ames went very still against him.

"Uh-huh. My poor cock is cold. You should touch it, warm it up."

One eyebrow lifted up, and Ames lips twisted. "I should, should I? But we wouldn't want it to get chilly."

Okay, that was positive. He would go with that. "I concur. No getting cold in the hot tub." He straddled Ames's thighs and pushed right up against his belly. Snuggling in.

Hopefully that was clear enough.

Ames grabbed his ass, holding him right where he was, and Nathan wanted to cheer. Hallelujah. The man got his play.

One hand slid up his back, Ames sinking strong fingers into his hair, then that mouth met his, Ames kissing him like there was no tomorrow. Hell, yes. Ames did know how to kiss, and he loved that, loved the heat of it, the soft, damp feel of Ames's lips and the scrape of his day-old stubble.

He started rocking, shifting his body in slow, steady thrusts against that amazing twelve-pack, the little bumps and grooves making his eyes cross.

"Mmmm. You got the advantage on me, babe," Ames told him, the hand on his ass slipping and sliding.

"I do, huh? Let me fix that." He shifted up and back, then tugged at Ames's swim trunks until they came off.

"Oh, much better." Ames grunted the words out as he scooted back up to rub them together.

"Yeah. Much, much better." Now they were cooking with a gas range. He circled his hips in slow-motion, letting them get full contact. Friction. He needed all of it.

Everything Ames had to offer.

His balls felt heavy, and he told himself this wasn't forever. This wasn't a marriage.

It was a hookup, pure and simple.

Still, it was here and now, and Ames was special, so he took it. Every inch. Every ounce.

"Damn, babe. That's—" Ames guided him where he needed contact the most, he thought. Because when he moved just right, Ames cried out, body bucking under him. He'd done that. He was the one making Ames crazy, and Nathan wanted more. The flushed cheeks, the swollen lips, the wide, fuck-me gaze Ames fastened on him...

Yeah, he was so taking Ames with him when he went over the edge.

He slammed their lips together because the last thing they needed was a curious teenager out here curious to see if someone was getting murdered in the hot tub.

Luckily, Ames got it.

Ames demanded entrance, their tongues fighting, both of them moaning into the kiss. Nathan wasn't alone in this need, and it felt so good to know it, proving he wasn't the only one who wanted so badly.

The bubbling water splashed against their skin, and it wasn't doing a single thing to cool their ardor. No, it seemed to be driving them together, the force of the water slapping them against one another.

Ames explored every part of him that he could reach, hands sliding down his back, fingers stroking his hips, his belly, his cock, grabbing both dicks in one hand and squeezing.

"Oh, fuck," he moaned, his eyes crossing. "Need you like breathing."

"Good." That single word was bit out like it hurt to say, like it had come from the base of Ames's spine.

He leaned forward, lips against Ames's ear. "Mean it. Need you."

And it was scary as fuck, to think that he was going to let someone else in, let Ames in. He bit that soft earlobe, hard enough to sting.

Ames arched underneath him. Right now this was enough, though. Right now, he wanted the callused feel of Ames's hand on his skin. The way that Ames pushed against him, the heat and the need. This was enough.

And it was close. Nathan was super close. He required Ames to be with him. He needed to make sure Ames was feeling the same thing he was feeling. He glanced up and met those shining blue eyes, and Ames stared right into him, humping up and begging with his kisses, with his hands. And his words, which were kind of jumbled, but they were sex words for sure.

Nathan dug in and hard and rocked down, fighting against the water, fighting against Ames so they could reach their climax together. He could see it in the way Ames grimaced, in the way those firm sweet lips pressed together, tight as a drum. He could see when it was coming, and he could feel it too. He could feel Ames shake against him, and Nathan knew it was time. His balls tightened up, his spine snapping as his head fell back, and he shot hard. And he knew it when Ames went with him right at the same moment, and it was somehow absolutely perfect.

He could really get used to this, and that was kind of a terrifying thought.

"Damn, Sam." He rested his head against Ames's forehead.

Ames's eye lines went deep. "Name's Ames, honey."

"Oh, you are a fucker, aren't you?"

"I can be." Ames chuckled, the sound full of deep satisfaction. Pure cowboy, that sound. "Mmm. We need to get you out of the bubbles, babe."

"We do?"

"Uh-huh. Between the orgasm and the heat, your blood pressure is gonna drop like a stone."

He glanced up. "Yours isn't going to do that?"

"Nah. I'm in the tub most nights. I'm used to it." Ames lifted him a bit, which was an impressive feat considering how lean and compact Ames was compared to his long, lanky length. But he was pushed and utzed and moved until he was draped in towels, and Ames was waltzing him inside.

At least it felt like a waltz.

They used the door that went into Ames's master suite, which was a nice feature. If he ever got another house, he wanted that. Hell, he would take Ames's house in a heartbeat if he could do a full inside and outside kitchen remodel...

He chuckled at the thought. Nope. No playing house with Ames. That way led to madness, right?

But Ames had a fantastic bed, and after Ames dried him off and they cleaned up, he found himself in it, the comforter pulled up over them, cocooning them in warmth.

"Hey." They were staring at each other, blinking nice and slow.

"Hey. You okay?" Ames asked, and he didn't know what to say.

Yes?

No?

"Better than that." Okay, his mouth knew what to say.

"Oh good. Because I'm so okay you don't even know." Ames palmed one of his ass cheeks and squeezed. "You're gonna stay here, right?"

"I brought a bag, so yes." He loved that Ames had issued the formal invite, though. Took out all ambiguity. "Thanks."

"Mmmmhmm." Ames took a kiss, patting him, and he could feel Ames sinking toward sleep.

He didn't think he wanted to sleep.

He wanted to stay awake and wallow in this quiet afterglow before it went straight to hell.

Chapter Sixteen

"You're absolutely sure we have to go by horseback?"

Ames laughed, grinning over at Nathan as he tightened the girth strap on his gelding's saddle. "Well, you're the one who suggested it again. And that's kind of the point of going camping. Roughing it a little. I mean, we could have taken the truck and gone someplace else, like the State Park, but I thought I'd ease you into it. So we're gonna go to one of the line shacks that has a shower and a grill."

Nathan chuckled. "Yeah, yeah, yeah. I guess all the lessons I've been taking from you in the last two weeks will help with the riding then."

Ames nodded. Nathan and horses were getting along pretty well so he'd decided they should ride. He had high hopes for the puppy he was going to pick up when they got back, too. Nathan needed a dog.

"I really appreciate all the hard work. I mean, I wanted to go camping with you before the school year starts again, and it's gearing up for that."

Sophie was going shopping with the grannies this weekend for school clothes, in fact. Even though she was homeschooling—he wasn't sure how that worked, but he guessed everybody got to go do fun things together, and nobody wanted to be left out.

It was really generous of the grannies to take Sophie along and let her experience a little normal.

He'd asked her if she wanted to go camping with them, and she said, "Oh God no. Please. I like outdoorsy stuff, but the grands are taking me shopping."

He laughed his ass off about that. And he was kind of excited about spending this time with Nathan.

Showing off. Doing his cowboy stuff, now that they were together and not kinda hating on each other.

He loved the idea of having this man to himself without any fear of interruption. Sleeping under the stars and scaring the wildlife with their noises.

"I brought a deck of cards because there's very few situations in life where cards aren't a thing."

Ames chuckled at the hint of nerves in Nathan's voice. "The bunkhouse will have games, too. It's a real nice setup. Not quite as good as the big house, but fine."

"So long as we don't have to sleep in separate beds," Nathan pointed out. "I'm not going out there to hang out with you in the great outdoors and have to sleep completely alone, unprotected from bears and scorpions and mountain lions and whatever strange things you have here in the desert."

"Man, you come from Texas. You don't get to complain about the strange things. You have Houston."

"Hell, we have the catfish the size of Volkswagens at Lake Ray Hubbard. They live under the bridge."

"Dude, anybody ever tried to catch them?"

"I'm sure they have, but I don't think it's ever happened. Surely that would be something in the news. Besides, who's gonna eat that? Nasty."

That got them into a long discussion about the difference

between giant channel cat and whales and the eating habits of different people and it managed to get them all the way through getting the tack on and loading the saddle bags, which kind of surprised him.

But then again, Nathan could ramble about some food.

"We ready to go?" he asked.

"We have blankets, right? And toilet paper. Did we remember toilet paper?" Nathan's eyes went wide.

That started him chuckling, "Come on. It's gonna be okay, Greenhorn. You're gonna survive this."

"Hey! I know about surviving. You're the one who put me on a horse for days. On my very first time. Days."

Nathan swung up into the saddle with relative ease for someone who was new to riding. His butt settled in the saddle, boots in the stirrups. "Did I mention days? It was days."

"Don't make me beat your butt."

"And here we are back on the kink thing. It's not a car thing, man. It's an on-the-road thing. We start going from one place to another and all of a sudden it's all about the kink, Moriarty."

"I think you inspire me. What can I say?" Ames loved that they always came around to the weird stuff. He had thoughts like that all the time, but up until now he hadn't had anybody to share them with, so it made Nathan extra special.

They headed off up the northern trail, the horses happy to stay at an easy walk, and while it was hot, it wasn't unpleasant

Nathan seemed much happier this time, his butt and legs way more used to being in the saddle. And Ames, well, he loved being outside. He loved being on horseback, knowing they were gonna go camp and maybe fish if he could convince Nathan to do it.

In fact, he didn't know Nathan's position on fish because they hadn't had a lot of it since Nathan started cooking. He wondered if Nathan didn't like it or if it was hard to get up here. Like, trout was one thing, but salmon and stuff, you kind of had to go to Santa Fe for that. Maybe to the Whole Foods, even, he wasn't sure.

"How far is it to camp?" Nathan asked about half an hour into the ride.

He grinned. "About another three hours. Let me know when you want to stop for a break."

"No, I'm good. I just wanted to know. This is actually not bad. The weather is good. The scenery is amazing. And the birds are pretty cool. I love the ravens."

"Me too. They're super smart. And up at camp we'll have magpies."

"Nobody that ever knew me back in Austin would think that I would be out here, you know?"

"No?" It wasn't a surprise. Nathan didn't seem to be the most outdoorsy of guys.

"No. I mean, I'm pretty attached to my phone and my Wi-Fi. And my knife kit. Not to mention my six-burner range— that's a pretty big one too." Nathan chuckled. "Seriously, I could go for weeks without doing anything more than restaurant, market, bar, and home over and over again."

It sounded like hell on Earth. "What kind of market?"

"Farmer's markets, of course!" Nathan wiggled in the saddle. "I love getting to meet vendors and seeing the different kinds of produce they grow through the year. That's something I learned to love in Spain. They're very big on markets."

"There's a large one in Santa Fe. We've gone to a couple here, huh? They're not too disappointing."

He hated thinking that Nathan was biding his time, waiting for a bigger, better opportunity. It frustrated him and pissed him off because he meant something, right?

"Disappointing? Dude, I have learned all sorts of things about indigenous food that I didn't know. Also that New Mexican food is a totally different bird than Tex-Mex or

Mexican or Baja Mexican or border Mexican or coastal Mexican. Oh my God."

Ames tried hard not to frown over because, one, they were starting on their vacation, as short as it was, and it would be ridiculous to start it off grumpy. And, two, because it was real bullshit that he was going to get his panties in a wad because Nathan said he liked it here. Just because he what? Wanted to get mad. No. Not today.

Nathan was trying. He was gonna try, too.

"Yeah, you like that prickly pear stuff, didn't you?" Nathan must have spent a hundred bucks on prickly pear syrup and jam and some sort of weird dried things.

"Yeah, buddy. Not only does it taste good, but it's such a pretty color. You eat with your eyes, you know."

"That's really a gross visual, Nathan."

Nathan tilted his head, and the horse started to follow the direction of the tilt, so obviously Nathan was clenching his thigh. "Oh, you have a point."

"Straighten up, man. Relax your legs. Heels down. Pay attention."

This was not a place to get dumped off a horse. There were altogether too many things that were going to poke the living shit out of a man that would prevent nookie later. No one needed an ass full of said prickly pear spines or yucca spears.

"Sorry." Nathan righted both himself and the horse. "They really are responsive, aren't they?"

"Yep. They feel what you want, and what you don't. They're curious enough to want to see what you see. And they'll take advantage of you if you lose focus."

"Kase says they're smart enough to be evil."

"Yeah." He patted his gelding's neck. "They so are. And they're way bigger than say, a puppy." He kept an eye on Nathan when he said it.

"Sophie says she wants a puppy. What do you think?"

"It's been a while since my last old girl passed. I would be ready to get a new one if one fell into our laps…"

"You don't have, like, trauma from losing her?" He could tell Nathan was curious in a genuine way.

"I smile now when I think about her. It was hard for the first little bit, and your heart has to be ready to try again. It's the hardest part of loving them. But I adore animals. And in general, we outlive them."

"That's so sad. I've never had a pet. I was always so jealous when I was a little boy. I'd go down to the park and watch."

"Are there a lot of parks in Austin?"

"Oh, yeah. It's a great city, really. Lots of green spaces, tons of lakes and such." Nathan grinned at him, shrugged. "It's funny, because it feels western, but it's not. It's sort of western-adjacent. The university keeps the liberal tone, the hippies are still there—have you ever heard about Hippie Hollow?"

"'Hippie Hollow'? No…" He imagined that was a head shop of some kind, where a seventy-something could score a joint.

"Clothing optional beach on Lake Travis."

"Clothing—well, go them!" He laughed, tickled at that thought. "We call them hippie pools here."

"I love it!"

"So…" He had to know. "Did you ever try it?"

"Hippie Hollow? God, no. I had investors, clients—that would never have worked for me. Dan would have died."

Well, that didn't make no sense. He thought that gay guys from the city were all out proud and shaking their thing at Pride events and stuff. He didn't understand.

After all, he'd seen Nathan naked. He'd explored every inch at this point. There were lots of tattoos—all of which were cool, if not something he'd want on his body. Fun to trace, real pretty in the whole package—Nathan was meant for admiring. He had all his important parts. They all worked.

Nothing smelled gross. Didn't have crotch rot. Had a beautiful cock. Ames didn't get it.

"Why? Was he embarrassed to go?"

"Oh no. He was very proper in all ways, but he was not interested in public displays of affection. He was interested in..." Nathan's mouth twisted a little. "Shit, man. I can't even tell you that he was particularly interested in me. He was interested in money, and I was the way to get that."

Jesus.

"I'm not interested in your money. That's for sure." He closed his eyes a second, because that had popped out of his mouth. This could go one of two ways, and one of them was really wrong. He couldn't believe he said that out loud.

"Well, thank God for that. I don't have a pot to piss in or a window to throw it out of." Nathan started chuckling, and Ames was glad that it had gone the right way. Instead of the I'm-going-to-kick-your-butt-and-it's-going-to-be-a-miserable-weekend sort of way. "You just wait. Ames. One day. I will get back to where I need to be."

"Where's that?" He didn't want know this answer.

"I'm going to have a restaurant again. You watch and see. I'm gonna make this happen."

"I don't doubt you one bit." It might break him, but Ames didn't doubt it.

"Thanks. My mom used to tell me that everything happened for a reason. Maybe she was right." Nathan took a deep lungful of air, blew it all out. "That's a dream for...not today. Today. I'm going camping. I'm on a horse. It's beautiful. I mean the sky just...oh, babe. I can't even tell you."

"You can see why all the artists come out here and fall in love, can't you?"

"The land of entrapment, right?" Nathan's expression made him want to tighten his thighs, feel Buck go and fly. It was wondering and open, and for a second Ames could see all the regret and shame and sorrow fall away, leaving Nathan young and happy. "But it's true. The sky goes on and on and on and nothing interrupts it. Not a cloud. Nothing. I've only ever seen one other thing this blue that wasn't fake."

"What's that?"

Nathan smiled up into the sky. "Your eyes."

Chapter Seventeen

Nathan had to admit two things.

The first was this little line shack was possibly the cutest thing he'd ever seen in his entire life. It was this wooden cabin, plopped right in the middle of nowhere, surrounded by mountains, seeming for all intents and purposes like it had grown there, willed itself into being.

There were two rooms—one for storage, the other one with the desk, a bed, and mini fridge. Even a stove with a propane tank underneath it to cook.

There was an ancient, rusty pellet stove for heating the cabin and a little well to draw water in the storage room.

The chemical toilet had been put at a good distance so that there wasn't a bit of smell.

It was clean. It was simple. It was adorable.

Nathan had never seen anything so far away from everything else.

There was also a tiny paddock for the horses, and a great big old fire pit for them to sit out at night along with folding chairs and blankets.

Ames had done good, that was for sure.

The second thing that Nathan knew?

His thighs hurt so goddamn bad he thought he was going to die.

At least this time, though, he didn't have to try to appear super brave and suck it up.

Oh no. This time he was gonna whine.

Whine and possibly pray for a massage, because it was Ames's fault he'd been on a horse for four hours.

"You doing okay, honey?" Ames asked. He seemed worried.

He ought to seem worried.

"Do I look okay?" He grinned and winked to take away some of the sting. "I don't suppose you brought any of that salve stuff? I might need that salve stuff." Nathan gave Ames the big anime eyes, hoping it worked. "Bad."

"I did bring Granny's salve, yeah, but I was talking about the line shack. This work?"

Nathan thought about giving Ames shit about it, but his lover looked so goddamn nervous that he couldn't tease.

"It's great, man. I mean, this is like a surprise out here in the middle of the high desert."

That must have been the right thing to say, because Ames gave him a smile that rivaled the sun before he ran his hand through that jet-black hair and plopped that summer straw hat back down on his head. "Good deal."

"But..."

"But?" Ames blinked, like maybe he'd blindsided him some with the qualification.

"Yep. But. If you want me to cook supper, you're going to need to do a little quid pro quo."

A little grin curved Ames's lips. "Am I now? What's that?"

"My ass and thighs are going to fall off. I need a massage, or I won't be able to stand."

Ames drew close, reaching up to put one hand on the back

of his neck and pull him in for a kiss. "See, we progress. Look at you, asking for help. Let me go take care of the horses, and then we'll clean up, and I'll rub you down. We can even have a nap before supper."

He moaned, because that sounded like heaven. He got it, though. He'd heard maybe a million times that cowboys took care of their horses first, then themselves, and their two were still tied to a rail out front, saddles and bridles on, the packs still loaded on the backs of their saddles.

"Can I help?" Nathan was afraid if he sat down he'd never get up.

"You can come keep me company if you want."

"Sure." Now that he could do. And he could help unload anything they needed, like the food and stuff.

They hadn't brought anything fancy—a pack of hamburger, some bacon, and sandwich stuff. This wasn't a busman's holiday. But he was so looking forward to Ames making biscuits over the fire for breakfast in the morning.

He'd channeled his mom's and her Girl Scout leader past and made a bunch of that gorp stuff—chocolate, cinnamon-glazed pecans, golden raisins, and homemade granola. Yum. He'd stuck a gallon bag in the pack and figured worst came to worst, they wouldn't starve.

It didn't take long to unpack and get the horses watered in the big trough.

Then it was time for the brushing.

Nathan knew Ames loved this part, because his cowboy could spend hours with a big brush in his hand, loving on whatever horse needed it.

He took Lobo, resting one hand on the big horse's hip, pushing the tail away as it flicked flies, starting to comb.

He could almost imagine being an Old West cowboy out here—riding along, coming across a place where you could sit for a few days, and really relax. Take shelter.

The use of these shacks hadn't changed in decades.

Obviously lots of people still came and went. Hell, there was even a logbook.

"You ever imagined being an Old West cowboy, Ames?"

"Only every goddamn day." The brush made a whooshing sound as it slid over the horse's hide. "I'm not like those rodeo kids attached to my phone or hunting for Wi-Fi. I'm not an athlete or a businessman. I was supposed to be a cowboy riding in the range. Just me and my horse."

There was a hunger in Ames's eyes that Nathan thought he could connect with.

"Just you, huh?" He didn't think he could go back. But of course, he couldn't. That wasn't at all logical. But if could somehow, he didn't want to go back even thirty years ago. He didn't like hiding, and he liked his fancy kitchen. Electricity.

Running water.

"Well. That's how I used to imagine it." Ames shrugged. "That's the romance tale, isn't it? The cowboy rides away, leaving his busty girl waiting in the saloon, waving at the balcony window. That's the way the story goes."

"All right. I thought it was a romance. That means it has to have a happy ending." He grinned at Ames's over Buck's back, admiring the way those muscles moved under a T-shirt that had been new ten years ago. "You do remember what those are right? Happy endings?"

Ames opened his mouth, then closed it, going for a grin. "Maybe. Maybe I do. Sure."

"I'll remind you lots." This was a vacation, their weekend off. This wasn't a place for deep thoughts.

He hadn't intended anyone to have deep thoughts.

"Oh, I like that." Ames kept brushing, so he did too. "I didn't mean to bring anybody down, you know..."

Ames shook his head. "No. No, but I do think a lot about the folks here had to come across from, like, Kansas City. Can you imagine the folks from the East Coast? They go from the East Coast to Kansas City, and they think it's the farthest, wildest thing that they've ever seen. Then they start out this direction."

Nathan nodded, tracing the long lines of Lobo's neck. "There's something unbelievable about thinking of Kansas City as the end of anything. It's the middle, you know? Smack dab in the center."

"Now, but back then? No way. I mean, most of the wagon trails are gonna go from Independence north on the Oregon Trail unless they were traders, then they'd take the Santa Fe trail. But those that came down this way?" The passion in Ames's voice rang out. "Or the ones coming across Texas? There's no wagons. No lines of settlers with everything in their Conestogas. They come across the Badlands on their mule trains, and all of a sudden, bang! They're in the land of arroyos and desert and mountains and..."

Okay, that was hot as fuck. Listen to that utter joy. It rang from Ames, and it made him want to hear more, if for no other reason than to listen to Ames speak.

"And they get to the top of those mountains, they stare out, and there's no ocean to be found. Not for hundreds of miles still. No proof that it actually exists at all."

"I can't even imagine," Nathan admitted. "I think I'd see that and quit. Put down roots and be all, here's where I'm from."

"That's how it worked, didn't it? People got as far as they could go, and then they sat down and they said, 'this is it. I'm home now.'"

"You have a point, I guess. I guess you go West, and when you get tired of walking, you sit."

"You know it." Ames sounded pleased, as if Nathan got it.

Nathan didn't know if he had, but he could sure fake it until he made it.

That was the story of his goddamn life.

Ames had listened to him wax poetic about food for hours. Had sat while he and Sophie menu-planned. Had peeled dozens of potatoes for them during the Fourth of July weekend.

The least he could do was cheer Ames on when he got his history buff on and talked about the Old West, right? And he did love a cowboy. Well, this cowboy.

Okay, that was also a Deep Thought, and now was not the damn time.

Ames gave each one of the horses a handful of sweet feed, then they walked them to the little fenced paddock and turned them out.

"You ready to go wash up, baby?" Ames asked. "I've still got plenty of energy for personal grooming."

He laughed out loud, the thought that he was going to get brushed tickling the shit out of him. "I'm game as long as that's a massage and not a curry comb."

"You know it." Ames held out a hand, and he took it, so they walked back to the cabin with their fingers curled together.

Warmth pooled in his belly. Not the kind that made him want to jump Ames's bones right now. That could wait. But the kind that told him he would spend days with this man, just enjoying the way Ames smiled at him, listening to that smoky cowboy voice rumbling on.

When they got inside the cabin, Ames unrolled their bedding on the bed, then got a big old pot of water on the propane stove, putting a lid on it.

"Washing up water," Ames said when he raised his eyebrows. "You need help with those clothes?"

He grinned wryly. "Not sure I can even get my damn boots off."

"Well, I live to serve. Have a sit in the chair there and I'll get them for you."

"Do I get to push your butt with my foot like in the old books?"

"Nope. You touch my ass with that boot, and I will beat you."

"Uh-uh. Remember, cowboy. Kink talk is reserved for traveling. You are banned until we're back on a horse." He winked and managed not to groan when he sat down. "Now, get with the boots."

Ames sat with Nathan by the firepit, the stars bright as hell overhead, the night clear and a little chilly like it always was up here, even in the late summer.

They'd forsaken the folding chairs in favor of piling the blankets on the ground and wrapping one around them. They'd had marshmallows on the heels of Nathan using up the rest of their supper supplies on a spectacular meal of grilled sandwiches and a weird salad that was an amalgamation of every vegetable he wasn't going to use to make a ranch hands scramble tomorrow morning...

Life was damn good.

He kissed the side of Nathan's neck, squeezing with the arm he had wrapped around Nathan's waist.

"A man could get used to this, baby."

"Eventually, you'd miss Sophie and your bathroom," Nathan shot right back, snuggling in. There wasn't any heat in the words, or any real tease, for that matter. "I have to admit, it is beautiful out here."

"It is. And I've had a ball." It wasn't just the scenery or the time off, though. It was Nathan. They'd learned each other these last few days. They'd made love endlessly, talked about movies and music and where food history and Old West lore intersected.

He didn't only desire Nathan. Ames liked the man, dammit. He was a trouper, and he was funny as hell. And kind.

Ames wasn't sure he wanted to go home.

"Mmm. I kinda do miss those things, but I've been damn happy here with you."

Nathan hummed, leaning harder into him. "I've had a great time."

"Yeah? I bet you're ready for a shower."

"Mmmhmm. And maybe a cinnamon roll."

"You do love your cinnamon rolls."

"I do." Nathan looked up at him, expression serious as a heart attack. "I feel the same way about you."

One of his eyebrows shot up. "I'm sweet and biteable?"

Nathan whacked his arm good and hard. "Don't make me hurt you. I just mean that I think I might be in love with you too. I have to admit I don't know if I want to be, but that doesn't have anything to do with you. That has to do with me being scared that I'm a giant screwup, that I'm not good at this relationship."

Christ on a pogo stick.

What was he supposed to say?

Ames could go with what he was feeling, which had a lot of jumping with joy and grabbing and squeezing and kissing hard involved with it.

He could go with what he was thinking, which was maybe he shouldn't get involved with some guy who wasn't sure if he was ready to get involved and who was fixing to run away and move to God knows where.

Unfortunately, or fortunately as the case may be, Ames was a cowboy down to the bone, and he'd never met a single cowboy on Earth who went with what he was thinking over what he was feeling. Not even once.

So he went with what he knew.

He turned to stare Nathan right in those eyes shimmering like sun through dark honey. "I got you, baby. You let go, trust that I have your back, and I promise that I'll never let you hit the ground. I'm a cowboy, balls- deep, and you got my word, you'll never regret loving me."

That must have been the right thing to say, because what he got was this big old grin and a kiss that liked to burn him to the ground.

He held on, because the whole world was spinning and dropping away, and the only solid thing to hold onto was Nathan. He kissed right back, because how could he not? He'd never said anything like that to a man before. Had never felt it.

He sure felt it with Nathan, and it scared him half to death.

Nathan clung to him, and he had a feeling they were sharing the same rush of emotions, the same crazy kaleidoscope of adrenaline and exhilaration.

When they broke for air, Nathan searched his face, lips parted, a little swollen. "I don't know what to say. I can't make any promises, because I'm terrible at—"

"Nope." He put his fingers over Nathan's lips. "I made my big speech. You say, 'Okay, cowboy.'"

"Right. Okay, cowboy."

"Good job." He chuckled at them. He guessed everybody who was in love was an idiot. It was part of the job.

Hopefully it got better, but he wasn't sure. The bosses sure still seemed to be stupid over one another, and he guessed, he hoped, he could be just as lucky.

"So what happens now?" Nathan asked.

He shrugged, kinda confused. "What do you mean?"

"Do we tell Sophie? Do we tell anybody? Am I allowed to

touch you? Or do I have to pretend like I don't like you? Do I get to spend the night every now and again? You know, what happens next?" Nathan rolled his eyes. "And nothing is an inappropriate answer. I mean, nothing could happen next."

"Don't be dumber than you have to be. Of course, we tell Sophie. She lives at the house, she's gonna notice. She also is not going to be surprised." He didn't know he was supposed to tell the boss. Did it matter? Bigger question was, did it matter to Nathan? "And you're welcome to spend the night any time you want. You could even put a toothbrush over at the house."

"Cool. About the toothbrush, I might do that because you know—I'm really in lust with your hot tub."

He snorted. "Yeah, yeah, yeah. Tell it to the judge."

"You think, Sophie'll be okay?"

"I think she'll be over the moon. You're her hero."

Nathan smiled and shook his head the tiniest bit. "That'll change. First time I tell her she did something wrong, or she makes something that's truly nasty, I'll be that asshole she used to work with. When she gets into culinary school, I'll be that asshole she used to work for because it'll give her street cred."

Ames couldn't stop his growl. "You're not an asshole."

"Not in the kitchen, no. I don't have that rep." Nathan rolled his eyes like dice. "But if I'm dating you and she's sort of my mentee, my intern. That could get weird."

"Families work together all the time." Didn't seem weird to him at all.

"Yeah, but I'm not family yet."

"We're working on that part. I think it's going to happen sooner or later, whether we want it to or not."

"You don't want it to?" He hadn't meant to put that hurt in Nathan's eyes.

"What? I mean, yes, but what am I gonna do when you go

back to Austin or to Dallas or Hawaii or wherever you have a restaurant?"

"Well, you could come with me."

Ames shook his head. "Oh honey, I belong here. I'm a cowboy."

"They do have cowboys in Texas, I am reliably informed."

"Yeah." He didn't want to talk about this.

Simple fact was that Ames loved his job. He loved his job as much as Nathan loved his, and whether or not this land was his, this was the place Ames could spend the rest of his life. He had his own place. He had his own horses. He had access to the best of everything on the ranch. Sophie was here. He didn't want to go.

"We don't have to talk about this. You said you wouldn't let me hit the ground, and I believe you. That's enough."

It was going to have to be enough for both of them, he supposed.

"Do you dance?" Nathan asked.

"What?"

"Dance. You know, two-stepping. Do you dance?" Nathan motioned toward the house. "There's a radio in there. It has batteries, I checked. Do you wanna dance?"

"I do." Ames nodded. He did. He really did. So he stood, and then hauled Nathan up alongside him. "Go get the radio. I'd love to dance with you."

God knew it was better than talking.

Chapter Nineteen

Falling in love with a cowboy was sort of like falling in love with a buffalo. It was dangerous, it involved a lot of shit, and about the time you did it, they ran off to deal with the herd.

They'd ridden down from their camping weekend to a ranch that was like a fire ant hill that somebody had kicked good and hard.

Cowboys had been running this way and that. Horses had gotten out somewhere, and in God knows where Montana there was a company transport trailer that had gotten broke into, and now there were animals running all over the damn roads.

Zebras or some such shit?

No one had the time or the inclination for a plated meal, so he spent all of his time making lunch sacks and things people could pop in and take.

Sophie helped about half the time. The rest of the time she was out being a kid, doing teenager things with other teenagers, which, he supposed was all right.

Sixteen wasn't an age to learn how to be a chef. Sixteen

was an age to go out and have a good time and learn how to be a human being. Still, it didn't help his feeling of loneliness.

It was kind of like having a full body Band-Aid on, and then having it ripped off. It stung like a bitch, but afterward it left you a little numb and you had to get back to work.

Ames hadn't been home because he was dealing with the zebra situation. So Sophie stayed up at the main house, and Nathan stayed in his little house, spending a lot of time thinking about what?

Shit.

Thinking about having bared his soul to a man who was terrified that he was going to do what he was meant to do in life?

He chuckled at himself.

Was that even a sentence?

He was sitting at one of the picnic tables outside the main kitchen, thumbing through his notebook trying to think of new menu plans, new recipes.

Daydreaming about God knows what.

He was thinking about being back where he had been, trying to get to where he wanted to be.

Nathan didn't know.

What he did know was that there wasn't a fucking thing he could do to help any of these people do any of the jobs they did because he was not a cowboy.

He was a queer chef from Austin whose idea of boots involved lots of buckles and black leather. He wore button-fly Levis and T-shirts that showed off his belly. His belt bore the buckle it had come from the store with.

He did not own any stretch jeans, however. He wouldn't go that far. He was still a Texan.

He wanted Ames to come home, so he could ask had he fucked up?

Were they fucked up?

It hadn't felt too terribly horked by the time that they had left the campsite.

But it hadn't felt like—there wasn't that romantic comedy magic you're supposed to have when you tell somebody that you love them, and then you find out that they love you back and there's all this future ahead of you and shit—but it hadn't felt bad.

It had felt like...like grown-up love.

He rolled his eyes at himself as if that was such a fucking thing.

This was his way of justifying the fact that they were not compatible.

At least their lives were not compatible. What they wanted was not compatible.

They were pretty damn compatible. They compat-ed along with the best of them. Not just in bed, either. He could talk to Ames for hours. That was part of the problem, right? They'd told each other some pretty deep stuff. Secret dreams. Real desires. What they both needed out of life.

Which was why he wasn't sure he could reconcile anything he knew about the two of them going forward...

"Hey, Nathan. How's it going?" Kase startled the shit out of him, standing maybe six feet away. He hadn't heard the man.

"Man, you scared me." He managed to find a grin for his boss, who stood there in a T-shirt, ancient Wranglers, and even older boots. For a man worth millions, he dressed in Walmart. "You need something?"

"Just to make sure that my chef isn't unhappy." Kase grinned at him. "We've gotten used to having you around."

"Oh." That was nice to hear. "Now, you all have Nanette, and you know it."

"She is a queen among women, and I love her with all of my

heart, but we all got to admit that at some point she's going to get tired of taking care of us all. Just like the grannies. Besides, you bring a certain je ne sais quoi to this whole ranch situation."

"Listen to you, using fancy French words." Nathan cackled because he could remember having been in France for the first time, working and thinking he was never gonna get this. He was never going to understand this damn language. He was too dumb, too Texan, too whatever.

But he did learn. You know, when the option was starving and losing your job, you learned a lot.

"I know, I know. I've got two of them taking French right now and needing help with lessons. I—I took Spanish. Why they're taking French, I don't know. They speak Spanish already."

Nathan shrugged. "Well, if they spoke one of them already, then they wouldn't be learning it, right?"

Kase gave him a patently fake glare. "Shut up, Nathan."

"Shutting up, Boss. What you need?"

Kase came to sit, stretching up as tall as his little bitty body would go, which wasn't very far. "I didn't need anything, really. You seemed so damn unhappy. So I thought I'd come see what was what."

Oh. "It's fine. I'm fine."

What was he going to say? Hi, I'm fucking one of your cowboys, and we may or may not be madly in love with one another. And we may or may not be already on the road to breaking up, which was going to make everything awkward, and I don't know. Yay.

It seemed a little inappropriate at best.

"You sure?"

"I'm trying to find the rhythm of the work here. It's totally different than the insanity I'm used to. It's a challenge—a good one, for sure, but I have a learning curve."

"I can see that," Kase admitted, hat shading his eyes. "Is there anything I can do?"

"Make zebras stop escaping?"

"Damn, that would be a trick, wouldn't it?" Kase shook his head, chuckling low. "Speaking of zebras, how's Ames? You heard from him?"

Oh fuck. "Yeah, he's out there herding and searching. They found all but one. I'm assuming zebras aren't particularly big on recall."

"Not particularly, no. Um, I don't suppose that you..." Kase stopped and sighed. "Never mind, I'll talk to Ames when I can."

Nathan arched an eyebrow. There was no way he was going to let his cowboy get in trouble. None. "Now look, there is absolutely nothing work wise that connects me and Ames. Ames is not allowed into my kitchen. I managed not to die on horseback, but that's really as far as it goes. I can't do anything rodeoesque, so... That's weird."

"I know." Kase twisted his lips. "I really know, but we've got a touch of a problem."

Huh. Odd. "This is a little worrisome and more than a little weird. Does it have to do with Sophie? Is Sophie okay?" He hadn't talked to her in a few hours.

"It does, but only on the most vague of...look, I can't get hold of Ames. You know, Montana is notorious for dead spots." Kase rolled his eyes. "But somebody dropped off two puppies. Today. And Sophie says they're yours. Y'alls. And I don't know what to do with them."

"Puppies." Nathan blinked, because that was a curveball.

"You don't know anything about puppies?"

Nathan shook his head. "I do not know anything about puppies. At all."

Like at all at all.

He needed to talk to Sophie.

"Hmm. Okay, well. They said they would have dropped them off at Ames's place, but no one was there. The kids and I can keep them until he gets back."

"Yeah, I have no idea what the plan is there." Puppies... "Can I come see them? Me and Sophie?"

"Of course you can. Hell, you can come sit with them in the X-pen and keep them company."

"What the hell is an X-pen?"

"It corrals them up some. Keeps them from running all over the house and peeing. And keeps our dogs from being all over them."

"So, what kind of dogs are they?" He didn't need a dog, but God, he was curious.

"Border collie and bloodhound." Kase's words were dry as dust.

Nathan blinked. "Is that bad?"

"No." Kase's head shake made him feel better. "No dogs are bad. Some are more stubborn than others, and some need a lot of work, but no dogs are bad. They're real cute. There's a black-and-white one and a brown-and-white one."

"And they're both mine?"

"That's what the lady said."

Oh, man. He had to find Miss Sophie, and he needed to talk to Ames, like right now.

He texted,

Call me. Need to talk

as they wandered into the little high school area Wat had set up, and found Sophie. "Uh. Can we chat?"

She gave him a wide-eyed stare, because he'd never shown up at school before. "Is something wrong?"

"No, but. It's your..." Dammit. "Mr. Kase here tells me that someone dropped off puppies. For me."

She clapped one hand over her mouth and stood, kind of dancing, like she had to pee or something. "Oh my God. Oh my God. Oh my God. It's puppies. The puppies are here. I didn't think they'd come until Uncle Ames got back."

"Would you like to explain?" Kase asked, as if this shit happened daily.

"Sure! Uncle said that...well, you see, I was going to get him a kitten because everybody needs a pet, and Uncle Ames said no, he needed a dog. Maybe a purse dog that he could have put bows on, and we couldn't find one, but we did find a passel of bloodhound border collie puppies and so Uncle said that we'd get two—one could be for Chef and one could be for him. And they could live together happily ever after."

"'Happily ever after', huh?" Kase grinned over at him.

"Shut up, Boss."

"Shutting up, I'm going to see the puppies."

Sophie made a squealing noise that could only be heard by dogs and other sixteen-year-old girls, obviously, because the teenagers came flocking, and they ran together through the house. They managed to make a beeline for the pen where the puppies were, because obviously she had a psychic connection with them or something.

When he got to the pen, he knew he was fucked, for sure.

God, they were cute. Seriously, little fuzzy balls of white with different-colored spots, and Nathan was in love like bang.

"Are they boys or girls?"

Kase picked one up, glanced at their bellies. "This one's a boy."

That was the little black-and-white one. Then the smaller brown-and-white pup was picked up. "And this is a little girl. So you got one each. You're gonna have to get them fixed."

"I don't know that that's up to me. I think that's an Ames question."

"You like him though, don't you? I mean, we get to keep them, right?"

How on earth was he going to tell this big-eyed little girl who'd lost so much that no, she couldn't have dogs?

He still wasn't sure how one of them had ended up being his.

He simply nodded. "Yeah. We'll talk to Ames as soon as we can and have him bring home supplies, I guess, or we can go out and get them later."

"Okay, I want the little girl to be called Honeysuckle," she said.

Nathan tilted his head, pondering that. "Then we should name the boy Thorn."

Kase rolled his eyes. "Well, there you go. Y'all have dogs. Like I said, we'll keep him over here until we get hold of Ames and figure out what's what."

"That's fair. I really appreciate it. I just wasn't sure." Well. This was unexpected. "And I do appreciate it."

He'd never had a boss keep puppies for him before.

Lord save him from cowboys, he had a dog.

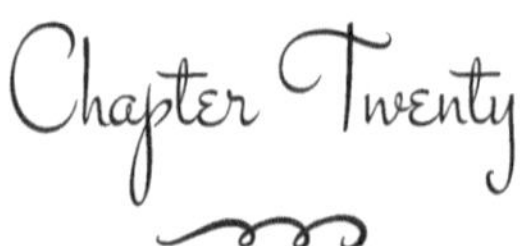

Chapter Twenty

Ames dragged his sorry ass back into the ranch at about two thirty in the afternoon on a Monday. At least he thought it was a Monday. He'd kind of lost track of time.

No one could even blame Big Jack, who had been the one driving the trailer full of zebras and oryx, ostriches and one kangaroo. They were rescues, destined for an exotic animal sanctuary run by one of the bosses' friends in Montana. And someone had T-boned the damn truck.

Ames had arrived to a full-blown rescue op, with about ten local wranglers already on scene. But he was the freakin zebra whisperer. And oryx. And kangaroo, apparently. No one whispered to ostriches, and sadly, one of them hadn't made it through the crash.

Big Jack had also needed some help with hospital stuff, and then there was the fact the truck and trailers belonged to the ranch...

But he was home now, and while he was a touch road-drunk and more than a little...crusty, all of the remaining animals had been delivered to the sanctuary, and he was ready to beg the bosses for a few days off for a job well-done.

As soon as he stopped in to see Sophie and Nathan, who should've been working at this time of the day. Sophie tried hard to finish her summer class early in the day to help Nathan with the supper stuff.

The new pups were in a small run right outside the kitchen door, and they set to barking as soon as Ames walked up.

Lord have mercy. Look at those beasts. They were goofy little fuzz balls.

Still, he knew Sophie was pleased as punch, and he figured that Nathan wasn't too mad, really. In fact, he'd seemed to like the idea of the puppies, and he was keeping them at his neat little house.

Ames had tried explaining that he didn't exactly mean to spring them on Nathan.

Except, he had, but not like that.

He had intended to be home and sort of go, "Here. Here's a puppy for you. I'll keep it over at the house, and you can visit it whenever you want to. That way we can get it all trained up, and maybe you could stay over here while I'm training it."

But, if wishes were horses...

"Hey, you hooligans." He reached down to them to let them smell. The little boy, Thorn, backed up, butt sliding on the ground, crying out for help. This little girl, though, that brave beast jumped right up on the side of the pen and growled, warning him away from her baby brother.

"Hey, why are y'all growling?"

"Since when did you say y'all?" he teased, and little Honey-suckle jumped a mile and peed.

"Hey, Uncle!" Sophie gave him a cheery wave, her eyes shining, then she bounced over for a hug, flour on the tip of her nose. "Welcome home. You need some food? Chef's teaching me how to make pie crusts, but we had calzones for lunch and there's still some left."

"Calzones, huh?" That sounded good.

"Yes, Chef says that people aren't coming in to be regular right now, with it being summer and all. So we're making things that people can take and eat however they need to. It's not as fun as making a plated lunch, but it's still good. We're working it out."

"Do I hear Ames?" Nathan peered out over the top of Sophie head. "Well, hey, stranger. Come on in, I'll get you a Coke. What kind do you want?"

"I'll take a Dr Pepper, if you got one. The rumor is there's calzones."

And also, I don't suppose that you're mad at me... He chuckled at himself. They weren't not talking, right? They'd talked a lot while he was gone. Sort of. In fits and starts.

"There are. I've got one pepperoni, one sausage and onion, and two—no three veg. Apparently veggie calzones are not the big seller this time." Nathan handed him a cold can of Dr Pepper, winking at him. "It's good to see you."

Oh now, that suited him down to the bone. "It's good to be seen, and I'll take a veggie and a sausage and onion, please. I'm hungry."

"Dude! Dude, you owe me five bucks." Sophie beamed at Nathan. "Seriously, I said the sausage should be gone first. Sausage are gone first, so hand it over."

"Oh, listen to you." Nathan didn't seem upset, though. He was laughing, and he handed over a crisp five-dollar bill without argument. "I thought for sure it was going to be the pepperoni."

"Sausage is big in these parts." Ames popped open the can of drink and downed a third of it. "Permission to enter the kitchen and wash up?" Ames asked.

"Granted." Nathan and Sophie moved to let him in. "I'll

get your plate done up. Sophie, you need to get that dough together before your butter melts."

"Oui, Chef!" She hurried back to the counter to do something with flour and butter and whatever. The only thing Ames knew about pie crust was that he loved it around fruit.

"We're having dough day," Nathan teased, artfully arranging calzones and sauce on a plate for him. Even when the food was delicious and simple, Nathan was amazing with it.

Well, okay, a turkey sandwich was a turkey sandwich, but these calzones looked and smelled amazing.

"Thanks, babe," he murmured, and he wanted a kiss. Badly.

"Turn your back, Sous." Nathan said, and Sophie turned around with a giggle. Then he got a kiss—not gross, but enough that he knew he'd been missed.

Ames took it and gave as good as he got because damn, he's missed this man. And he'd been worried about spending so much time away when all of this was so new.

They pulled apart, and he grinned. "So how's it been going?"

"Well, like Sophie said, it's been pretty slow. Miss Nanette would like a weekend off soon, so I think I'll be at the big house for a weekend."

"Wow, look at you. You gonna make them eat kangaroo?"

"I understand King Ranch Casserole has been requested, but I have cooked kangaroo, believe it or not. A number of times, in fact. It's all right. I prefer venison, though. It's more versatile."

"King Ranch Casserole, huh?"

"Yeah, it works out because that way I can make up the casseroles, leave them over there, and the guys can throw them in the oven whenever they're ready to eat. As opposed to me actually missing an entire weekend, for instance. From what I understand, both Ryder and Kase can make a mean omelet, and one of the two of them makes pancakes."

"That makes sense." It seemed to him that most cowboys could, at least, make one breakfast meal and one thing that they could cook on the grill without seeming like an idiot. It didn't have to be anything fancy, something solid enough to work if you were having a cookout nobody would tease you and if you were wanting to get married they wouldn't run screaming.

Also, he supposed that it was a good thing to be able to feed yourself. "Everybody's got their one thing, don't they?"

"They do. So tell me. Mr. Ames, what is your one thing that you can cook?"

He tried to think. He did pretty good with basic stuff, and he never was going to starve, but hmm, what was the special thing that he did?

Maybe his breakfast strata, although that was on the fancy side and he didn't want anybody to think he was uppity, but still... "Well, I am the king of midnight pancakes. But I make this breakfast thing with meat and bread and—You kind of put it together the night before and then you eat it the next day. My mom taught me to make it. We always had it Christmas morning." This was weirdly embarrassing.

"Granny's Christmas breakfast casserole!" Sophie's eyes lit up like he'd promised her diamonds. "You know how to make that, too?"

"Yeah, yeah, I do."

"So can we have it this year? I don't know how to make it. I mean, I'm sure there's a recipe online, but you know, they're all different. And I want it to be like hers."

"Well, I can do that." Now, somehow it didn't feel quite as ridiculous. It felt sort of important.

"Food memories, man, those are some strong things." Nathan grinned at him. "I mean, part of it's just that it's about smell, right? Not to mention because smell memories are the strongest. The food's got that, plus the taste, the sight. It hits all the all the sensory buttons. It fucking rocks, man. I can't wait to taste it."

Okay, so that meant that Nathan intended to be there until Christmas.

He'd take that as a win.

"Well, then, breakfast strata for Christmas morning it is. I'll have to go into Santa Fe to get the fancy cheese." He winked, trying to share the joke with them both.

These were the things he wanted to share with Nathan. He wanted to share them with Sophie, too. Remind her where she came from without being an ass about it, because sometimes where she'd come from wasn't a great place.

But that was a lot to think about right now, considering that he'd just gotten back from a zebra road trip. He had plenty of time, and it wasn't necessarily this moment that he had to think about Christmas, although Christmas had a way of sneaking up on a man if he wasn't careful. So he'd have to think about it a bit.

"What else can you cook?" Nathan asked.

"Oh, I don't know. I guess I can do things like eggs and bacon?"

"Eggs are proof that there's a God and we're loved," Nathan said. "Good egg cookery is a great skill. What else?" That steady gaze sort of burned right into him, so intent.

"Biscuits."

"You do make fine biscuits. On a campfire, no less," Nathan pointed out. "What else. Wow me."

"You mean things that I have to like season? Believe it or not, I'm really, really good at fried potatoes."

"Oh." Nathan gave him this glance. This sort of not-quite-sexual look, but it was close.

"Like, hash browns, or—"

"No, no. Well, sure, I can do hash browns too. That's easy. They're already cut for you, and you open a bag. But no, I'm talking about the kind of big kind of potatoes where you have to chop them up and put them in the oil and fry them yourself. Season them up good. I could do that."

"Yum." That was the expression he wanted to see on Nathan's face. A little admiration, a little laughter.

"Wait, can you make Granny's enchiladas?" Sophie asked.

He kind of laughed. "Well, that one you might have to help me with, but I bet together we can come up with something to make them taste like they're supposed to. I can make your mom's spaghetti sauce too."

Her eyes went wide. "Wow. That's cool. I mean, your mom only opened a jar of Ragu."

"Yes, your mom was the one who made the really good sauce." And he'd taught himself how to do all that because to begin with he'd missed home like a sore tooth. They grinned at each other, and Nathan laughed.

"Well, I can see that we have all sorts of things to put into the personal rotation," Nathan said.

"Sounds good, man. Sounds really good after maybe I take a nap. I don't suppose you'd be interested in hot tub and a nap?"

"After Sophie gets done, makes her pie crust, and we clean up, I would love to."

"I've got the bottom crust in the pan, Chef, and the apples are ready to go. I used cinnamon, butter, brown sugar, allspice, and a little pink peppercorn in the filling."

Pepper? Good Lord and butter...that sounded, not pleasant.

"All right. Well get it in the pie crust, top it off and let me see." Nathan winked at him as he wiped off counters and straightened things as they waited. The man was never still, not even when he was sleeping, and Ames loved that he knew that.

Loved that he understood that Nathan needed to be held at night, so he could snuggle in and get rest.

"You ready to get home?"

He nodded. "How long will the pie take to cook?"

"Too long. Y'all can take it home and she can cook it there."

He nodded, because he knew that Sophie would want to come to the house tonight. Hopefully Nathan did too. They could all ride over together with the puppies.

Oh man, the puppies.

Thank goodness he'd been putting in bibs and bobs of everything since he found out he was going to pick them up. He had pens and beds and crates and bowls—all of it stored back in his garage. He'd have to grab enough puppy food to last until tomorrow morning when he ran out to the feed store.

"Pop the pie in the cooler bag. We'll take it to the house to cook for dessert if you want," Nathan said, shooting him a quick curious glance. "I can make supper tonight. If you'd like."

"Whatever you figure, babe. You know what is in the fridge. You've been stocking it." He offered Nathan a grin. "Why don't you pack a bag for a couple days?"

Why don't you just come and stay? He didn't say that one out loud, but he wanted to. He didn't want to think about the whys and the wherefores and all that because moving in was a big thing, and he had Sophie now, and...he didn't know what to do.

He did know what he wanted to do, and that was to bring Nathan home where he belonged.

He wasn't sure that Nathan with all of his cosmopolitan

Austin ways would appreciate that primal urge that he had to wrap him up and keep him forever, but that was the truth.

"Hey, babe, where you at?" Nathan's voice was warm, and...loving. The word was loving.

"I was thinking about bringing you and the puppies home to stay."

Those words fell out of his mouth. They plopped onto the counter like a turd in a punch bowl, and he couldn't believe it.

This wasn't him. He didn't just say things.

But he *did* mean it.

Nathan didn't even hesitate, simply gave him a nod like he was on the back of a bronc and wanted the gate to open. "Yeah, you think there's room for us there?"

"I think there might be. Does this mean that we're dating?"

Nathan shook his head. "No, no, I swore off dating."

That wicked little grin sure enough flipped his switch like nothing else. It said all the things—all the things they were never going to say out loud in this kitchen with Sophie sitting right there and watching them like a hawk. That little grin made private promises right out in public.

"Well then, I guess we won't be dating, but there's room for you. How long will it take you to clean out your tiny house?"

Nathan's eyes rolled like dice. "Approximately seventeen seconds. All my stuff is in storage."

"Excellent. Let's grab whatever we can in seventeen seconds and head home, huh?" That prospect made all the shit from the last little bit worth it. All the zebras and ostrich bites and worry.

"I'll get a bag, really. I can grab the rest tomorrow. You're tired."

That he was. "You're right about that."

"Pie is in the bag," Sophie said. "You need me to clean anything else, Chef?"

"Just start the dishwasher, kiddo, then head for the truck. We'll be there in a moment."

"Okay." Sophie suited actions to command, starting the dishwasher, then grabbing her phone and making her way outside.

"Want to come help me pack a bag?" Nathan waggled his eyebrows, and Ames hoped that meant a few more quick kisses while they were tucked away from prying eyes.

"I do." He took Nathan's hand, and he got no resistance as they walked to Nathan's tiny house.

They got inside, and Ames reeled Nathan in to take the kiss he so desperately wanted. He'd never asked anyone to move in with him before. This was a first, and it seemed to him like he needed to mark the occasion somehow.

"Mmm." Nathan wrapped both arms around his neck. "We both need a shower."

"Well, at least it's even, then." He thought Nathan smelled damn good. Like apples and spices.

"I fucking missed you, man." Nathan nipped at his bottom lip. "I started worrying. It was hard not knowing. I mean, you know, we'd just walked in from our weekend together, and we hadn't even put the horses away when you were gone, you know?"

"I know. It sucked. That's how it works, huh? This is a ranch. There's always something." He prayed Nathan could get used to it.

"Not too different from a restaurant, maybe more animals. Well...alive ones." Nathan winked at him, then dove back into another kiss. The way that Nathan's tongue pushed between Ames's lips made him shake inside.

His cock filled, his balls heavy with how bad he wanted.

"Babe, you keep pushing me like this, and I'm going to embarrass myself."

"I just wanted you to understand that—" Nathan stared into him, so open, so eager. "I didn't come here to fall in love. None of this was what I expected. And... I'm glad you're home, I guess. I started to imagine that things were—I swear I'm not clingy."

Ames wasn't sure that he agreed with that. He'd held the man while he slept, but that was okay. Everybody needed the secrets they kept from themselves.

That was part of what a lover did, he reckoned. Get those secrets and honor them.

"I'm glad I'm home too. I don't mind traveling, but I prefer it to be a little bit more planned out with fewer ostriches." He stole another hard kiss, and then swatted Nathan on the butt. "Come on, let's get your stuff together. I really want to get you and those puppies home. I want to get into a shower with you and love all over you."

"I am in. Just let me grab some clothes." Nathan grabbed a big duffel bag and started emptying drawers. "What did you think of them, the puppies? Were they amazing?"

"They're gorgeous. I'm glad that you didn't completely short out when they showed up." He'd already hashed this all out over the phone, of course, but it was different face-to-face. "They were supposed to be this neat surprise all set up at my house. Congratulations, we have puppies! Then suddenly I'm gone. They need the whelping box back, and Kase is coming to you and handing over dogs."

"It was an amazing thing," Nathan agreed. "I mean, I've had more fascinating situations with my employers here..."

Ames snorted, tickled. "You are a good sport."

"Even if I hadn't liked dogs—which I didn't know that. I mean, maybe I don't like dogs, but puppies are awfully cute—but at any rate. Sophie was so excited." Nathan shook his head, peering from the closet. "It was... I couldn't disappoint her. She's had some hard blows, and she deserves the good stuff." Nathan headed for the little bathroom. "Did you know that she's got a girlfriend?"

"What?" Ames didn't know how to feel about that. She was awful young to have a girlfriend. "That seems pretty fast. Who is it? Is she nice? Have you met her? Have they been alone together? Have you explained that this is...there are certain ways that I mean..."

"Oh, Uncle Ames. Breathe. She doesn't live here. She lives two towns over. It's about a fifteen-minute drive. They all met when the bunch of them went to the movies. They have been on two group dates. She's going to ask you if they can come and spend the night maybe sometime next weekend. There's also a...some sort of a trail ride thing that's going to be happening right before school starts, officially. A bunch of the kids are going on it with the bosses, and she would like to go on that with her friend as well. Cool, huh?"

He stared at Nathan, tongue stuck to the roof of his mouth. "Whoa, whoa. I don't know that I'm ready for her to be sixteen."

"Good luck with that." Nathan winked at him. "Uncle Ames."

"That's some kind of evil, springing that on me," Ames groused.

Nathan gave him a big old grin. "I am. I can't help it."

"So what *are* we gonna have for dinner?" Ames asked Nathan.

"I don't know. I guess that depends on the puppies."

Ames squinted at his lover. "We're gonna eat the puppies?"

"Don't make me beat your ass, man," Nathan threatened. "It's a lot of work, and my arm's tired from chopping all day and rolling out dough."

"Did I ever eat?" He couldn't remember. He thought he'd had a plate in his hand at some point, but...

Nathan shook his head. "No, you handed it to Sophie. She wrapped it up for you along with the pie crust so that you could take it home and eat it when you got there."

"Oh well, no wonder I'm hungry." Ames figured he'd gotten so excited about the conversation with Nathan that he'd forgotten everything else.

"Anyway, we're not going eat puppies, but if they take a long time to get settled, then we're gonna have something like sandwiches or an omelet. But you know, if they're out like a light from playing all day, then I'll make you a steak or something." Nathan was nothing if not practical about everyday food.

Ames moaned. "You know, there are precious few steaks in Montana, considering that it's supposed to be cattle country and all that. I would love a steak." And he would take care of the puppies.

"Well then, that's probably what I'll make. We'll see."

Ames would take a 'we'll see'. In fact, he figured he would take that for the entire situation. Nathan was coming home with him tonight, and they were going to have a shower together, and that was all that mattered.

Even if he wasn't ready for Sophie to have a girlfriend.

<h1 align="center">Chapter Twenty-One</h1>

"And that, y'all ladies, is how y'all make a southwestern lasagna, where you freeze one, and you serve this one. You can ramp the heat up and down, you can go fruity or smoky. Not only that, it didn't cost the Earth! And y'all take notice, how long did it take us to make? Totally a weeknight meal. Now, everyone come grab you a plate, and I hope that y'all have a wonderful afternoon here at the ranch." Nathan waved the Lions Club-slash-Ladies Auxiliary Club-slash-Baptist Women's Coalition-slash-St. Francis Books and Snacks- slash whoever, whichever class he was teaching today, off.

It didn't matter what the group was. They all wanted the same thing—a chance to get together, relax, eat some good food, and listen to him flirt in Texan.

He loved it.

Kase had come up with some sort of plan where he taught one class a month to one of these social organizations, and these social organizations in turn ended up doing some sort of a scholarship for one of the foster kids.

It was a win-win situation for all concerned. The women

got what they wanted. Kase got the money they needed for these scholarships so it wasn't coming out of their pocket. The kids got practice applying for the grants.

It didn't matter. Nathan was having a ball. He enjoyed teaching, he enjoyed cooking, and he could talk to trees. So why not?

He nodded to the couple of hands Kase had allotted him for the cleaning up. "There's not a whole lot to do, guys, just the bowls. We used recyclable compostable pans for the food. Just take the extra one over to the big house. The family will eat it later."

He'd fed the cowboys this meal yesterday.

He got a quick grin from one of the cowboys. "You and Ames aren't going to eat it?"

He shook his head. "Nope. Ames is cooking. I didn't ask what. I am totally in."

The other cowboy—Greg maybe, or Gorgon, or George? He couldn't remember—looked at him with huge, wide, very, very young eyes. "Mr. Ames cooks?"

"He does for me." And that was that.

He laughed, going to table touch a few of the women who were lingering before taking his leave and stopping by the office to peek in at the bosses.

He knocked on the door, and Ryder opened it, eyebrows rising.

"Nathan, how'd it go?"

"Fine, fine it was lasagna. You all have that for dinner. Everybody enjoyed it, but if we're gonna keep meeting outside, you're gonna have to get me heaters." It was only September, and it wasn't bad yet, but he could tell. The Texan in him knew cold weather was coming, and it wasn't going to be pretty.

"Oh man, it's gonna be too chilly for you to do classes outdoors. No, heaters are not gonna work. I'll have to put you inside. I mean, heaters could maybe cover you for October's class, sure, and…" Ryder's eyes went wide, as if a light bulb had gone on. "Also, so that you know, the Halloween party is… You do know about Halloween, right?"

He stared at Ryder. Had the man lost his marbles? "No, no, they don't do Halloween in Texas. What day is it?"

"I will hit you over the head with a shovel."

"You sure could try, Shorty. What's the deal about Halloween?" He had finally figured this out. This was less a boss situation and more a say you won't situation. And he was beginning to fit in with this whole thing. These guys had realized he was going to provide food that was going to fill them up and give them energy and taste good. And the guys had stopped telling him how to do his goddamn job.

He was overjoyed, and so were the bosses.

"So you see, Halloween is my—our—anniversary, and also we have a huge haunted hayride. Oh, and there's trick or treating. So there's gonna be the anniversary party. That's sort of the family party with the kids, and you know, everyone cheers. There's the food for the hayride, so if there's anything you want to put together for that, it would rock. And then there's the fact that I'm leaving town with Kase and taking him on a cruise, which he doesn't know about. So we'll be gone for ten days."

"Okay, so. Haunted hayride. Scary haunted? Cute haunted?" It was an important distinction, and his mind raced.

"One of each."

"I can do that." He grabbed the pad and pencil that lived in his jacket pocket, jotting down notes. "Family party—real family, potluck catered family party, what?"

"I want chili and cornbread with all the fixin's. I'll provide the cake; expect seventy."

Jesus. All on the same day? "Fair enough. What do you need for when you're gone?"

"Backup for Nanette, mainly." Ryder winced. "Can you provide say five of the ten suppers that we're doing? Don't have to be fancy. You don't have to be there. Just something that the grannies can throw in the oven, or Charlie can. Plan for fifteen per meal. That should cover it."

That was easy enough, no problem. "Do you need me to make sure Sophie stays here, like here at my house, here, not here, here where I'm standing, which is the exact opposite of what I was asking. Let me start over." He took a deep breath. "All right, do you need me to keep Sophie at home?"

"Please. We've got more teenagers now than we have little ones, and another teenager isn't going to help."

"Okay, next question. Do you need me to bring any teenagers to our place? We could keep a couple more for two or three days." He hoped. He assumed he probably should ask Ames first, but he hadn't. So there was that.

"No, we have a system. We're good to go, and Charlie's coming home, so… Charlie is like the hammer of death. I think that I would probably choose her over the grannies at this point to run the kids roughshod."

Damn. That was impressive. "Right, well, then I will deal with the food part. I will send over a list of supplies and things, also heaters. I want heaters for outside, because it's cold. Or it's going to be?"

Regardless, heaters were important.

"Good deal. What are you gonna do for the October class?"

"Green chili pumpkin soup." Duh.

"Ooh, I like that. Make enough for that we can all have some after, please?"

"You get me the pumpkins, I'll get you the soup."

"We can do that. Corn, beans, and squash. Staples around these parts." Ryder reached out to clap him on the shoulder. "Good to have you on the team, man."

He grinned, feeling as though he were part of a brigade. Somehow that made things easier. His feet were on solid ground again.

It didn't hurt that he had Ames at his back now, and a real place to go home to.

"Okay, I'm on puppy duty this afternoon. Y'all holler if you need me, but the kitchen is cleaned and closed."

"The guys will deliver lasagna?"

"You know it." Ryder did love his Italian food, even if it was a New Mexican hybrid.

"Cool. Hey, can you tell Ames I texted him? I swear, he's the only cowboy I know who's not glued to his phone twenty-four-seven."

"Tell me about it." Nathan rolled his eyes. Ames was so old-school it was kinda cute. "Is it bad?"

"Nah. Just herd maintenance."

"Got it." He headed out to his SUV, shivering a little. He and Ames were heading down to Santa Fe this weekend to get him winter boots and socks, sweaters, and a coat.

Maybe long johns.

The clothing kind, not the doughnuts.

Hmmm. Doughnuts. He had some extra time...

He got to the house, which now proudly held all his shit too. It was kind of hilarious, all his kitchen stuff in Ames's kitchen.

The smell of some kind of red sauce hit him as soon as he walked in the door, and he sniffed hard, heading for said kitchen to see what Ames was up to.

"Something smells good."

Ames was in the kitchen. It was adorable—he had on a pair of tissue-paper thin jeans and an ancient retro Tim McGraw T-shirt with holes in it, and his feet were bare.

Nathan couldn't be more in love if with the fine son of a bitch if he tried.

"I am making spaghetti sauce. Not weird green chile spaghetti sauce. Not basil pesto sauce that goes on spaghetti. Not anything with artichokes or sunchokes or choking anything. No sunflower seed-based spaghetti sauce, just spaghetti sauce with hamburger."

"That sounds amazing." He wasn't going to argue. He wasn't cooking. He didn't have to. That was fine. "Do you need any help?"

Ames stared at him. "Well... Sophie made bread. The sauce is already cooking, so you can't touch it. Um. Salad?"

"I can totally make a salad. I like salad." Silly cowboy. "Let me get changed."

"How was your class?"

"It was great. I had a ball. They loved the lasagna, thank you very much. The boss says that he texted you."

"I'm not at work," Ames stated.

"Okay." That was not his circus. Not even marginally his monkeys.

Ames followed him into the bedroom—into *their* bedroom, and it felt damn good to be able to think that, didn't it?—those hard hands on his hips, his ass in the cradle of Ames's body. "Well, hello."

"Hey, I'm glad you're home."

"I'm glad I'm home too."

Ames kissed the back of his neck. "This is Sophie's mom's sauce recipe."

"Ah, cool. She'll be so tickled." He grinned, rocking his hips some.

"Evil man. Do it again?"

"Mmmhmm. I thought I was on salad and then puppy duty."

"Oh, God, Sophie and Gracelyn took the puppies over to puppy training with Hansen. You know, the hand that does the flyball and stuff?"

"That's cool." That meant an empty house for a few minutes... That sounded like fun.

"The sauce can sit and simmer for a bit." Ames swayed, almost dancing with him, one hand sliding to his belly. That made things below that hand pretty happy.

"I do like a sauce that can simmer." He stretched, reaching up tall and then putting his hands behind Ames's head.

That move brought them even tighter together and gave his belly the perfect, long arc. Oh, he liked that.

Ames responded by tightening his fingers and rocking that heavy cock against him, making a promise that had his dick filling.

It was a rare thing when the two of them were alone together at the house—no teenager, no puppies. He loved their life, but this?

This was necessary.

"Did you close and lock the door?"

"I did."

"Good man." Ames began to unbutton his chef's coat.

"You're getting good at that."

"Weeks of practice." Ames pinched one of his nipples, making him gasp. "Arms down, babe."

"But this stretch is so good." He chuckled, and Ames tickled his ribs, getting his arms down straight away.

"I can show you some other things that feel good."

"Better than a stretch?" he teased.

And Ames shot back with, "You'll have to tell me. We'll take a poll."

He did love this relaxed Ames, the one who was willing to tease and play and make him shiver on a bone-deep level.

"I can do polls."

"I know. You're a smart puppy." Ames bit at his neck, which made his hips buck in the best possible way.

"Damn, babe. That's fine."

"Mmmhmm. Salty." Ames licked his skin as he shoved off his chef's jacket and started on his undershirt, tugging it out from his checks, baring his belly.

"You got the best hands, babe."

"Do I?" Ames laughed, the sound deep and husky. "I like to use them on you, that's for sure."

"Well, I'm all for that." He turned, sliding his arms around Ames's neck. "So, what are you going to show me then?"

AMES GRINNED AT NATHAN, THEN TOOK A KISS, figuring he would go with actions over words. God, he loved to kiss Nathan, because those soft lips and that stubbly face were the best kind of contrast.

He ran his hands over Nathan's bared skin, wanting to touch every inch, then taste it too. This was his new favorite pastime.

Nathan grunted when he hit a particularly sensitive spot, going up on tiptoes to press against him. They broke for air, then dove into the kiss again, and he got to work on Nathan's pants. He wanted to see and feel the rest.

"So what is it with the weird pants? I thought chefs were allowed to wear like, jeans and shorts and stuff now."

"Checks were designed to resist heat, give air flow, and the black and white pattern hides stains. I like them better than jeans and cargoes because cotton is the death fabric."

"You sound like a rafting guide."

"Well, it's the same idea, right? You get cotton wet and it clings. This checks stuff, awful as it is, doesn't."

Ames pushed the pants down and off. "Well, I'm not complaining, since I get to make them disappear, right?"

"You do. And I can wear what I want. I like to go full bore

with the students." Nathan leaned back, stared at him. "Do you really care about that right now?"

Ames chuckled, fluttering his eyelashes, going for silly. "Only because you're not naked."

"I can arrange naked." Nathan didn't tease—there was a shiver, a wiggle, and the briefs under the pants hit the floor. He did love a willing man. This man in particular.

"Fucking beautiful," Ames murmured, running his hands over all that hot, bare skin.

"Mmm. I'm glad you think so."

"I know so." He kissed and licked and danced Nathan over to the bed an inch at a time, his whole body ready for the main event.

"You are wearing entirely too many clothes, babe." Nathan sat on the bed, then tugged at his belt buckle, getting it popped loose so he undo Ames's jeans.

Ames shrugged out of his shirt, nodding. "I am at that. I like that you're a solution kind of guy."

"I am. I work with my hands." Nathan didn't glance up from his work, and Ames stared at those amazing hands, scarred and peppered with little burn marks. They looked like heaven against his skin, and he was bare in no time.

"Oh, now, there we are." Nathan bent forward to nuzzle his belly.

"God. Your mouth." He stroked Nathan's shaggy auburn hair, the thick stuff clinging to his fingers.

"I love the way you smell," Nathan nuzzled in, that cleft chin with the barest hint of stubble brushing the tip of his cock. Someone had shaved before teaching his class, otherwise it would have been more rough, more raw. As it was, it was the barest hint of a tease.

He would have answered, but his mouth was dry, just from watching this, being able to feel those scarred-up hands on his skin. He'd never imagined how physical a chef's job could be until he'd seen Nathan at work.

Until he'd seen how sharp those knives were and how fast they could move. That didn't even count the fact that, from the elbows down, Nathan's skin looked like he'd been in a war.

Burns and cuts had caused thousands of scars. And each one of them felt different on his skin.

Ames loved it.

Nathan's touch slid around his body, the heat moving across his waist and down until Nathan cupped his ass, fingertips digging in as he tugged him up into that hot waiting mouth.

If Ames had ever doubted there was a God, he knew now that there absolutely was, and then He'd offered Ames this amazing guy.

"Focus." Nathan's fingertips dug in and dragged along his butt cheeks, making him give an uncontrolled thrust up as his glutes tightened.

Nathan grinned up at him, eyebrows gesticulating like mad. "Somebody likes that."

Ames's lips twisted as he fought his laugh. Lord have mercy, he was stupid for this fine son of a bitch. "Don't you have something better to do than to give me shit?"

"Not a thing."

He winked down, tugging that heavy hair real careless. "Then get back to it, man. You make me crazy."

Nathan chuckled and went right back to his work. He licked and sucked until Ames was grunting and panting and trying not to lose his shit, and then he had to pull away, because he wanted more.

He wanted full-body contact sports here.

"Need to be with you." He pushed Nathan back gently so he could crawl on the bed.

"I can get with that." Nathan scooted back, then opened

his arms so Ames could slide up between those wide-spread thighs and take a desperate kiss.

Nathan cradled him, kissing back with all that want and need, and Ames rubbed hard against him, pressing them together as much as he could from head to toe.

Breaking away, Nathan stared at him with those sherry-colored eyes. "You got lube, babe?"

"And a brand-new box of condoms. Top or bottom, honey?"

"Mmm... I catch and pitch, but right now, I could use a nice hard fuck."

Ames's eyes crossed and he shorted out a little bit, because damn. Damn, he loved to hear Nathan talk like that.

"I can do that," he said once he got his breath back. Oh, yes. He could so do that. Ames sat back on his knees so he could grab the condom and lube from the bedside table.

"I do like that you're all prepared, babe," Nathan told him, eyes on his cock.

"And you will be soon." He grinned, feeling more equal to the task now. He set the condom on the bed, then opened the lube. "Let's get you slick, huh?'"

"I'm ready." Nathan spread wide and planted his feet, lifting his hips up off the bed.

That was going to give him heart palpitations.

Hmm, wasn't that pretty?

He got the lid off the lube and slicked his fingers up. Telling himself not to be clumsy but knowing he wanted this bad enough that his hands were shaking good and hard.

Nathan started stroking his prick, showing off some, giving him something to focus on, something to watch, and damn, that didn't make the shivers any better.

It did make him feel as if he were the hottest cowboy on earth, like Nathan didn't want anybody but him.

Those pretty eyes were laser-focused on him, and when he

touched Nathan's hole, his lover gave this long, low moan that was pure need.

Yeah, he could handle this.

"Need you, dear. Been aching for it."

"All you have to do is ask." Hell. Nathan didn't even have to ask. He'd give Nathan anything, whenever.

He hadn't quite gotten used to the idea there was somebody here with him. Not just to help with the day-to-day shit of life.

Ames had a lover, someone to share his needs with.

He grinned. That was a fine damn thought, and he didn't rush the preparation. He gave Nathan time to feel every sensation, to know that he cared about getting Nathan open for him, slick enough to take him easily.

When Nathan was squirming and panting, chest and belly flushed the same deep rose as his face, his cock bobbing, Ames tugged his fingers free and muscled up between Nathan's thighs.

"You ready for me, babe?"

"Fuck yes." Nathan offered himself up, nice and easy

And Ames couldn't resist that for anything in the world.

He lined his cock up and slipped in, the scrape making his eyes cross. His breath caught, and he stared down at Nathan, holding that gaze as he sank in all the way.

"God. That's it. Just like that." Nathan arched up, moving him closer, deeper.

Nathan's body was the tightest, hottest place on earth, and he didn't want to be anywhere else. So Ames began to move, pushing in, then pulling back, and every time he rocked away the tiniest bit, Nathan made this hungry noise...

He wasn't going to last long at this rate.

"So fucking full." Nathan levered himself up on his elbows and began moving with Ames, grinding them together.

"Tight, honey. Tight and hot. Fucking perfect." Words

kind of failed him then, because Nathan squeezed down and all he could do was grunt and rut like the animal he was right now.

Nathan made a noise that he took to be one of approval, because Nathan's eyes crossed and that sweet ass tightened unbearably.

That was about all he could take. He grabbed hold of Nathan's prick and started jerking it fast and hard, watching the open need flash in Nathan's eyes with fascination.

"Come on, baby, I need it. I need to feel you come on my cock." A sensation of pure power poured through him as Nathan writhed and arched underneath him.

"Fuck. Fuck cowboy. Please." Nathan had barely hissed the words out before he was shooting. The spunk splashing over that tight, hot little belly.

Ames was going to die if he didn't get to come soon. He needed this more than he needed to breathe. He managed to kiss Nathan, tongue slamming into those lax, parting lips before his rhythm became clumsy and awkward. He had to fight to keep his eyes open while he shot, needing to watch Nathan float down as he went over the edge.

"Mmm." Nathan stroked his back, letting him know he was right there with him. "That was the ticket."

"Uh-huh." Was he expected to talk right now?

"Your sauce smells great."

He grinned. "Thanks. It's a good recipe." A family one. And he was pleased that Nathan seemed receptive to him cooking.

"I can't wait to try it." Nathan hummed low, smile peaceful and easy. "Love you."

Oh.

He did love to hear that.

"Love you too, babe."

He didn't mind saying it either.

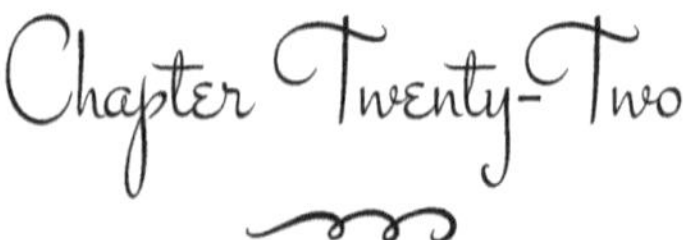

Chapter Twenty-Two

"Is it always this bad?" Sophie seemed exhausted.

"One, yes, and two, you don't have to do this. You're a sixteen-year-old kid. In school, you don't have to help so much. I will understand. I will."

Nathan held his hands up in sheer exasperation. "The cooking will always be here. The kitchen will always be here and it is open for you. You don't have to work yourself to the bone. That's my job."

She was a sweetheart and passionate, the good Lord knew, but it was the holidays, which meant finals. And projects. And parties. And dates and sleigh rides and carriage rides in all of this strange nonsense that these people who were now home from the rodeo decided to do.

He'd dealt with Halloween. He'd struggled with the week of anniversary. He'd coped with the lead-up to Thanksgiving, and then the sheer involved, unadulterated hell that was Thanksgiving, which he had never personally experienced before because chefs took Thanksgiving off. And now? It was the holidays.

And Nanette had announced her retirement.

So he was going to have a stroke. But that did not mitigate the fact that Sophie was a teenager who needed to do teenage things. Like go and find a girlfriend and dance around and stuff whatever girls did.

He didn't remember being sixteen. He needed to talk to Charlie. Charlie could speak to her.

Actually, Ames was her Cousin Uncle Father. Ames could do it, he was the live-in.

Okay, that wasn't fair. Ames had never treated him like the live-in. It was really something evil and mean to think when he was feeling all aggravated. Thank God he never said it out loud.

"I know, I know Chef. I'm just—I feel bad. You have so much to do." Sophie gave him a very earnest look, pushing her hair back behind her ear.

"I do. And this is really not my shtick. But that's okay. I'm thinking about doing some sort of a plated dinner around Christmas, and then I'm going to take a month off. And everyone can starve."

That kind of thing he said out loud.

"You're a dork." She grinned at him. "I do kind of have plans for tonight. Uncle Ames said that it was cool. But I want to make sure you didn't need me."

"I don't need you tonight. Tonight I'm going to go home and I'm going to let your Uncle Ames order us a pizza. Is it a good date?"

"It's less a date and more just plans. We're gonna go ice skating. In Santa Fe there's a place. There's a bunch of us. And we're going to go."

"I think that sounds amazing. Did your Uncle Ames give you some money?"

She nodded. "Yeah. I've got cash, and I've got a cute sweater, and there's a cute girl."

"Now that is what I wanted to hear." He winked at her, and she giggled, and then his damn phone buzzed.

"Hold on." He answered the phone. "Hey, Kase, what's up?"

"You have a visitor."

"Who?" No one visited him.

"Says his name is Dan."

"Do not let him any farther in the property. I'll be right there." Nathan hung up the phone and gave Sophie his most serious expression, one reserved for raw chicken and car accidents. "I need you to lock up here and then I need you to call your Uncle Ames and tell him that Dan showed up. He'll know what that means."

"You mean the evil ex Dan?" she asked, eyes wide and lips parted with shock.

"Yeah." God, she heard everything. "I mean, I—I don't want—I'm going to make him go, okay? But let your Uncle Ames know."

"I'm on it." She pulled out her phone. "I'm on it. You—he's not gonna hurt you."

Nathan let one of his eyebrows rise all the way up to his hairline. "Excuse me, I am the chef. I will cut him to ribbons, serve him to the dogs, and no one will even miss him."

"Oh, cool. Be careful. Call me if you need to. I'm here for you."

Jesus Christ, that was the sweetest little girl on earth, and he loved her more than was reasonable.

"Thanks, kiddo, I know you have my back." Then he headed off to the office.

Nathan seethed the whole way, his face hot, his hands clenched. How dare Dan show up here? Hell, how had Dan known where he was? Whoever had ratted him out wasn't getting cookies from him this Christmas.

He slammed into the ranch house through the kitchen, making Nanette and Mrs. Chiara jump.

"Sorry, ladies. Where is he?"

Nanette's face crumpled in sympathy. "He's in the formal living room."

He chuffed out a laugh. He'd learned that the formal living room, which he'd been swept through that first day on the way to Kase's office, was where the family kept people they had no intention of sharing their house with.

A space to put people in their place, so to speak.

He stopped outside the door, taking a deep breath. Calm. Centered.

He was not going to pop anyone in the nose or start screaming like a banshee when he walked through the door.

In. Out.

Okay, he was ready.

Dan was sitting there, big as you please, wearing a turtleneck and the sports jacket he always called the man's management tuxedo.

Once upon a time that would have been sexy. Now it was just irritating.

He strode over, skirting the edge of the room. He wasn't even giving Dan a chance to stand and get close. "What do you want?"

"Nathan, baby, you look..."

"What do you want?" He wasn't talking to this son of a bitch. He wasn't dealing with this son of a bitch. He wasn't doing anything here.

"I've been talking to some investors. It's important that you listen to me here. We can get the restaurant going again. I know a lot of people who want to do this. I know how to do it this time."

Oh, Nathan didn't think so.

"Fuck off, man, leave me alone." He didn't want to deal

with this shit right now. "You're a liar and a thief. You need to go back to your little fuck star in Houston."

And he needed to watch his mouth.

"We broke up. He's not you."

"Of course he's not me." Nathan knew that. It was fucking amazing how Dan had figured it out. "You need to leave the Chiaras alone."

"You don't belong out here. This place is ridiculous."

He stared, his arms crossed, trying for expressionless. Whether or not he was supposed to be here was none of Dan's fucking business.

Maybe he didn't belong here, but that didn't matter. He was building a life here, one way or the other.

He didn't fit in completely, no, but Ames did, and that was important.

That was the big part.

There was no way he was going to have a screaming fit in the Chiaras' house. No way.

The kids were in here. Who knew who else was in here. He simply wasn't going to do it. "Excuse me? I think you need to leave."

"You don't understand. I can get the restaurant started back up for you. I have investors. They came to me in private, and they wanted to work with you. And we're not talking Dallas, we're not talking Austin, we're talking New York. They want you to open up in New York."

Jesus Christ. He swallowed hard, because this was the dream, right? This was the whole thing. This was what everybody wanted.

Nathan found himself standing there staring at Dan because this was the most backhanded awful piece-of-shit situation in the history of piece-of-shit restaurant situations.

Here, let me offer you a chef's dream, but it's attached to

an asshole you hate, that you can't trust, and you'd have to lose the family that you were in love with to get it.

Fuck him.

Fuck this.

Fuck everything.

"You have to go. You're bothering these people."

"Well, I didn't know how to get a hold of you."

"Well, thank God and Greyhound, that's good. You've got to go. This place has children. I don't want them even to know that you exist. You make this place filthy by standing here."

Dan gave him a hands up, placating smile. "That's right, baby, get it out. I know you're mad. You have a good reason to be mad."

"I'm going to fucking show you mad," he snarled. If he'd had one of his chef's knives is his hand? Somebody would be bleeding.

"Well, there you are." Ames came strolling into the parlor as if he had nothing better to do, hands loose and ready at his sides. He curled his lip at Dan. "Who's this?"

"Just someone I used to know." He tried hard for casual. "Don't care to anymore."

"That's that, then, ain't it?" Ames moved in between him and Dan. "I reckon you've outstayed your welcome."

"Who are you, John Wayne?" Dan sneered.

Ames never blinked. "No, sir. I like to think I modeled myself on Doc Holliday in *Tombstone*. You know. About the huckleberry?"

Oh shit. He'd never seen this side of Ames, and while it was kind of hot, he didn't need the impending bloodshed to come from Ames any more than he wanted it from himself.

Dan gaped. "I—Well, I have business with Nathan, not you."

"Oh, no, sir. You got no business here. Nathan already said so."

"I did. And I meant it. I want you out of here." Dan was a little disease.

"Don't be an idiot," Dan snapped. "We're talking about New York City; we're talking about Manhattan. We're talking about a flagship restaurant. You've worked for this your entire life, and I'm offering it to you on a silver platter. I have the investors. I have everything, I have signatures. All I need is you."

Fuck, his heart hurt. "You have to go. You don't belong here."

"Neither do you. You belong where you can be celebrated, not trapped in this dusty, cheap redneck wet dream."

"Now. Out. Ames. We need to make him go. And without the kids disrupted. I don't want them upset, or the Grannies."

"Listen to yourself. You are a chef and you're what? Babysitting. Running an old age home? Catering to the masses? Are you a chuck wagon cook?"

"No, her name is Layla. Ames, please. Quietly."

"I can do quiet."

He turned his back on Dan. And went to stand in the hallway so that no one saw whatever it was that Ames did.

He didn't care.

This whole thing was so fucking stupid.

And he wanted to lie down and cry.

Chapter Twenty-Three

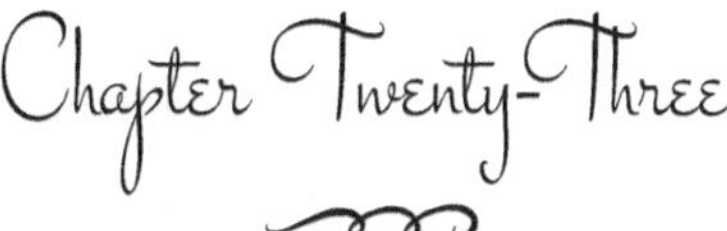

Ames took a moment after the man drove off, standing on the porch of the big house. He had to take a breath before he headed back in to see what Nathan needed from him.

Because this was about Nathan.

He unclenched his hands and his jaw, because Lord it had taken everything he had not to smack that smarmy bastard in the face.

"You know this is not what he's meant to do. He'll come back. He's a star, and he's meant to be in the New York market, you little pissant."

That was what that fucker had said to him.

He took another deep breath. Then he headed inside.

Kase met him in the foyer. "You need anything, Ames?"

"No, sir. I'm sorry if that ruckus disturbed your house."

Kase's lips curved wryly. "Not the first ruckus in this house. Now, go on and find Nathan. I think he was in clean-up time, so why don't y'all take the rest of the day off?"

"Sounds good." In fact, it sounded like the best idea ever.

He'd once found a deer caught in a snow fence, that poor young buck caught in a million different places, all tangled up.

Ames had put his physical safety on the line to untangle that deer one antler at a time. This situation felt like he was walking into that all over again.

He headed back to the drawing room to find his man.

He found Nathan with Dani under one arm, Dani feeding him cookies and patting him. "It's okay, Mr. Cooking Man. It will be okay."

"Everything's fine, Dani. Thank you for the cookies; they're very good."

"I made them with Mimi. Did you know? I did. I make them with Mimi all the time."

"You are a lucky girl to have a Mimi." Nathan hugged her. "Thank you very much. I have to go now and finish cleaning up the kitchen, all right?"

"Okay, Mr. Cooking Man. Hi, Cowboy Ames."

"Hey, Dani."

"Do you want a cookie?"

No, he didn't want a cookie, but he of course nodded and said yes. She handed him what was either oatmeal chocolate chip or oatmeal raisin.

Either way, he didn't care. He said thank you and stuffed it into his mouth.

Then he grabbed Nathan by the arm, and they headed out together toward the kitchen.

"Was Sophie helping you clean up?"

Nathan nodded. "I told her to go. Lock up. She was going out with some friends. I'm sorry, but I don't remember what she said she was doing. Skating? Was it skating? Do they even do skating here?"

Ames nodded. "Ice skating. She was going to Santa Fe to go ice skating with a bunch of kids. I think she has a girlfriend that she's interested in. I caught her putting on some makeup the other day and kind of gussying up. Which is good, since she broke it off with that girl from church camp."

"Good to know."

Nathan unlocked the kitchen and glanced around. "She did a great job cleaning up. She's working awfully hard. I wish she'd go and do things. I was tickled that she said she was going to Santa Fe. I think that's good…"

He nodded. "It is. It's great. How are you?"

Nathan shrugged for him. "Have no idea. Like I literally have zero idea how I am."

"That's fair. You don't have to have a clue." Ames wanted to know though. He wanted Nathan to tell him that it was all going to be okay, that there was no way Nathan was going to leave them and go to New York City and be famous.

He didn't think he was going to get that conversation, but he wanted it.

"Thanks. That was so unexpected. I never want to see him again."

"Are you telling me you're not gonna leave me behind to have a wild happy, thieving bastard life with him?"

Nathan looked around and stared at him and then obviously saw his smile, because he relaxed. "Don't make me beat you, man. He makes me want to barf. I mean that literally. Like gag, like my stomach is upset, and I have acid now. Like I don't even know if I can have a glass of wine because I'm so acidy."

"That's pretty bad."

"Right? This is the nastiest thing that has ever happened to me, except for the other things that he's done to me which are equally nasty." Nathan's eyes flashed, and his fists clenched. "You know, I mean, at least this way nobody else really is involved in his nastiness. I don't have to go to a bunch of investors and apologize because they think that I screwed them over. Can you imagine? Do you even understand?"

Ames shook his head. "No, no. I don't, I'm sorry."

"Well, the idea is, you know, we...we have these investors. They hand us money, we do the work, we pay them back as we can. Like literally as we can. We take care of the business, so if somebody just bought in, we pay them off until their investment has been repaid. At the end, the restaurant would be ours, and everything would be hunky-dory."

Nathan began to shake. "Except that's not what happened. That son of a bitch took the money. So he wasn't paying people back, and I didn't know. I thought that this... I mean, there were checks going out. They were going out into his pocket. That's not legal, by the way, and at the end, I had to sell everything to pay those investors back. I lost my whole world and ended up here."

The fury in that statement hurt his heart.

"And it's not even the being here that's the big step down. I was running a restaurant by myself. It was my place, and now I'm working for somebody else again. I'm just another chef again. And it's his fault."

Ames reached out, hoping Nathan would take his hand. But he made it Nathan's choice. He wouldn't push.

Nathan grabbed his hand as if it were a lifeline.

"I'm sorry, honey. I am. It sucks, and I wish I knew what to say." Especially when he wanted to ask how this could possibly work, then. How could it, when Nathan wanted to be in his own place again as soon as possible?

How far would he go? Could Ames go with him, or would that be a mistake? Fuck, he had no idea.

"I do too. I don't even have anything. Do I have to have something to say right yet? Can I just be like shell-shocked and wigged-out?" Nathan glanced at him, so obviously worried.

"Yes. Yeah, you totally can. I... Do you want to go riding?"

"There's snow out there." Nathan pointed out. "It seems odd. Do people go riding in the snow?"

"Yeah, sometimes they want to clear their heads, and the horses need exercise, and it's not too cold."

Nathan shook his head. "I really don't want to go riding. It's cold." He paused for a second. "You want to go to the barns with me instead? I could brush a horse."

Nathan's suggestion shocked the hell out of Ames.

"Really?"

"Yeah, I mean, we could go home and brush the dogs too. They probably stink. You know they've been romping round in the backyard like...puppies because, you know, puppies."

"I've got the afternoon off. So do you. Let's go home and towel off puppies." Because as cool as it was that Nathan had suggested going to the horse barn, if he went, he knew he'd have to get work done. Someone would need him for something.

This way they were off, and if Nathan wanted to play with animals, he could.

"Hell, if you really want to go brush a horse, we can go brush up the guys in our barns." His barns were filled with older rescues, ones who just needed a home and someone to love on them.

He found Nathan out there sometimes, talking to some of the old horses about nothing at all, kind of visiting with them.

For a guy who'd never even had a pet up until a few months ago, Nathan was quite the animal lover, if not a cowboy.

Ames didn't think that Nathan would ever be a cowboy.

"That sounds good to me. We can go down to the barn and brush out the horses, then clean up the dogs, because you know that they'll be outside watching for us." Nathan offered him a warm smile. "Then maybe... I was hoping maybe you'd buy me a pizza. We could sit together and eat pepperoni and olives. I promise not to bitch about the ex and how evil he is.

Instead, I'm gonna be incredibly grateful that my studly new lover escorted him out."

Nathan turned and hugged him, holding on tight. "It was kind of hot, by the way. Thank you. I didn't even ask if it was all right to put you in that situation. I just—I told Sophie to call you because I knew that you'd come."

Ames squeezed Nathan good and tight. "I wanted to clean his damn clock, but I was in the bosses' house." Ames chuckled. "Come on, honey. We'll order pizza and play cowboy, and then maybe we can have hot tub time."

That Nathan was willing to do no matter how cold it was. They'd bought a towel heater together.

Bubbling with Nathan would let him gather his scattered chickens and figure out what to do next. They had some hard discussions coming up, but now wasn't the time.

Now it was time for him to support his lover, to let Nathan know it was damn okay to feel how he felt.

However that was.

Chapter Twenty-Four

Nathan sort of went through the next few days in a fugue state. Dan had come back twice, and the second time Ryder and Kase had met him at the door.

And that had been that.

No more Dan. No more trouble. And no one had really said anything about it.

It was wild. It was as if Dan had never really existed.

He didn't even know how to feel.

Usually he didn't know what to think, but he had feelings down to a fine art. He knew if he was angry. If he was worried. If he was scared. Whatever. But he didn't this time.

He didn't know.

Was he mad about losing this opportunity, or was he stupid for considering it? Was he worried about what was wrong with him? Was he worried that there wasn't anything wrong with him? Was he getting old and settling? He didn't know.

So he wandered around and cooked things. It was Christmas, so it wasn't like there wasn't enough to do.

In fact, he was in the middle of a batch of biscochitos right now.

Cookies.

Christ.

"Chef?"

He looked over at Sophie, head tilting. "What do you need, kiddo?"

"Where did you go?"

"Huh?"

She nodded down at the bowl on the counter. "You wandered off on me."

He realized he was sitting there with the spoon in his hands, like the spinning of the earth would stir the cookie dough. He'd been staring out the window, in his own little world. "God, I don't know. I was woolgathering, I guess. Sorry."

"So the rumor is that guy, your ex, offered to get you another restaurant. That's what he was yelling when the bosses asked him to leave." Her bright blue eyes speared him.

Damn it. He nodded. He wasn't gonna lie. "That is what happened."

"Like in New York City, huh?"

He nodded. "Like in New York City, huh."

"Are you going?"

Nathan shook his head. "No. I can't work with him."

She leaned back against the counter, that blue gaze fastened on him. "So what if it wasn't him? What if it was a real thing, a real person. Investors, I mean. Would you go?"

He knew that this was somewhere he needed to be careful, somewhere he needed to actually pay attention to the words coming out of his mouth.

"Could you see me in New York City?" That was fair, right? It wasn't a lie because he didn't know. He was so Texan he might not make it in Manhattan.

But it was the dream, right? To go and have a five-star restaurant in a big city with fine dining and an upscale clientele and...

"You can do anything you want to do. You're amazing. Like you're the real deal." Her eyes filled with tears. "We're just—"

Oh no. "No, girlfriend, you are not *just* anything. Don't you ever say that. You're not just anything to me, and you're not just anything in general. Neither is your Uncle Ames. Y'all are not just *anything*."

"It's easy to say that."

"No, it's really not." In fact, it was the hardest thing to say, ever, because the simple fact was he wasn't going to leave Ames. He wasn't going to head to New York City, or Austin.

Or Los Angeles. Or Chicago. Or London. Or Paris. Or Milan. Or Tokyo.

Not without his cowboy.

"But you can work anywhere, Chef. You could go *anywhere*. You wouldn't have to stay here. Not now."

"Soph, I didn't have to stay anywhere. At all. I didn't have to come here. I'm an adult. I wasn't forced to come here. I chose this place, and if I stay, I choose to stay here. That's all."

"Yeah, I guess. I mean." She shrugged. "Whatever."

"So what's wrong? Talk to me." Nathan wasn't sure what the hell was going on. He thought he'd said the right things. He'd said he was staying, hadn't he? That was good, right?

"You're like this guy. You're the chef. We all know you're not happy, and that's not cool. Is that what you'd tell me? That it's not cool to give up what I want to do for some girl? You would say that to me. You would say 'Sophie, cooking is your passion. You matter so much, and you have to follow your passion'. That's what you would say to me. So are you lying?" She threw up her hands, clearly torn about the whole situation.

He was going to kick something or throw a bowl of cookie dough.

"I'm not lying." Nathan was confused, he was hurt, he was a little sick to his stomach. He was afraid. He was overwhelmed, and he didn't want to do this anymore. But he wasn't lying.

She stared at him, lips parted for her next salvo, when the dogs—who were outside in the new covered pen that the bosses and Ames had come up with—set up a wild barking like he had never heard before.

Saved by the puppers.

"Let me go see what's what. You watch the cookies."

"Yes, Chef." She nodded, her chin set in a determined line, and he fled.

Nathan didn't think he was up for anymore hard discussions today.

"What are you two hooligans—" He broke off, squinting. Okay, what had they cornered?

"What are you puppers doing? Get over here." He whistled and three of the four dogs that were in the pen came right to him, and he was tickled. Two of those three dogs belonged to him, which meant that the one dog that was being an asshole didn't.

That meant he couldn't get blamed for whatever the fuck was going on.

"I'm serious. Get your butt over here right now, whoever you are."

Sure as shit, Whoever You Are came right over and plopped his or her fuzzy little butt on the ground, next to Thorn and Honeysuckle.

"Good dog. Now, what did y'all have?" He wandered over, frowning deep.

Oh Jesus.

He scooped up the three little kittens in one hand.

"Sophie! I need you to call your uncle and bring me a couple of kitchen towels right now."

"On it, Chef."

He nudged the puppies out of the way, encouraging them gently not to jump on him as he tried to make his way out of the pen.

"Oh, sweet little fuzzy beasts."

The kittens were adorable. There was a black one, a white one, and a yellow one.

Orange.

It was probably closer to orange. Definitely more mango than lemon, but with a hint of actual, like, tangerine in there.

Sophie came out of the kitchen, towels in her hand. "Oh my God, oh my God, oh my God! Babies!"

"Kittens, three of them. We need to get them out of the dog pen."

"I'll help."

He managed to get up without falling in the snow or letting any dogs out. "Do you see the mom? Have you seen a pregnant cat around here?"

She shook her head. "I don't think so. I mean, not that I've noticed. And they're not teeny. I mean, their eyes are open and everything."

Yay? "Call your uncle, tell him what is what, and he'll know what to do."

Nathan assumed that meant calling the vet, getting them warm and dry and de-fleaed so they could be fed, because that seemed to be all of the things that one did.

Then they could take them home.

"Are we gonna keep them?"

"Well, right now, yes, and I don't see why not, I mean. Cats are good, right? They catch mice."

Sophie went wide-eyed and she nodded. "They absolutely catch mice. Can I have the black one?"

That worked for him. "Yes, but I want the yellow one."

"Marmalade."

"Pardon?" Nathan didn't follow.

"They're called marmalade, the yellow ones."

That made sense to him. "Dude, cool. I would like the marmalade one. I'm going to name him Tigger."

"But if it's a girl—"

"Then her name can be Tigger. It's a gender-neutral name."

Sofie grinned him. "And that could be a gender-neutral kitty."

"Oh honey, I guarantee you after it's old enough, it's going to be neutered, one way or the other." He winked, and they giggled together, like Honeysuckle and Thorn weren't enough.

Ames came jogging up from the barns, his hands full of work towels. "What did y'all do?"

"We are heroes. The dogs had these three cornered in the dog pen. I don't know, maybe she moved him into the covered area to keep him out of the snow. I don't see her. The dogs had hold of them."

"Oh damn it. Let me call the vet, get her out here to cast eyes at them. We'll see what the bosses say, whether or not they want them."

Sophie shook her head. "No, no, no. Chef already said we could have him. We saved them."

"We're keeping them. The marmalade one's name is Tigger, and the black one? Her name is Wacky. You can name the white one." Nathan was feeling magnanimous.

"I can, huh?"

"Yes. I don't know if it's a boy or a girl yet, but you can totally name it."

"Go for gender-neutral," Sophie interjected.

"All right, but we still have to get them to see Tygh. He'll check them out. I want to make sure they've not been hurt. I want to know how old they are, all that. What if we find mama?" Ames asked.

"Then she's obviously not been well taken care of, and we're going to bring her home and love on her and get her fixed." Nathan didn't have any problem with that. "Nobody needs to be just...a baby factory."

"Sometimes I worry that you don't know how a ranch works, honey," Ames told him, and then winked, the expression wicked as hell.

"Shut up and take care of our new kittens. I've got cookies in the oven."

"Dude, cookies, right? I'll go save them," Sophie raced inside.

"Wash your hands first!" Nathan called after her.

"Kittens." Ames kind of stared at him a little bit.

"Yep, kittens. Wacky, Tigger, and whatever you decide to name this one."

"Obviously it's a Snowball."

"Obviously." Why hadn't Nathan thought of that himself? It was a perfectly logical name for a white cat, and he could have saved Ames the entire seven seconds it took him to think of it. "Excellent idea. Do you think they're okay?"

"They seem healthy. I think you're probably right. I think that the mom took him into the doghouse to get them warm, and then when the dogs came barreling in, they got frightened and went hunting for Mama."

Oh, he did like being right.

"Speaking of dog runs, what are all these dogs doing in here that aren't our dogs? In fact, our dogs are pretty equally matched in number at this point. At some point, we're going to have fewer of our dogs than just dogs."

Ames rolled his eyes. "Well. Sarah Jane owns the little white fluffy one. Her name is Frenchy, and her dog sitter crapped out on her. And then? Charlie brought that bigger hairy mutt. His name is Leopold. Don't ask. She's training him to be a service dog, I think. Or maybe he flunked out of service dog school. I don't know. But anyway, he's here. He's a bruiser. Super sweet, but a little dumb."

"Oh, sort of like you?" he teased.

"Shut up." Ames said it with no heat.

Nathan winked at Ames. He did love making his lover smile.

"I was thinking if you wanted..." Ames's tone was careful. "We could put up a Christmas tree this afternoon after you're done with the cookies. I've got some stuff. We've got the decorations that you got brought over with your storage container. I got lights. There's all this stuff from Sophie's house..."

Oh, how sweet. "I'd love to. I love Christmas." He glanced over at Ames. "What is it you want for Christmas, little boy?"

Ames didn't even hesitate. "For you to be happy."

Damn, this man made his heart ache. He chuckled, though, keeping it light, shaking his head. "That's not something Christmas can do."

And Nathan didn't want to talk about that right now. He didn't want to think about the fact that he had to figure this out.

And quick.

Maybe he needed to get investors in Santa Fe. That wouldn't be a terrible drive, right. It would be long, but not terrible. People had commuted way longer for way worse.

He wasn't super interested in doing private cheffing.

Of course pop-up restaurants were another option, and they didn't need investors. He simply had to figure this out, but he was going to.

"I'm not leaving," he told Ames.

"What?"

"I'm not leaving you. I'll figure this out, but I'm telling you now, I want to be with you."

Ames stared at him, blinking like he was a goat looking at a new fence. "Look. I want to be—"

A cowboy came out, hand waving as he hollered. "Ames. Ames, we need you back over here. What the hell are you doing?"

"God for fucking bid these kids do one thing on their own. I swear. I want to talk with you. I do, but—"

"But this isn't the time." Right. They were both on the clock.

Ames blew his hair off of his forehead. Someone needed a haircut. "Can you hold these kittens and deal with the vet? Is that something that you can do?"

He was becoming a master of handling the vet. "Yes. Sophie's on the cookies. I'll deal with the critters."

He sounded so official when he said that. He knew he did.

"Thanks, I appreciate it. Time to go play cowboy."

"You do that; I'll play Kitty Father." It was less archetypal, but way more descriptive.

"Oh, I like it." Ames pulled out his phone. "I'll call the vet on my way." He winked. "We'll talk."

"We will." He waved Ames off, because he had wiggling kittens to wrangle. They always had later to deal with them things.

Chapter Twenty-Five

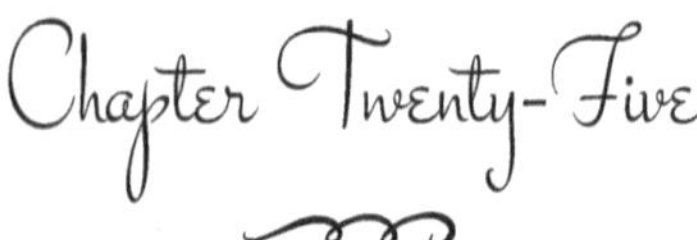

Nathan was staying.

Not Nathan was thinking of staying or Nathan might stay, but Nathan had looked him right in the eye and said, "I'm not leaving."

He'd never been so fucking happy and so scared in his entire goddamn life.

They had dogs together.

Apparently they had cats together too, especially now someone had found the mama cat. She was getting a check-up at the moment and was about to be fixed.

Her name was going to be Sally. He didn't ask Sophie why, since everyone else had a genderless name, or whatever.

Even all his stuff was out of storage and here at the house. Nathan was staying.

So Ames was going to figure out a way for his man to have a restaurant. He'd been thinking on it, and he'd been talking hard to Sophie, who seemed to be a little mad at him for ruining Nathan's career. As if he was asshole who'd done Nathan dirty.

He was gonna figure this though, damn it.

He wasn't sure how. He had no real idea how restaurants worked. But surely between the Chiaras and all the rest of them they could figure this out.

Today though, today they were going to put up a Christmas tree.

He had spent the last hour making a space for it, and Sophie had started stringing lights around the windows. Nathan was making chili and cornbread. The house smelled amazing, and it had never been so bright and sparkly.

He was proud of them—all of them, even him—because this was going to be Sophie's first Christmas without her mom, and his first Christmas with Sophie, and Nathan's first Christmas at the ranch, and Sophie's first Christmas at the ranch, and his first Christmas with the Christmas tree in so many years he couldn't count.

Wow.

This one. This was a big one. And Ames wanted to make it right.

He wiggled the tree in its stand. "Is this better? Does this work? Is this straighter?" he asked Nathan, who leaned over and looked.

"Oh, much better."

"Yeah, cool."

Those simple words shouldn't make him feel like a million bucks, but they did. They made him feel solid. Somehow the cowboy in him needed that, to know he was solid as rock.

He hadn't been sure that it could happen outside of being on the back of a horse, but it seemed that it could.

Ames tightened the tree stand, remembering all the years he had done this for his mom, crawling under the tree because he could fit.

Really, when they thought about it, it hadn't been all that

many years. He'd left home at sixteen, and he'd gone back a handful of times since, and none of those had been good.

He guessed he ought to be sad about it a little. It was what a person was supposed to do, right? Be all nostalgic about what had been and obsess about all the traditions that were not his to have, but, well, they were decorating in rainbows.

Rainbow lights.

Rainbow ornaments.

There was even this silly rainbow tree skirt to hide the stand.

He'd let Sophie pick it all out, and by the time they were done, it was like rainbow Christmas had exploded in the shopping cart.

Sophie came over to him, hand on his shoulder. "It's going to be the perfect tree."

"Yes, ma'am."

"This is the first Christmas tree that doesn't...that doesn't feel like a lie since I was a little girl." Her voice was low and soft, and she spoke so damn fast.

It killed Ames to hear the shame she was hiding in there.

"Everything felt like a lie. And I know—" Her voice trembled, and tears filled her eyes. "I know that momma's gone. But I feel like... I feel like I get to live now. Does that make me bad?"

Did it? Hell if he knew, but if it did, then they were all bad.

Fuck it.

"No, ma'am." He shook his head. "Makes you human. It means you're home with the folks that want you."

And that was that.

He had the man he loved, his sweet Sophie, the Chiaras, and the horses and critters and his bit of land. Everything he needed in this one spot, and he knew it.

Sophie grabbed him, and her storm of tears was fierce, but fast, and Nathan met his eyes over her head, a sad little smile on his lips.

Ames hugged her tight. "We got you, kiddo. I swear it. We're all here, and this is going to be the best, most real Christmas."

"It is." She hiccupped, but he could feel the storm passing. "Love you, Uncle Ames."

"I love you too, kiddo." He'd learned, though it was a recent thing, to give the words freely. People needed them. Shit, he needed to say and hear them. He might be feeling his way blindly in all this, but the words were damn important.

Nathan held up the wild, sparkling rainbow star that lit up. "Tree-topper first?"

"Yep. That way we don't have to tilt the tree once we get everything on it." He would swear Sophie had bought out both the Walmart and the Target in Santa Fe of ornaments... He patted Sophie's back. "You ready for this, kiddo?"

She sniffled, nodding. "I am."

"Good deal. Kleenex up, and we'll get lights and garland on." The kittens and mama cat were still confined mostly to the kitchen, so he didn't think he needed to gate off the tree, but they'd see. The pups might get a little too rambunctious for it.

Though they were both training up a treat considering they were half hound...

Sophie grabbed a tissue, blew her nose, then got back to work, humming with the Christmas music they had streaming.

"You okay?" Nathan asked softly.

"Yeah. Yeah, let me get that star on, huh?" He smiled, going in for the casual kiss. He loved being able to touch and love on Nathan at will.

"That sounds perfect," Nathan smiled at him, rubbed their noses together. "Chili is ready when we are too."

"Mmm..." Nathan's chili was the best, and he got to doctor it with onions and cheese and Fritos. Whatever he wanted.

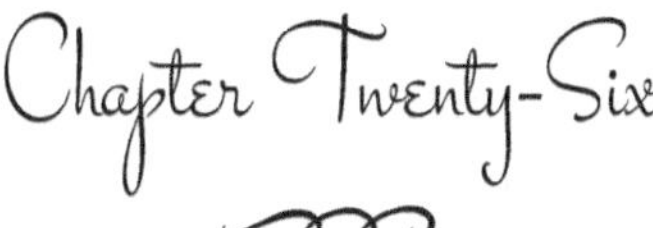

Chapter Twenty-Six

Nathan sat in the little office he'd been provided at the main house, which was a nice thing, because man, it was damn cold everywhere else.

He'd thought December was cold in Northern New Mexico.

January was downright frigid, and without all the new clothes Ames had gotten him for Christmas, he'd be losing his will to live. In fact, since the floor was Saltillo tile in the office, he was wearing his fuzzy-lined slippers instead of his boots.

The pups were allowed up in the big house now that they were potty-trained, too. That kept his feet super warm, since they fought to sleep under the desk.

He was working his way through ordering food for the whole ranch, which was his job now that Nanette was training a replacement housekeeper.

He kind of loved that, because provisioning that many people with that many moving parts was a real challenge. It made him think.

The pups both stood, tails wagging as they padded to the door, so Nathan glanced up to see who was visiting him.

"Hey, honey. You got a minute?" Ames bent down to rub long ears.

"Uh, sure. What's wrong?"

Ames smiled, those blue eyes alight for him, the way they crinkled at the corners so amazing to see. "Nothing. But I need you to come to Kase's office."

"Sure, babe." That he wasn't worried about. He hadn't done anything wrong. "Is he having another party?"

He grabbed his phone, his notebook, and his pen, then he stole a kiss because what fun was it having his man in the office if he couldn't steal a kiss?

"Come on, you." Ames patted his butt, and Nathan felt his lover vibrate against him.

Weird.

"Coming."

They wandered deeper into the house, and Nathan couldn't help his smile. He could hear kids doing their schooling along with someone singing and music playing.

It was one of the things he liked best about this house. There was always something going on.

They got to Kase's office, and he was shocked to see Ryder sitting there. He didn't deal with that cowboy much—not out of meanness or anything, because it seemed like he ended up being on Kase's to-do list.

"Hey, y'all." He waved and sat, surprised as all get-out when Ames came and sat with him.

"Hey, Nathan, how's it going?" Kase asked.

Nathan nodded over, still wondering what Ames was up to. "I am the king of menu plan building and acing food cost for all of us. It should work out real well. I've got it set up to where we've got the regular meals, and y'all have five breakfasts, three lunches, and four suppers fresh made along with four bag-type lunches and three suppers a week that are stick in the oven and warm up, stick on top of the stove, that sort of thing. So that gives you both some flexibility, keeps me not completely swamped all the time, and gives everybody their weekends free." It was damn good, his plan, and he knew it.

"How's Sophie doing with her prerequisites for culinary school?"

Nathan glanced over at Ames. Where on earth had that come from?

"Uh, fine." He switched gears. "She's working with Wat on some of the math stuff. You know, food costs and inflation. He's more patient there. And since I got the manual they sent, we've been working through lessons like champs."

He actually liked it a lot. It reminded him of going to culinary school himself, and some of the little refreshers were kind of cool.

"Do you think that she could take over some of the planning work and things by next year?" Kase asked.

So that was what this was about. Promoting Sophie.

"I'm gonna be honest here." Nathan took a deep breath. "Is she capable of it? Absolutely, and I think that it's totally reasonable for her to spend some time doing that." He held up one finger. "But I also think it's important that she does kid things. Restaurants will always be around. Always. But this is an isolated situation, right?" Nathan shook his head, warming to his subject. "Just that being in the commercial kitchen, there's no other kids doing it. She's not working in a team like she would be in a restaurant. That's a huge part of this whole thing. Of her learning how to work with other people, how to lead other people, how to run a kitchen, how to run front of house. There's more to this entire thing than simply learning how to cook."

Ames grabbed his fingers, squeezed and nodded, encouraging him, so he kept on.

"Which? You know, I'm loving, but she needs—If this is what she wants to do, she needs restaurant experience."

Ryder grinned, one corner of his lips quirking up and it made the little roping scar that he had really noticeable. "So would you hire her?"

"What?"

"If you had a restaurant, would you hire her as a line cook?"

"You bet your sweet ass. In a second." He thought she was brilliant. Easy to work with. Smart.

And that was just in restaurant work.

"But you think it's important for her to be a teenager, right?" Ames prompted.

"Like I said, she's still a kid." He took a deep breath. "I grew up fast. Went to work early. I don't regret it, and I didn't have a choice, but Sophie does. She's got a good situation here. She needs to let it come naturally."

Ryder and Kase glanced at each other, and Nathan frowned, his eyebrows drawing down. "Okay, what the hell is going on? Is somebody trying to accuse me of overworking Sophie? Because I guarantee you, I'm not. I am following the rules of her homeschooling and of the child labor laws absolutely. She's getting paid for some work, she's not getting paid for the work that's schoolwork, and both of those added up together does not go over what she's allowed to do. And trust me, I'm getting enough shit from her about that. So I know that it's right."

And why wouldn't Ames come to him and tell him if there was a problem instead of doing it this way? That seemed fucking mean. And Ames hadn't been mean to him since that first week.

"Dude. Nathan. Chill." Ryder shook his head. "There's nothing like that. Nothing at all. You're an amazing mentor to Sophie. Amazing. No one is accusing you of anything."

"Well, good, because I haven't done anything wrong."

And he didn't like feeling like he had. It pissed him right the hell off.

"No. Okay, look, let's lay our cards on the table." Kase looked at Ames. "You want to talk first?"

"Yeah." Ames took his hand. "So I was spit-balling with Kase the other day. About Sophie. About some of the kids who come through here. About you."

He blinked. "What about me?"

Ames leaned forward. "You're so good with Sophie, and with the kids who work the events. You know, kitchen help. Wait staff. And Kase came up with this wild idea."

Nathan glanced at Kase, his eyebrows climbing. "You did?"

Kase chuckled. "Well, I'm the grant writer around here, oddly enough. So when it comes to the not-rodeo stuff, I have all the wild ideas."

"I don't understand." He wasn't a teacher. He wanted a restaurant. Not this year, maybe, but soon.

"Well, I was thinking."

"Which is always dangerous," Ryder put in.

"Right." Kase grinned. "Anyway, I know you want to do a restaurant."

He stared back and forth at the three other men.

"Well, I was thinking Ryder and I could invest in a destination-type restaurant. It would have to be something five-star to get folks to come, but we know a shit-ton of high rollers in the rodeo world at least, who would be happy to throw money at you."

His mouth opened. Closed with no sound. Opened again. "What's the catch?"

"You'd have to take on kids who need to learn a vocation who don't have a chance of getting into culinary school without work experience. Or at all. They would learn on the job with you."

"I couldn't do this job and run a five-star restaurant. Not and give it what it needed."

"Of course not, but we would ask that you help until we can hire people. We need to feed the cowboys."

"Okay." Okay, fine. He needed to think, and fast. This was everything—literally every single thing he wanted in the world. Ames. Sophie. The restaurant. Management. Freedom. The mountains.

He could work this in a way that might help more than one person and the kids. "I want at least two other trained adults there. I don't want any possible accusations of impropriety. If you can give me three trained employees, I can cover the ranch and the restaurant."

Please God. Please.

"Shit. We can give you an army if you need it. But we want the right people, so we can start with three. Make it a place folks want to come work." Ryder beamed.

Nathan thought Ames might squeeze his hand right off.

"I have some phone calls to make, but I have some solid contacts—amazing people that I trust." And all of them were hunting a solid place to land. He searched Ryder and Kase's eyes. "This is real, right? This is a real thing?"

"It's as real as it gets. Kase can get the contracts drawn up in less than a week and y'all can decide where to break ground."

He was going to pass out. Just boom. Dead. "Ames?"

"It's serious. It is. I need you to be happy. I want that to be here with me."

"You did this?"

Ames shrugged, cheeks pink. "I asked about the possibilities. It was Kase who came up with the business proposal to put to you. I couldn't even imagine it."

"You—It's not a guaranteed investment, guys."

"Maybe not, but there are a lot of poor kids in New

Mexico, and the state depends heavily on tourism. If they have training, they can lobby for better jobs in an industry that's having to catch-up to competitive wages." Kase had really thought about this.

"And he has opened up so many things for Sophie. He knows so many people in the industry. This could be something super special. I know it could." Ames stared into him. "And I want you to stay. I need you to be happy."

"I want that too." He felt like he might pass out. "This is —You. Sophie. My own restaurant. The ranch. I could have it all."

"You could." Ames looked right into his eyes. "We have dogs and cats. I can't let you move on."

He shook his head. "Oh, Ames. You giant dork. That wasn't ever going to be a thing. Restaurants come and go. You're once in a lifetime."

Ryder jerked his head at Kase, and they rose. "We'll talk to you in a bit, Nathan. Feel free to not use the office for anything weird."

"Yeah, yeah. We'll go to my office for weirdness."

"Nathan! Ew!"

Oh, Kase did an amazing Sophie impersonation.

They laughed, but when they were alone, Ames pulled him to his feet and into those strong arms. "You mean it? You'd stay no matter what?"

"What made you think I wouldn't?"

"Sophie was so mad about you giving up your career for me, as she put it."

He held Ames's gaze. "I would have, at worst, started a restaurant in Santa Fe, but I'm in love with you. I'm your lover. I'm with you."

"I love you too, honey. So much." Ames kissed him hard. "And I thought I wasn't gonna like you at all."

"That's because you hadn't learned how good my chili is

yet. You hadn't figured out how much I love you and Sophie." He hadn't either.

"Nope. And you hadn't gone camping or mopped up after puppies." Ames chuckled. "And I hadn't cooked for you."

"Right? That's when I knew you were a cowboy, down to the bone." He cupped Ames's jaw. "You got me a restaurant."

"I helped you get one. You impressed an entire ranch of hard-core cowboys into investing in you." Ames kissed his fingers.

"And you. You're investing, right? Like for the long-term?"

"You know it. I can't get better black and bleu burgers." Ames gave him this shit-eating grin and wink. "Wanna go get weird?"

"Fuck yes. Let's go home." They could call it a long lunch hour. The bosses would understand.

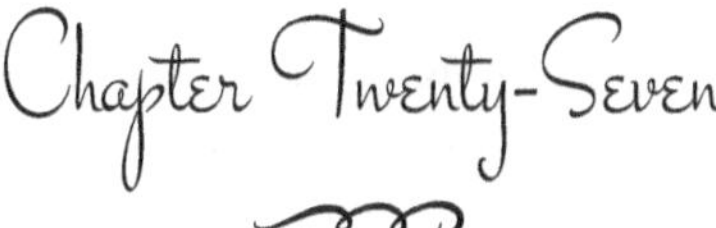

Chapter Twenty-Seven

Ames watched the hustle and bustle of opening night of Nathan's new restaurant, Cholla.

It was a gala evening at God knew how many dollars a plate, but it was limited to fifty covers, as Nathan called them. That way the wait staff, who were all squeaky and new, and the line cooks, who were just as green, could keep up.

Nathan's two sous and his front of the house manager were on the ball, and had trained these kids, including Sophie, within an inch of their lives.

He felt less than comfortable in a jacket and tie, but Wranglers and boots were allowed in this fine-dining establishment, and if it wasn't for the ring box burning a hole in his pocket, Ames would have relaxed by now.

Nathan had been in the kitchen all night, cranking out Nanette's enchiladas, Granny's lasagna, and the dessert special of a trio of Mimi's cookies. It was the prettiest food he'd ever seen, and everyone was over the moon.

Soon, though, the chef was due to step out and say hello to his guests.

Ames could wait. He had the little two-top toward the back to himself, so Nathan could get to him last.

Applause struck up as Nathan and all the kids came out, leaving the two sous and the dishwashers in the back. Look at Sophie's grin.

She had blossomed in the last year, becoming a high school graduate a year early, and was leaving for New York for culinary school in the summer.

New York.

Shit.

"I'd like to welcome y'all and introduce my brigade. I can tell you, I've never worked with better. These are some brilliant folks." Nathan showed off the kids, who were blushing and beaming.

The applause got louder, and the kids all turned to clap for Nathan.

Ames felt the same way. That was his damn man.

"I hope y'all enjoy your food, and please, be careful going home." Nathan waved, eyes obviously searching for him, lighting up when they found him. "Ames! You made it. Did you enjoy?"

"God, yes." He'd ordered one of everything, which had made his waiter, Jaime, call him Gordon Ramsey. "It was amazing, honey."

"Thank you, love! Did you see I put enchiladas on there just for you?" Nathan leaned down for a kiss.

"I did." There was another little spattering of applause as they kissed, and he figured it was now or never. "It must be love."

"It so is." Nathan grinned at him. "It'll be a late night, but I'll bring Sophie home."

He'd already talked to Angela, Nathan's front-of-house manager. She and Nathan's chef de cuisine, Markus, were going to handle the breakdown of the restaurant, and Sophie had her car.

Nathan wasn't staying late.

"Mmm. Nope. We have a thing. You'll come home with me."

"'A thing'?" Nathan's confusion was perfect and so, so sweet.

"Well, I sure hope so." He wasn't wanting to upstage Nathan's big night, but everyone they cared about in the world save the dogs and the cats was here, so he pushed out of his seat to one knee, pulling out the ring box.

Nathan gasped, and that scarred hand went to his mouth, and those amazing sherry-colored eyes filled with tears. "Oh, my God."

"Is that good?" Panic spurted through him. Please be good.

Nathan nodded his head. "Only if you're asking me to marry you."

"I am. Will you marry me, Nathan? I want the whole world to know how damn proud I am to be with you."

Nathan nodded, pulling him up to standing. "I will. Yes. Absolutely."

The whole restaurant exploded in cheers.

Ames took the kiss he wanted to take, not worrying a bit if someone got offended. They wouldn't be at Kase and Ryder's ranch if they were gonna be bothered.

He had everything he'd ever wanted—a lover, a home, his job, and a great relationship with a kid he'd almost missed altogether.

Ames figured that was about as good as it got for a cowboy.

Well, that and the occasional hamburger.

Interested in learning more about BA's cowboys? Want free fiction and news? Join my newsletter or follow me on Ream!

About BA

Western to the bone and an unrepentant Daddy's Girl, BA Tortuga spends her days with her hounds and her beloved wife, having mother-daughter dates, and eating Mexican food. When she's not doing that, she's writing. She spends her days off watching rodeo, knitting, and surfing Pinterest in the name of research. Following their own personal joys, BA and Julia heard the call of the high desert and they now live in the New Mexico mountains. BA's personal saviors include her wife, her best friends, and coffee. Lots of coffee. Really good coffee.

Having written everything from fist-fighting cowboys to rural single dads to werewolves, BA does her damnedest to tell the stories of her heart, which is committed to giving everyone their happily ever after. With books ranging from heart-warming stories of found families, to rodeo cowboys that are fighting to make a mark, to fiery passionate love affairs, BA refuses to be pigeon-holed by anyone but the voices in her head.

Also Available from BA

Gay Romance

BA's Cozy Cowboys (cowboys w/ kids novels)

Back in the Saddle

Cowboy Haven

Cowboy in the Crosshairs

Cowboy Logic

Cowboy's Law

In the Morning Light

Ranch Manny

Security Detail: an AusTex novel

Silver Buckle Linings

The Cowboy Contract

The Cowboy Guardian

The Meaning of Life

Trial by Fire: an AusTex novel

Two Cowboys and a Baby

Two of a Kind

The Banished Series

In Wulf's Clothing

River's Edge

Aspen's Song

The Border Crossing Series

Bombs and Guacamole

Ammo and Enchiladas

The Cereus Series

Cereus: Building

Cereus: Opening

Cereus: Training

Cereus: Rescue

The Cowboy Wanted Series

Cowboy Healing

Second Chance Cowboy

The Foster Ranch Series

The Cowboy Contract

The Cowboy Guardian

Leanin' N Ranch Series

Commitment Ranch

Finding Mr. Wright

Whiskey to Wine

Come Back Around

This Old Wind

Perfectly Seasoned

Love is Blind Series

Ever the Same

Real World

Midnight Rodeo Series

Welcome to the Pack

Tails and Whiskers

Above the Fold

Brownie's Sway

Thack's Angel

Here, Kitty Kitty

The Recovery Series

Refired

Slip

The Release Series

The Terms of Release

The Articles of Release

Catch and Release

The Road Trip Series

Racing the Moon • Steam and Sunshine

Under Pressure • Walking on the Sun

Roughstock Series

Blind Ride

And a Smile

File Gumbo

Back to Back

Pulled from All Sides

Coke's Clown

Leading the Blind

The Sanctuary Series

Just Like Cats and Dogs
What the Cat Dragged In

The Spirit Quest Series
Crossing the River

Chasing the Moon

Breaking the Ice

The Stormy Weather Series
Rain and Whiskey

Tropical Depression

Hurricane

Two is Never Enough Series
Claiming Their Mate

Needing to Breathe

Contemporary Standalones
Adding to the Collection

Back Forty

Best New Artist

Boys in the Band

Broken In

Elite Connections

Fighting Addiction

Latigo

Living in Fast Forward

Mud, Movies, Bullets, and Bulls

Needing To

Old Town New

Rainbow Rodeo

Rough in Wranglers

Say Something

Seashores of Old Mexico

Soft Place to Fall

Stetsons and Stakeouts

Truth or Consequences

Wicked in Wranglers

Historical Standalones

Cabin Fever

Hammer and Tongs

Oranges and Peppermints

Paranormal Standalones

Baker's Dozen

Calling His Bluff

Forged in Magic

Long Black Cadillac

Luck of the Draw

Redemption's Ride

Roman and Cage

Setting His Sights

Things that Go Bump in the Night

Unearthed

Wolf Run

Lesbian Romance

Summit Springs Series

Christmas Bizarre w/ Jodi Payne

Honeymoon in the Cards w/ Jodi Payne

Tipping the Barrel

Contemporary Standalones

Bright Lights and Boobjobs

Games Girls Play

Historical Standalones

Bustles and Doeskins

With Jodi Payne

The Collaborations Series

Refraction

Syncopation

The Cowboy and the Dom Series

First Rodeo

Razor's Edge

No Ghosts

The Soldier and the Angel

The East Meets Westerns Universe

Temptation Ranch

Les's Bar Series

Just Dex

Hide Bound

Wholly Trinity

Merry Everything Series

Window Dressing

Cowboy Protection

Cowboy and Cupcakes

On the Ranch Series

Tending Tyler

Roped In

Diamonds in the Rough

Wrecked Series

Wrecked

Flying Blind

Special Delivery

Seeds and Sunshine

Pick Up Man

The Higher Elevation Series

Land of Enchantment

Keeping Promises

Bigger than Us

Heart of a Cowboy

Home Free

The Sin Deep Series

Sin Deep

The Trouble with Cowboys

Hey, y'all!

Thank you for giving The Cowboy's Texan a try. I hope you enjoyed the story, and will consider leaving a review at the eBook retailer website where you made your purchase.

Don't forget to "like" my BA Tortuga page on Facebook to keep up with new releases, author news, special discount codes and sale announcements. And if you're interested in sneak peeks, rodeo pictures, and general fun, please come see the BA's Cowboys on Facebook. We'd love to have all y'all!

Yeehaw!

BA

www.ingramcontent.com/pod-product-compliance
Lightning Source LLC
Chambersburg PA
CBHW061431150726
47987CB00001B/176